PRAISE FOR RABINDRANATH MAHARAJ

"A sprawling, colourful epic . . . This novel's allure comes from its comic energy and its plucky, determined characters . . . The book is charming."

— *New York Times Book Review* on *A Perfect Pledge*

"Part comedy, part tragedy, the book is Dickensian in scope, creates a detailed world of characters a la V.S. Naipaul and evokes the allegorical qualities of Chinua Achebe or even John Steinbeck."

— *Montreal Gazette* on *A Perfect Pledge*

"Imagine Don Quixote staying home in Trinidad, and you've got something like the wandering, witty, ultimately devastating story that Rabindranath Maharaj tells in *A Perfect Pledge*."

— *Washington Post Book World*

FATBOY FALL DOWN

RABINDRANATH MAHARAJ

Published by ECW Press
665 Gerrard Street East
Toronto, Ontario, Canada M4M 1Y2
416-694-3348 / info@ecwpress.com

Editor for the press: Michael Holmes/ a misFit Book
Cover design: Troy Cunningham
Cover image: K.V. Maharaj

This is a work of fiction. Names, characters, places, and incidents either are the product of the author's imagination or are used fictitiously, and any resemblance to actual persons, living or dead, business establishments, events, or locales is entirely coincidental.

LIBRARY AND ARCHIVES CANADA
CATALOGUING IN PUBLICATION

Maharaj, Rabindranath, 1955-, author
 Fatboy fall down : a novel / Rabindranath Maharaj.

Issued in print and electronic formats.
ISBN 978-1-77041-452-5 (softcover)
ISBN 978-1-77305-312-7 (PDF)
ISBN 978-1-77305-311-0 (ePUB)

I. Title.

PS8576.A42F38 2019   C813'.54
C2018-905341-0   C2018-905342-9

The publication of *Fatboy Fall Down* has been generously supported by the Canada Council for the Arts which last year invested $153 million to bring the arts to Canadians throughout the country and is funded in part by the Government of Canada. *Nous remercions le Conseil des arts du Canada de son soutien. L'an dernier, le Conseil a investi 153 millions de dollars pour mettre de l'art dans la vie des Canadiennes et des Canadiens de tout le pays. Ce livre est financé en partie par le gouvernement du Canada.* We acknowledge the support of the Ontario Arts Council (OAC), an agency of the Government of Ontario, which last year funded 1,737 individual artists and 1,095 organizations in 223 communities across Ontario for a total of $52.1 million. We also acknowledge the contribution of the Government of Ontario through the Ontario Book Publishing Tax Credit, and through Ontario Creates for the marketing of this book.

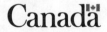

PRINTED AND BOUND IN CANADA   PRINTING: FRIESENS   5 4 3 2 1

MIX
Paper from responsible sources
FSC® C016245

WHEN HE WAS FIFTY-EIGHT years old and preparing for his retirement in a slumberous cocoa village nestled within a valley's crook, Orbits would look at the parakeets, so tiny and green they could be mistaken, from a distance, for skittering leaves, and he would recall his dream of reading the weather report with a macaw perched on his shoulder. The bungalow, its walls wrinkled by vines that trailed from the lemon and guava trees and seemed to glide into the open windows, he had coveted for half his life, and his ease in acquiring it at an affordable price encouraged him into speculating about other long-delayed pursuits.

He would visit his daughter, whom he had not heard from nor seen for over a decade. He would populate the pond at the back of his house with red tilapia and augment the yard with fruit trees — cashews, mangoes, custard apples, cherries and plums. He would attend to his growing vision problems and finally finish his meteorology course. All of this, he mentioned in letters to Wally, his old friend from the Ministry of Agriculture. It was Wally who, before his relocation to Toronto, had introduced him to life in the capital and who had explained how aspects of the island's past had ingrained themselves into a culture of lime and unexpected generosity always twinned with reproach. Wally, too, had noted that the faddishness of the boom years did not completely displace the old way of thinking: the refusal to be persuaded, the childish presumptuousness, the nursing of grudges, the fear of competition, the absolute dread of being ignored.

Wally's heart attack had preceded Orbits' by a few years, and in a letter, Orbits had joked about both men resting side by side on hospital beds. But Wally had survived his heart attack.

In the evenings, Orbits walked across the yard of the old shop where tufts of knotgrass sprouted from concrete and asphalt and he mentioned his plans to the sceptical shopkeeper. "Just a few months again for my pension," he told the shopkeeper. "I have my bucket list."

The shopkeeper, offended by Orbits' optimism, replied, "Careful the bucket don't tumble down the hill and take you with it. Remember what happen to Jack and the other miserable little one." The shopkeeper knew Orbits only as a local politician of negligible importance, an unremarkable man trying to be remarkable. If Orbits, in an uncharacteristic burst of candour, had described the torment that marked his childhood and which had left both scars and a faltering imagination; if he had spoken of the events that had forced him to return to his parents' house following his brother's suicide, only to witness the life squeezed out of both; if he had mentioned that for most of his life, always expecting rejection, he was forever preparing for it; if he had confessed any of this, the shopkeeper, a tiny man with an unevenly shaped moustache and bristly eyebrows that gave him a harried and reflective look, would not have seen Orbits as any different from anyone in the island.

But Orbits had grown to see himself as different, and separate. For most of his life he had little idea of what the future might bring; he never planned for anything and when a little slice of luck fell his way, he briefly imagined it was the world settling itself, balancing the turmoil of his early years.

～

YET, AT THE BEGINNING of his life, before the birth of his brother, he never suspected there was anything unusual or shameful about himself. There was nothing unnatural about the rolls of supple fat that hung from his waist and which his mother pinched and tickled whenever he fell from the sofa or the front stairs. Or with his father's amused comment, "Clear the road, Mamoose. The steamroller coming through." He assumed the responses of his parents to his weight and clumsiness were normal and that in every house in the village, there were little fatties like him rolling around to the amusement of the adults.

Then, a few months prior to his fifth birthday, his slim and perfect brother was born. And shortly after, he was sent off to school. He expected he might find there some variation of his parents' jolliness, but he discovered that school was a place of hardened bullies and frustrated teachers waiting patiently for students like him while they nursed their hangovers. He also learned quickly that it was a bad idea to run away from the other boys because invariably he tumbled on the road, drawing even more ridicule. One day while he was trying to pull himself from the slippery mud, a group of boys pretended to be applauding his effort. As he rolled back and forth to get some traction, one of them said, "It look like Fatso rocking himself to sleep."

"Like a little piggy."

"Oink oink."

When he came home, his blue shirt was smeared and there were

3

two clumps of hardened mud like horns on his forehead. "I not going to school again," he declared.

"And where exactly you want to go?" his father asked genially.

Orbits had always believed that if a genie or *prate* granted him a single wish he would ask for the power to float. Not to swoop across the sky with his hands punching the air and one calf raised like Superman but to gently glide on cushions of air, feeling the warmth of the feathery clouds as they tickled his toes. He didn't care about shooting beams from his eyes or web from his fingers, and he was unimpressed by super strength or dazzling speed. He just wanted to float above everyone.

Before he could answer, his mother said in a joking voice, "Look at your clothes, boy. You playing steamroller again?"

"Only frogs does play in the mud," his father said in a reflective voice as if he were introducing a solemn guest. "Or maybe is toad. To me the two is the same. Don't know why they have to give different name to the exact same things. Halligator and crocodile. Turtle and morrocoy. Goat and sheep. Toad, frog and—"

"Crappo!" the mother exploded. She hoisted her son into the air and asked with each catch, "Who is a crappo? Who is a little crappo?" Orbits was certain his brother in mid-air pointed to him.

In Orbits' second year at school, a teacher brought a bottle filled with squirming tadpoles and instructed the class, over the following days, to watch the bottle while he slept off his hangovers. The girls seemed both entranced and disgusted by the big heads and the little flicking tails and Orbits, alone among the students, wondered whether these ugly little things would transform into dainty creatures the way the subject of another project, a lumpy caterpillar, had metamorphosed into a butterfly. He was deeply disappointed to learn the tadpoles' future was the frogs kicked around by the boys when a football was not handy. He felt no grief when the teacher emptied the bottle beside one of the latrines. Maybe the slimy tadpoles deserved

4

their fate. He got that notion from the principal of the school, a man whose habit of scratching his crotch had landed him the nickname Master Crab. During an assembly, following the closure of the school for a week because of an infestation of bats, the students returning to twitching, bloodied mammals on the floor and desks, Master Crab had tried to soothe the disgusted girls by saying that it was okay to kill animals like bats and pigs and frogs because they were ugly. "God made them ugly for a reason," he had said. "That is why is a capital offence to interfere with a peacock."

One year later, Orbits got the nickname which would stick for the duration of his life. His mother was breastfeeding his brother who, at four years, was half Orbits' age, and his father was at the table vigorously attacking a bowl of gizzard, shaking his head like a shaggy dog to get a proper bite. Both parents were listening to a radio news item about the unplanned crash landing of a Russian satellite. His father said, "I wish that thing could land right in the backyard. We could salvage the radio and seatbelts and all the rows of bulbs. Or if it still good, we could paint it over and sell fruits from it. Everybody will rush to buy. Eh, Mamoose? Big fancy sign saying fruits from outer space. Moon mango and Pluto pineapple."

Orbits' mother never knew whether her husband was joking or serious, and in both instances, she used the same rejoinder, "You and all your fancy ideas, Papoose."

Orbits wanted to say that it was a stupid idea because the lab would be destroyed before it touched ground, but his little brother beat him to it. He loosened his lips from around his mother's nipples and recited in a clacking voice, "Papoose-Mamoose-brother-moose."

Orbits could predict the stupid bantering that would ensue. He hated the stupid nicknames his parents used for each other, and he was fed up of his little brother, who seemed to be conniving with the entire world to make his life miserable. And his mother said, "Hush, baby. Your daddy not going to do anything but settle on his hammock."

His father, who had finally defeated his plate of gizzard, placed his meat-eating dentures next to the pile of rugged rubbery bits that had his resisted chewing and looked like a tattered bolt of canvas. While adjusting his thinner and lighter dessert dentures, his father said, "That is where I get my best ideas, Mamoose. Like for instance, how this thing that floating for dozens of years suddenly decide to drop to earth. Sometimes, is one little nut or bolt that cause the big problem. Something that didn't tighten properly. I wonder how much nuts and washers a helicopter have? More than a washing machine, you think? The two is nearly the same. Uppers and lowers."

The father was an impractical salvager who packed junk all around the house and in every corner within, but recently, most of his ideas had begun to revolve around local materials for his business as a denturist, for which he had gotten the name Swallows. The name had been given because of a series of denture accidents, but it suited the father who, with his narrow chest above his gently pushed-out belly and his thin feet, looked like an elongated bird. The feeder, birdlike too with his insistent beaky lips, looked at his mother expectantly, but before she could say anything, Orbits cut in. "I want to float."

"Boy, you too fat to float," his father said. "You have the correct round shape for floating, but you too heavy." The feeder giggled and Orbits felt, as he had so many times, the urge to pluck him from his mother's breast and fling him straight through the window to land on the banga tree outside.

"But didn't the Buddha used to float?" his mother asked mischievously. "That is a nice name for you. Little Buddha." The mother, who had a sturdy body set upon thin legs, more yard fowl than flight bird, glanced down at the feeder. "Boo Baby Bumkins. Buddha gone a humkins." The feeder gurgled malevolently at his mother's jumbled joke.

Orbits recognized the mood and regretted saying anything. He should learn to keep his silence at home, as he had at his school, where protracted bullying by the other boys and the teachers had stiffened him into an almost mute butterball. Still, he couldn't resist saying, "Anybody could float. Is different from flying. Look at all these big goose. I thinking of it a long time now."

"Float like the . . ." His mother began to convulse like a fowl shaking off dirt and the feeder's head was thrown left to right. Orbits watched his brother's fingers clutching air and thought of a frog climbing a wall. "Like the . . ."

The father offered a pre-emptive laugh. "Like the . . ." he encouraged.

"Michelin man!" the mother exploded.

After the laughter had died, the father said, "Boy, your head always in the cloud. You have to come down from that orbit."

"Look who talking now," the mother said. "You and Orbits no different."

And so, he got his name.

It was not a name he disliked, and because he preferred it to his nicknames at school, he was relieved when word got around and everyone began to call him Orbits.

~~~

HE HAD ALWAYS LIVED in dread of the walk from his house to the school, and each morning and evening, he tried to forget the nicknames and the bullying by focusing on the buildings rather than their taunting inhabitants. If he were older and less traumatized, he might have noticed that every house had a different shape: some were tall and angular like lighthouses, others squat like pillboxes and yet others were roundish with many windows and doors or rectangular with multiple pillars and arches. He may have noticed not only the profusion of fruity, flavescent colours that tickled his appetite but the range of building materials. Houses were built from concrete and brick, brick alone, cedar and teak, corrugated aluminium and ply-board. All were incomplete, even the elaborate structures, and this incompleteness gave the street the air both of stagnation and progress. As he hurried along, he wished he were living on another street, in another village. I wish Mamoose and Papoose could move somewhere else, he thought, as he struggled up the slight incline before his house. Even a small house.

But Orbits' street was no different from those in all the other villages in the island. Here as elsewhere, wealth was displayed as prominently and with the same pride as grinding poverty, and a house was the most visible representation of status. The house in which he grew up was of middle size and ambition and a passing traveller might see it and know that its occupants were not farmers or tradespeople, nor were they contractors or proprietors. The traveller might guess at a profession, perhaps teaching, and he or she would not have been far off the mark.

Orbits' father was a self-taught dentist. Every village had its own quack and they were expected to extract teeth, install fillings and scrape tongues as well as fashion dentures. His father's lab was not in the village but in a town about five miles away. To get there, the father had to get a taxi at the junction, which was an intersection of parlours and a small dry goods shop opposite two rumshops. When his father had opened his office eighteen years earlier, the town had been a place of family-run stores, but over the years, all the gaps and spaces between the buildings were stuffed with parlours and stalls, some just eight feet wide. These cubicles were congested with limers smoking and *sooting* the passing schoolgirls. Orbits' school was in the opposite direction and on his way there, he felt he was sinking deeper into the village, the opportunity for escape lessening with each footstep. After some brutal day, he would say, "I finish with school."

And his mother would reply, "Don't worry, Chunkalunka, that baby fat will melt off just now."

It increased every year. So Orbits was relieved when the new nickname stuck, and to ensure it would not be displaced, he would stop suddenly on the road and look up. Once in a while, he shaped his hand like a gun and shot away the birds that were obscuring his view of the sky and of the clouds. Occasionally, a housewife would watch him from the window and ask, "What the fat boy staring up at the sky like he crazy?"

And the husband would reply, "Oh, that is Orbits. His father is the quack. Swallows."

As the years passed and he went from one school to the other, skipping classes and failing most of his exams, the name suited him even more. Teachers were especially cruel to him, and it was because of this group that he missed classes. During his first year at a high school, the teacher, an aristocratic whiskered man who walked like a general, lectured the class about students who had failed all their exams and who were herded into private schools like this, clogging up the classrooms. These students would forever be burdens, to their parents, to teachers like himself and to the island. "Look at this beast here hiding something in his hand and eating." The teacher, nicknamed Snakebelt because of the way he smoothly slipped off his belt, pointed his rod at Orbits. "Come up boy and let me see what you gobbling."

A month earlier Orbits had developed grainy warts on his fingers. His father's sulphurous concoction, rather than removing the warts, had hardened them into thick brown scabs. Orbits had discovered that each time he bit off the scabs the warts grew smaller.

"What is your name, boy?" When Orbits remained silent, he added, "You don't have a name? Eh." He swished his rod against his pants.

"My name is Orbits."

"What you say, boy? Horrific? Orifice?" With every mispronunciation, the class bellowed.

"Orbits," he said quietly.

"Who give you that name, boy?"

9

"My father."

"Is it him who patched up that shoe to resemble an alligator?" Orbits' father's penchant for inventive repairs extended to shoes, bookbags and uniform. Orbits tried to hide the offending shoe by crossing his legs and almost fell again. The class erupted.

"Yes, sir," he said, his eyes burning.

"You know why he give you that Orbits name? Is because he wish you was far away from him. Is because he know that gobblers like you will bring down the entire family because of your *lickrishness*. Now open your hand and let me see what you was eating. Both hands!" Reluctantly Orbits pushed out his hands. The teacher got up from his desk. "You blasted little cannibal. Is flesh you like to eat? Well, I going to help you with that. What you waiting for? Continue eating." Orbits looked at his fingers and at the teacher and at the howling class. "Eh? Your belly full." He repeated the sentence each time he brought down his rod on Orbits' hand, on the scabs he had been gnawing at. "Go and stand at the back of the class." When Orbits was walking to the back, a boy pushed out his leg and he tumbled. The teacher's annoyance changed to amusement. "Fatboy fall down," he said, and the class erupted.

Orbits' warts eventually dropped off, but for months afterwards, he heard the taunt, "Fatboy fall down," in the corridors. Followed sometimes by, "Gobble gobble."

～

DURING A BRUTAL MORNING in school he packed his bookbag and headed for the taxi stand. On his way he stopped by a street vendor. While he was eating his fifth aloo pie, he noticed couples streaming to a nearby cinema for the day's matinee, a double feature. He realized his parents would ask why he had returned so early, so he joined the group. On his way home, he recalled how wiry the heroes were, how fat the comic extras, how gluttonous the villains, and he wondered if those were the only two options for him. Clown or villain. He glanced at himself in the taxi's rear-view mirror and saw a face that seemed to be disfigured by a flurry of short jabs and then hurriedly fluffed and patted back into place. He saw himself as grotesque, but somewhere within the swelling and bumps, there was an okay-looking young man. Perhaps it was his eyes, alert, sensitive, whispering. But his eyes were always clouded with shame whenever he passed anyone of his own age

High school brought other types of anxieties. He gazed longingly at the pretty girls, noticed how they flirted demurely with the boys, hitching up their skirts and looking up so their eyes appeared rounder, the way their expressions soured whenever he approached, their relief when he walked past them. Even when he transferred to another private school, he imagined the students murmuring among themselves, "Fatboy fall down." In each new school, he looked around for limpers, lispers, stutterers, other fatties, boys with missing toes, girls with extra fingers, those who were cross-eyed or rabbit-eared — anyone who could take the focus off him. In the aftermath of these moments, struck with guilt and ashamed that he would wish his torment on others, he began to get a whiff of the sly, conniving cowardice of the weak and the picked-upon. He suspected the other misfits had likely felt the same way about him and had held off on any friendship for the same reason: they would just make a bigger target.

Maybe they, too, were sustained by little fantasies, he thought. One afternoon, a boy everyone called Sixtoe Changoe, who claimed that his extra toes gave him the ability to land on his feet like Beast from the *X-Men* comics, was seized by a group and dragged to a mango tree that inclined above a shallow muddy ravine. There he was swung like a bag of potatoes by four boys and let loose on the ravine ten feet beneath. He landed on his head, and when the boys saw his limp body floating downstream, they ran away. He reappeared in school two days later with a missing tooth and a deep gash on his cheek where he had hit a rock. For a short while, his disfigurement was forgiven while the boys speculated as to how he had managed to survive. There was even some grudging admiration. One boy said, "Six toes and a mashup face. Maybe he have some kind of catfish gill too." When Orbits heard the talk, he wondered if he would finally be accepted if he floated down from the school's roof or one of the telephone poles. But he could never extend this illusion because his fantasy had always been floating from rather than towards everyone.

Whenever he was struck by this particular thought, he was reminded of the teacher's comment that his father wished he were far away. He made an effort to please the older man, listening to his dinner table conversation, which was mostly about teeth. Although his father spoke in his usual solemn manner, his mother laughed at all his descriptions, and when she eventually got up to clear the table, his father would still be mumbling about ownway teeth, blocky donkey teeth, pointed *guabeen* teeth and gums that had hardened into an enamel consistency. One evening Orbits heard him murmuring about a man called Gramophone.

"Why was he given that name?" Orbits asked.

His father replied absent-mindedly, "Because he have only one teeth in the middle of his mouth like a gramophone needle. But he don't want to pull that out so I have to make a denture around it."

"You could do that?"

From the kitchen, his mother said, "Like Orbits following you in the profession. Just now everybody will call him Swallows Junior."

Orbits briefly considered the name and decided it was associated too much with eating and weight. "I prefer Orbits," he said softly.

His brother came out from his room to say, "Quack and Son. You could put that on the sign outside the office."

"Hush, boy," his mother said, chuckling.

Two months later, Orbits was apprenticed in the dental lab. He was horrified by the clamps and rusty pliers and little mallets that looked like medieval torture implements, by the clinging odour of resins and crazy glue, by the bawling of the women as his father tugged and grunted and the bloody wads of cotton they spat from their swollen cheeks into the bin. The dentures his father boiled in a big pot resembled frantic crabs, and Orbits imagined them unexpectedly crawling around the mouths of their new owners, pinching and biting. One morning, he saw his father bent over a woman rocked back on the chair, her eyes huge unblinking balls. His father's foot was between her legs which were twisting in unison with his wrists. "Hand me the pliers, quick-sharp," he said to Orbits. But Orbits was frozen by the sight of the woman's legs now flapping with pain and imprisoning his father's foot. Afterwards, his father told him, "Boy, you have to come down to earth soon. You not good in school and not good in this business. What will happen to you? What is it you really want to do?"

Orbits briefly considered all the professions he associated with floating, but he recalled the derision of his various teachers when he had mentioned astronaut, pilot and explorer. He thought of a teacher in primary school, a blue-black man with a bald head so smooth it appeared malleable. The teacher had told him in a reflective voice, "An explorer, eh? Take care you don't land up in some jungle. The cannibals will like that. Fat to last a whole month." The class had exploded and Orbits, as always, had headed straight to the roadside vendor when the bell rang. The only people who displayed anything other than contempt were the vendors who began slapping their doubles in place whenever he approached. "Tell me when to stop, Fatboy." The comforting experience of the oily doubles gathering saliva, fluffing out, trailing down his throat and filling his stomach temporarily displaced his shame. He usually asked the vendors to stop after six or seven doubles.

One day a visitor to his father's lab, a dark-skin man with a Bermuda hat and a yellow floral shirt, told Orbits, "You have good teeth. You know how I guess that?" Orbits began to smile but the man added, "Your belly tell me that. You must have good teeth to pitch all that material down there." Later, the visitor mentioned to Orbits' father a business he was beginning. "Lots of tourists just walking around in short pants and slippers like if they lost. In the meantime, it have all these wonderful sights all over the place."

Later that night, the father repeated some of these sights to his family. Botanic gardens brimming with exotic plants. Parks with waterslides and picnic sheds overlooking streams filled with leaping fishes. Bird hiking trails filled with musical surprises. Beaches where the leatherback turtles lumbered like behemoths in the nights to lay their eggs. "The man make me want to see these places with my very own eyes," the father said.

"That man just showing off," Orbits' brother, who had grown up to be a remarkably critical teenager, said. "Nobody going to waste money to see a place with only rubbish and dead dogs."

"I think they keep these places clean for the foreigners," the mother said. "Just like how they push all these people from the shanty town behind the big wall whenever it have some fancy event."

"I would like to work with that man." Orbits was not sure why he made the bold statement. He was seventeen years and eleven months old and he had no discernible talent. His brother, the former feeder, was the opposite of him in every way. He was forthright, confident, censorious and thin. His mother claimed it was the breast milk, and she doted upon him in a way that made Orbits, who could not recall any similar treatment, wonder if he had been adopted.

The brother said, "None of these places up in the clouds, you know."

"Don't say these things, Starboy," the mother said, trying to hide her mirth.

"The man will be coming next week for his teeth. Five uppers and six lowers. He asked for the two front teeth to be bigger than the others to take the pressure off his jaw. I will talk to him. Rabbit is his name."

AND SO ORBITS BECAME a tour guide. The first week he was sent to the swamp. The boatman said, "Watch all the overhanging branches for snakes. And don't hang your hand outside the boat. The alligators will like that. We going full steam ahead in search of the fabled pink flamingoes." Two hours later, he said in a grumbling voice to the passengers, none of whom were tourists, "These birds getting too smart. Is like they playing a cat and mouse game with humans now. Laughing at us. I have a good mind to wring the neck of the next flamingo I see." By then Orbits and everyone else were scratching the mosquito bumps on their bodies.

When the riverboat was docked, the boatman asked Orbits, "What kind of tour guide you is? You didn't say one single word for the entire trip."

Orbits thought of what he could have said. The sun is hot. The water is muddy. The mosquitoes and bugs must have eaten the flamingoes. The boatman wouldn't shut up. But as usual, he said nothing.

On the second trip, he improved to one utterance. "The lady vomiting," he shouted to the boatman.

"Lady, please lean over and vomit in the water. Not in my clean boat."

"What about the halligators?" the husband asked.

"Halligator? What is a halligator? I never see one of them in my entire life." His sarcasm spluttered as the woman issued a stream of green matter. Later, as Orbits was cleaning the boat of vomit and mud, the boatman told him, "Mahatma Gandhi rightly say that human animals far worse than animal humans." Orbits was certain he had just made that up just as he had invented all the ibises and flamingoes and golden ducks that somehow managed to remain hidden during the trips. When Orbits was finished with his cleaning, the boatman told him, "You have to give these people hope. These people don't care if they don't see the thing they come to see once it have a small chance that the thing they come to see is not the thing they didn't come to see. You understand? Why you shaking you head for? As Mahatma Gandhi rightly say, the two eyes of a doubting man could never meet at the same spot because they forever travelling in opposite direction."

"He really say that?"

"What the hell you asking me? You think I is a liar? Why you don't go and ask him yourself."

"I think he dead," Orbits said timidly. "A long time ago."

The boatman shouted to a group gathering for a trip. "Everybody listen to this. This fatboy here gone and kill Mahatma Gandhi." They began to laugh, and Orbits felt a familiar shame bubbling through his fat. The mangrove looked like spindly limbed beasts snickering at him.

During the following trips, he kept his eyes on the clouds. They seemed so soft and malleable and fluffy. He watched as the furry bits joined and became something new and how at the end of the day, a little portion seemed to catch fire. He thought of a big pot hidden behind a curtain and frying all sorts of delicacies. At the end of one trip, the boatman told him in a low voice, "I notice you looking up in the sky whole day and I have to tell you that is not really bird season now. Is mosquito and sandfly season. If you didn't figure that out, then you is a bigger backside than I first thought. Furthermore, you not doing your job properly. I tired tell you that every time we pass a bend, you must shout out, 'Ibis ahoy.' And when people start watching tell them it dive in a hole for no rhyme and reason. Tell them it shy. Tell them it pregnant. Tell them any damn thing you want but tell them something."

The following week, they came across a snake sliding across an over-hanging branch. "The fabled swamp cobra," the boatman said.

"A cobra? In this place? It don't have any cobra here. Who put a cobra here?"

Orbits felt he had to say something because the speaker, a man with drooping whiskers and eyes, was looking at him sleepily. "It look like a horsewhip," he said softly.

The boatman glanced darkly at him. At the end of the trip, he threw his cigarette into the swampy water and lit another. "I don't think you cut out for this job. You is just ballast. How much you weighing? Two hundred? Two fifty?"

"I don't know." Orbits was close to tears and he turned away to clean the opposite end of the boat so the boatman wouldn't notice.

Later that evening, he stopped at a street vendor and ordered three doubles. He moved to another vendor and asked for a shark and bake sandwich and a sea moss drink. He topped off the sand-wich with a six-inch wedge of *pone*, a sticky cassava cake. When he was finished, he bought a calabash mango and a bag of governor plums that he ate in the taxi. As always, the fullness in his belly spread throughout his body and displaced the shame and uncer-tainty. The next morning, he decided to fortify himself by stopping at the street vendors before he arrived in the swamp. An hour later, he felt the undigested food churning with the boat's rocking. He heard the boatman saying, "That bird over they is the famous Canadian goose. They build for winters."

"So what they doing in this hot swamp?" a man with his lower lip hanging over his chin asked. The man's protruding lower lip made him appear short-tempered and erratic.

"Vacation," the boatman said testily.

"You think maybe one of them tourist leave a pair behind and they breed here?" A short chubby man with his arms clasped tightly around a frightened girl asked.

"They have wings. They does fly," the boatman said abruptly as if he wanted to finish the conversation.

Orbits wished the trip would end. The muddy water and the acrid aroma of the swamp added to his nausea. He heard someone saying, "If you ask me is a ordinary common duck."

"Time to go back," the boatman said. He turned the boat suddenly and Orbits was flung to the side. When he got up, he vomited on an old woman. The woman, who was loaded with gold bracelets and who had been badgered by her husband into making the trip, was gripping the sides of the boat nervously when Orbits' vomit landed on her head.

At the end of the trip, the boatman displayed a surprising equanimity. He delivered a rambling account of Mahatma Gandhi's allergy to salt and his periods of fasting during which he was joined by Richard Attenborough and Ben Kingsley. Orbits had already figured out that following each trip, the boatman drank liberally from a bottle of Puncheon rum, so he listened quietly. His belly was grumbling again and as the boatman added other notables to the fast, Orbits was forced to rush away. The last words he heard from the boatman were a familiar assessment: "You don't belong here, Fatboy. You useless. Go and learn some fat people trade. Making basket or something. Tailoring. Selling toolum."

That evening for the first time, he passed the street vendors straight. And later in the evening, as he stared at the bowls of fried plantain and curried goat and at the aloo pies and other oily delicacies his mother usually cooked for dinner, he felt his queasiness returning. "What happen, Orbits? You not feeling well or what?" his mother asked.

Orbits continued staring at the food.

Starboy said, "He probably filled up at one of these nasty doubles place."

"I hope you didn't pick up anything from the swamp. All these mosquitoes could be spreading dengue and Ebola and leper and god knows what else."

The father flicked away a piece of gristle caught in his dentures. "This swamp work don't suit you, boy. I will talk to Mr. Rabbit and tell him to send you some other place."

And that was how Orbits landed in the caves after seven months in the swamp. The swamp tours were undertaken mostly by bored couples and men trying to work out their hangovers and people who wanted to escape the bustle of the cities for an hour or so. But the cave tours were filled with schoolchildren whose detour there was part of a trip that involved the soft drink factories and the botanic gardens and the zoo. They were rowdy and rude and Orbits' job was to meet them at the bus parking area, about a half-mile downhill, and escort them to the caves. They were always accompanied by one or two teachers who constantly shouted to the children about running ahead and who, once they got into the caves, lost control entirely.

The crystallized limestone caves were filled with slushy water and the chinks and pockets between the jagged stalagmites were teeming with hidden life. The boys and girls scampered around, pelting the bats and oilbirds and squealing when they flew too close. Eventually, the children were forced out not through the bawling of the teachers but because of the bat guano. On their way down to the bus, they were all peaceful and subdued from inhaling the noxious dust. Orbits discovered two serious fears while deep in the caves: first, he was claustrophobic, and second, he was afraid of creatures flapping about in the dark. These phobias grew by the day. But there was another transformation taking place, one that he had fantasized about all his life. This change had begun on his last day at the swamp when, overcome by the effect of the rocking on the oily street food in his belly, he had vomited on a passenger's head. That nausea never left him, and it was compounded by the queasiness induced by the bat guano. He realized that street food — greasy, salty, fatty — intensified the feeling while fruits lessened it somewhat. So entirely by accident, he fell into the habit of healthy eating.

The fat melted and it was quite dramatic. His mother noticed and pestered him about diseases and routinely examined his neck for bat bites. She extended her examination to his hands and shoulders when Starboy said that only vampire bats from movies chose the neck. His father said, "The boy passing through some sort of *tabanca*, Mamoose. Just now he will get back nice and roly-poly."

During the trek to the cave, Orbits felt his body loosening as if the blood vessels, bones and tendons, imprisoned for so long by layers of lard, had sprung free. Once, he had been forced into a wide-legged gunfighter's walk to prevent chafing on his inner thighs, but now his steps were longer and occasionally he surprised himself by nimbly stepping over a crevice or boulder rather than laboriously navigating his way around. The pimples on his face and neck grew smaller and smaller until he no longer felt the urge to squeeze and pick them.

About ten months after he began his work as a tour guide in the caves, a pack of unruly children was released from a bus. Orbits heard shouting from within. "Everybody make sure you remember the rules. If anybody get lost, they damn well lost for good. Furthermore, if anybody get bite, don't come running to me but walk out of the cave and look for the bus. And finally, we leaving at three sharp and who not here will spend the night in the cave. The bats will like that."

When the teacher from the bus emerged, Orbits recognized him as a student from one of his high schools. He had been in a higher form and had been a relentless bully. He would stand outside the school compound with a group of other boys smoking and *sooting* the girls. Whenever he saw Orbits, he would say things like, "Run, is a earthquake," or, "How you does iron you clothes, Fatboy? With a steamroller?" Orbits felt some of the old shame, but the teacher did not recognize him. "You is the guide?" he asked. When Orbits nodded, he fished into his pocket and withdrew a pack of cigarettes. "You better go up with them. I will come later." He lit a cigarette, inhaled and immediately coughed into his elbow.

Orbits noticed the teacher's nicotine-stained teeth and his red stale-drunk eyes. "Okay, but is against the rules to enter the caves without the teacher. We will wait for you on the hill."

"Don't bother with that. You have my permission."

"Okay. But I will have to write it up in my report book."

"Eh? Report book? What the hell this country coming to now?" The teacher quarrelled with his students the entire time they were in the cave and when the group emerged, Orbits noticed the teacher's trouser muddy at the knees. He had fallen somewhere inside, and there was a patch of mud on his nose, too. Orbits wondered how he had been so terrified of this person. Some of the other teachers pretended allergies to avoid the muddy descent into the cave and there were times when, remembering how he had been treated at school, he could not help feeling some glee as they emerged from the tunnel miserable and muddy.

It took a while to adjust to the smattering of respect given to him, and he still felt a kinship to the occasional fat student sulking in a corner, pretending to be allergic to the guano or muddy water or sick from the bus trip. He tried to urge these students and was confused and even irritated by their sturdy defences. During one trip, a girl he had encouraged into the cave emerged in tears. Her hair was streaked with mud. The teacher told her, "Is your fault for going in places that you not suited for. Who tell you to go?"

"I did," Orbits said. "We couldn't leave her by herself out here."

The teacher looked Orbits up and down. "I see. *You* encourage her to go but is *I* who have to explain to the mother why the little . . . the little thing come back nasty like a hog." That brought a fresh burst of crying from the girl. Orbits felt all of his old hatred of teachers rising to the surface as he walked towards the bus. He tried to keep this anger in check during other trips. One evening on his way back to the taxi stand he thought of the job at the swamp, where the sky was always blue and clotted with clouds of every shape, and his current job, which obscured everything but the jagged walls and the muddy water. Yet he enjoyed this job far more and once, while he was striding to the taxi stand, he thought that if someone, just two years earlier, had mentioned that he would be sprinting up and down the hill, skipping over boulders, breathing naturally, not wheezing, he would have seen that vision as close to impossible.

≻⊶≺

A YEAR AND A half after he began working at the caves, a young female teacher told him, "This is my first excursion, so please help me keep an eye on these students." Orbits was surprised because even though he had been commanded or tricked into common tasks, no one had requested his help so respectfully. So he spoke to the students firmly and when they strayed too far, he reminded them of water snakes or if they lingered at the end of the tour, he told them that bat guano in large doses was poisonous. "It will stunt your growth to three feet," he said, repeating a teacher's warning a month earlier. "And your ears will begin to resemble bat wings." He added another teacher's invention.

While they were walking down the hill, the teacher asked Orbits, "Will that really happen? They will change into bats?"

"No . . . I was just . . ."

"I know it's not true," she said with a tinkle in her voice. "And thanks so much for the help, Mr. . . ."

He hesitated for a while before he said, "Orbits."

She smiled and stroked her hair. "This country and its nicknames! Even I have a nickname." They continued walking and she added, "You not going to ask me?"

"Ask you what?"

"What is my nickname, silly? Okay, don't ask. I will tell you." She leaned closer and whispered, "It's Miss Teapot."

Orbits looked at her. He saw a slim woman with a puckish nose and big eyes in a perfectly framed face. "But you don't look like a teapot."

She giggled. "I should hope not. It's from a poem I used to recite at school when I was a child. Little children can be such bullies." Orbits looked at her again; he was struck by her wisdom. She returned his gaze and he looked away. "Why do they call you Orbits?"

"I wanted to be an astro— wanted to be a pilot."

"Oh gosh. That's amazing. Everyone here seems to have such limited ambitions. A pilot! Goodness."

A student shouted, "Miss, hurry up. The bus ready to leave. You could talk to your boyfriend later."

"These children!"

Orbits and Miss Teapot were married fourteen months later. He was twenty-two, one year younger than her. During the courtship, conducted mostly in the cinemas and chicken and chips joints, she spoke of her family, her school, the other teachers, the island and the world outside. She was in constant motion, stroking her hair, leaning forward and backward, rubbing his wrists, laughing at something she had just said, rolling her eyes. Orbits always felt shy during these sessions and he said little.

But Miss Teapot didn't seem to notice. In the cinema, she guided his hands to her breasts, pinned her lips against his and forked her tongue into his mouth. She misunderstood his shyness and awkwardness for decorum and once during a movie, she told him, "You just like one of these gunslingers who hardly say a word. Strong and silent and never cracking a single smile. Like John Wayne, who always looks as if he is ready to turn a corner the way he walks. No, not him. He looks like a bully. Maybe Clint Eastwood. My parents will like you for sure."

Parents? Later, his tongue felt limp in her mouth.

Her parents' house was the last in a lane. It was a light-blue concrete flat with a paved driveway and bordered on both sides by zinnias and petunias and with a lawn that was uniformly cut. Inside the T-shaped structure, there were bedrooms on either side of the living room, which was separated from the dining room with an arch directly above a three-foot partition on which were little curios, delicate looking china dolls and other figurines. The kitchen was partially blocked off with a screen of diamond-shaped crystals. Orbits noticed that the house had been built in a modern fashion with none of the abutting cupboards that came in the way of doors and no electrical wires snaking around plumbing pipes as in the house of his parents. He noticed, too, that the minimalism also applied to the furniture: a couch and a recliner on one end of the living room and on the other end, a desk. At his parents' house, every inch was choked up with safes, tables, and shelves. Above the desk, he saw three rows of books, all neatly stacked. There were placemats and rectangular pieces of carpet beneath all the furniture and a rug beneath the glass-topped table in the dining room. Remarkably, the interior was of one colour, a pale yellow that made Orbits think of a quiet Mexican villa.

During his first visit, Miss Teapot told a man who was seated at the desk, reading a newspaper, his glasses low over his face. "Dad, this is the boy."

Orbits felt trapped by all the mats, wondering whether he should step over those that led to the sofa or to the father's desk. The father glanced up and motioned to a nearby sofa. Orbits sat and prepared himself for questioning, but the father returned to his newspapers. A woman emerged from the kitchen and said, "Teepee said you are the quiet kind so don't feel you have to make conversation." She had the same mannerisms as her daughter. "We know everything about you." Orbits considered what they might know but couldn't think of anything other than his former life as a fatboy.

During dinner, served with cutlery and on china plates and cups, mother and daughter chatted about her lesson plans at school and about the students. Orbits was glad the focus was not on him because he was trying to navigate his way around all the tiny bowls of food and properly use his knife and fork. The mother must have noticed because she asked him, "I hope the food is okay. What's your name again?"

"Orbits," Miss Teapot said, and mother and daughter laughed. The father glanced up from his newspaper, which he had brought to the table. He had thin, downturned lips, crinkled like the rim of a broken saucer, and he seemed to be perpetually squinting. "It's not the food. He is a health nut."

"That's good. There are too many lickrish people in this place. When I was still working, I used to pass this doubles vendor and see all these obese people eating doubles after doubles and licking their wrists clean," the mother said. "This country is a feeding ground for diabetes."

"Eew," Miss Teapot said. And to Orbits, "Mom was a teacher. Dad, too, but they retired earlier this year."

"What work do you do?" the father asked.

"He is a field guide and researcher," Miss Teapot said quickly. "He is thinking of opening his own business."

"Business?" The father folded his newspapers slowly.

Orbits could not recall ever mentioning anything about business to Miss Teapot, and he was relieved when the mother asked him about his "studies."

"I am doing a few courses," he said, which was true as Miss Teapot had signed him up for a correspondence course in meteorology, the only thing that caught his fancy in the myriad booklets she had presented him.

"In meteorology," she said. "He always wanted to be a pilot."

"A pilot, you say. 'I know that I shall meet my fate / Somewhere among the clouds above.' It's a line from Yeats. Have you heard it? Or this: 'I sweep the skies with fire and steel / My highway is the cloud / I swoop, I soar, aloft I wheel / My engine laughing loud.'"

"Dad is a true romantic," Miss Teapot said. "That's why he hasn't gotten a phone. Mom is just happy with her books."

"My imagination is my carriage," the father said. "It takes me hither and thither. That is why I surround myself with Russian novels." He gestured idly to a shelf stacked with books so thick Orbits wondered who would have the patience to read through them. "Pushkin. Dostoevsky. Nabokov." He pronounced each word with a little flourish at the end as if he was patting these writers on their backs. Everything was strange about this house: the inhabitants, their language, the furniture, the order. Orbits felt completely out of place and was comforted only by Miss Teapot's ease as if there was nothing unnatural about a stranger finding himself in the middle of this organized cell. At his parents' home, the dinner conversation was confined to his father's elaborate descriptions of dentures followed by his mother's chuckles and her intermittent shouting to Starboy, who always ate in his room. Here, the father continued to talk of his Russian novels. "Pushkin was mixed race. Did you know that?"

"Everyone knows that, Dad," Miss Teapot answered in an amused way. "Dad says the most obvious things," she told Orbits.

Pushkin sounded like a pet name, maybe for a fluffy cat or a sleepy baby. Come Pusskins, come here for some milk. But Orbits nodded. He continued to nod during the dinner and surprisingly felt a bit sleepy. When he was leaving, Miss Teapot asked him, "So when are we going to meet your parents?"

Orbits had not planned for nor even thought of this. He went along with Miss Teapot's invitation to visit her parents only because she had allowed him to feel her up and he had no idea where this was leading or if there was a particular protocol. At that time, marriage or even a permanent relationship was the furthest thing from his mind. "When do you want to come?" he asked, trying to think of some roadblock.

"Next weekend."

"Okay," he said, but the minute he stepped into the taxi, he felt trapped. He contrasted his parents' place with the neat house and landscaped yard he had just left. His father had junk all over the place, his mother still treated him as a fat little child, and his horrible brother was always waiting for an opportunity to condemn. What if his father casually took off his dentures during dinner? What if his mother revealed the reason for his nickname? What if his brother just opened his mouth? Over the following days, he tried to think of some way out. These ranged from telling her they were all struck with dengue or some other contagious disease to avoiding her altogether. He realized these were just temporary measures.

Each day she reminded him of how eager she was to meet his parents, and each day when he got home, his horror grew at what he saw. He tried to clean up the place, adjusting the linoleum to cover the holes on the floor, straightening the safe and the cupboard that jutted out so close to the door he had been forced to pass sideways during his fat period. The day before her visit, he brought doilies that he placed on every piece of furniture.

His mother asked, "Orbits, you feeling alright? Don't tell me that you and all hearing voices." She was referring to the postman who claimed that voices in his head had been directing him to regularly throw the mails into a river. The voices stopped after he received a solid licking from the villagers.

"Maybe the boy have a little chick that he invite over, Mamoose. A little chickadee," the father said. "A nice little craft."

Starboy's sarcastic comment about the unlikelihood of a girlfriend was drowned by the mother's laughter. "A nice roly-poly little girlfriend." She still made these fat jokes although at that point, Orbits was the slimmest and healthiest in the family.

"Yes, I invite somebody over so please behave like civilized people for a few hours. Then you could all go back to being savages. Pusskins would be ashamed of you." They all stood still. His father began to tongue-swish his denture in his mouth as he usually did when he was thinking deeply, and his mother's mouth was open, but nothing came out. Orbits went into his room and pulled the blanket over his head.

The next evening in the taxi, he tried to prepare Miss Teapot. His parents were simple and honest, he said. They were frugal and hard-working. Then he changed his mind and said they were always joking. He recalled a word used by her father and said they were addicted to bantering. He tried to think of other plasters, but his family seemed irredeemable. He visualized multiple scenes, each more embarrassing than the other, but when he entered the house he was dumbfounded.

His father was in his lab coat stained red and green, with his legs crossed, his mother was wearing some kind of wedding gown, and Starboy was in short pants and socks like a tourist. They were arrayed on the sofa as if they were posing for a photograph. Worse was to come: in their effort to appear cultured they had adopted confusing accents that ranged from Indian to Cockney to southern American.

"It is veddy nice to be meeting you," the father said. Orbits noticed he was wearing a new chalk-white denture, prominently displayed because of his fixed smile.

The mother got up and held out her hand limply. "Most pleased to make your acquaintance, I can assure you." She, too, had a frozen smile that, coupled with her makeup, gave her a corpse-like appearance.

Thankfully, Starboy remained seated, scowling at nothing in particular.

"Would y'all care to join us at the table," the mother said. "It would be my utmost pleasure."

The food, too, was a surprise; instead of oily fried vegetables, the bowls contained wedges of boiled pumpkin and breadfruit, macaroni threaded with sliced meat, and an array of fruits. After each gulp, his father said, "Veddy nice."

Miss Teapot, who had been stunned into speechlessness so far, recovered to say, "Wow. This is very good. You must have taken ages to prepare all of this."

"It is mah pleasure," the mother said. "Try some of the soufflah."

"And the ghote meat," the father added. "Veddy nice ghote."

Orbits began to feel a slight relief.

Then Starboy asked, "So I hear you are a teacher. Is that correct?"

"Yes, at a primary school. Common Entrance class."

"Veddy nice."

"I think exams are a waste of time. Just rote learning. Does nothing to improve the mind."

Orbits knew his brother was being contentious, but Miss Teapot said, "I can see your point. All the students suffer from stress. It's so competitive, especially among the parents."

"I am waiting on my A-level results. The first in the family, but I don't care if I pass or fail. This country doesn't respect originality."

"What subjects did you take?"

"Chemistry, biology and physics. Useless."

Miss Teapot turned to the mother. "You all must be so proud. Such bright children. One a scientist and the other almost a pilot."

The two most frightful scenarios Orbits had imagined were his brother showing off and his father having a denture accident. And that was exactly what happened, but one disaster cancelled out the other. When his father's denture fell on the table, Miss Teapot began to giggle.

The father replaced it in his mouth, stretching his lips this way and that and smacking his tongue. "Isn't that ironic?" Miss Teapot said. "Orbits told me you were a dentist."

"Irony is in the eye of the beholder," Starboy said sourly. But his moment had passed. Miss Teapot began to act in a more familiar manner. She mentioned her parents, who were retired, and her worry that they would lose interest and fade away. Because of that concern, she had forsaken the opportunity to do a postgraduate course at the local university. She spoke of her job and how she had automatically followed her parents' profession. After each statement the father said, "Veddy good," and the mother, "Mah-vellous."

She helped the mother clear away the dishes and apologized for leaving so early. "Dad doesn't like me to travel in the dark," she said.

"I will walk you to the junction," Orbits said.

When they were about to leave, the father asked, "Can you be telling me what is the next step in this grand adventure?"

Orbits realized his father was just talking in his exaggerated way, trying to show off, but Miss Teapot said, "That is all up to your son. He hasn't asked me as yet."

"Boy, what wrong with you?" his mother said, slipping into the local dialect. "You better move fast before this bright pretty girl come to she senses."

"Mango season will be in a few months. The best time for a wedding," the father said.

"House wedding or church wedding?" the mother wondered aloud.

"All unions are a farce," Starboy said.

And so was the marriage broached and settled.

During the twenty-minute walk to the taxi stand at the junction, Orbits was quiet. He felt the pressure of Miss Teapot's head on his shoulder and her nails digging into his palm. A pothound followed them before it ran off barking at a car. From a house came the sound of a family squabble. The black sky was cloudless.

Orbits' parents discussed the wedding each evening, and its size and scope grew to magnificent proportions. With Orbits sitting silently between them, they asked each other: Should Orbits enter riding on a horse? Was it possible to borrow an elephant from a zoo? Could the reception be held at a seaside village instead? But what if the wind blew over the shed and carted off the bridesmaids? Should the father post his "Bad Pay List" in tiny letters in the wedding invitations? Or maybe a tiny advertisement for his denture lab? Was it possible to ban the girl's relatives from the wedding? That last question had been prompted by the one meeting between both sets of parents, during which occasion they had taken an immediate distaste to each other. Orbits had been disappointed when the pair of parents parted with stiff and steady smiles instead of quarrelling down the place and calling the wedding off.

"If it was me I would just elope," Starboy said. "Wedding is just a big pappyshow." For the first time, Orbits agreed with him.

"Dowry and all that backward nonsense."

"That is the next thing," his mother began. "Some people insist on it."

Orbits felt as if he was rushed into battle. (Years later, when he described his mood at that time, his friend Wally used a cricketing analogy that felt right to Orbits. "Is like walking to the pitch without properly padding up.")

The pair were married at a small ceremony in a temple situated between an ice cream parlour and a mortuary. Clients of both establishments wandered out to observe the commotion, the beating of drums that seemed unnecessarily loud and fancy for such a small gathering. Apart from the teachers at Miss Teapot's school and a couple clients from the denture business, there were just a few relatives from Miss Teapot's side. The relatives, perhaps imitating Miss Teapot's parents, sat glumly in one corner, occasionally glancing at the ferociously smiling denture clients in the other corner. Orbits' mood, too, ranged between these two extremes during the ceremony. Everything had happened too quickly; he had no say in the entire process and had just been swept along. Then he looked through the smoke at his bride-to-be sitting demure and satisfied, and he considered his mother's injunction about marrying quickly before the girl came to her senses. The priest fanned away the smoke with a mango leaf and commanded Orbits and Miss Teapot to walk around the fire. Orbits was uncertain how many times they did this, holding hands, but each circle felt longer, the fire in the centre fiercer and his feet heavier. He felt as if he were walking into a blazing oven. The priest threw more incense into the fire, provoking the nipping flames with a mango leaf and seeming to guide the curling blue smoke in a solemn dance up to the ceiling. Orbits heard the priest saying in his accented English that he now had to protect, love, honour and satisfy his wife and bring glory to her family, and he imagined himself escaping up the swirling smoke to a cushy overhead cloud. He tried to recall if he had seen a drawing or a movie of a genie performing this trick. During the closing prayer, he noticed both his mother and his new bride's mother trying to outdo each other with their frowns. The fathers just looked impatient. He could see no sign of his brother.

Following the ceremony, Mr. Rabbit, Orbits' employer, walked up to him and said, "Now that you are a married man, we can't have you walking around caves and thing. What if you fall and break your neck? Who will take care of your little wife?" He seemed to be waiting for an answer, but Orbits was considering the appellation. Little wife. It sounded as *wittle life*. He heard the other man saying, "Your father tell me that you doing big-big courses in matter-rology. So from now your job will be in the main office. As a matter-rologist you will have to plan the schedule for all the trips depending on the weather."

Orbits did not differentiate this offer from the congratulations of the other guests, but when he mentioned it to Miss Teapot during their honeymoon in a neighbouring island, she was thrilled. "This is so great," she enthused. "I know how much you were unsuited to the caves." She teased him by adding, "Now that you are a meteorologist, we have to get you a parrot." She was referring to a television weatherman who did all his forecasts with a macaw perched on his shoulder.

The unease Orbits had experienced during the ceremony faded during the honeymoon. His new wife was assured, lighthearted, chatty and more experienced than he was in every way. In the late evenings and nights, she positioned herself on top of him or laid back and guided him all the way to her final muffled moans. She sounded as if she was suffocating and Orbits tried to be gentler, but she would have none of that. He was constantly surprised whenever she casually walked past him naked into the kitchen, and one morning, she told him in a teasing manner, "I don't know why you are constantly covering up that nice body you have. There's no one here but us."

All he could say was, "It really nice?"

She pushed him onto the bed.

During the following days as they explored historic sites and beaches and waterfalls, Orbits felt a confidence he had never previously experienced. And so one morning in the hotel's pool, watching the overweight and mostly older guests jumping effortlessly into the water, he did the same. He sank quickly. During his first resurfacing, he waved his hands frantically, but the other guests felt he was playing. On the second resurfacing, he remembered he could not swim. Before he went down, he heard someone shouting, "The bloke's drowning." He was swallowing water and his chest and stomach felt as if they were about to burst. Someone or something was coming towards him. It looked like his wife. Then everything went black.

He awoke coughing out water. His wife was astride him in a familiar position, but her face was different and she was pounding his chest. Behind her, far above, a ragged cloud formation looked like two armies of squirrels preparing for battle. He giggled and coughed up more water. All around him were watchers. They were moving closer and seemed to be wagging their fingers. Some of the men helped him up.

33

"Are you okay, buddy?" one asked.

"Do you want something to drink?"

"The man nearly drink out the whole pool and you asking him if he want anything to drink."

"I have seen this happen a hundred times. Once I had to dive into a waterfall in Borneo to rescue an idiot. Two days later, he got knocked down by a motorcycle."

"The girl's a good swimmer though."

"Yeah. She ain't bad."

He looked around for his wife. Where did she go? Did she leave the hotel and the island out of shame? Then he saw her walking out of the hotel past the bar to the pool. Why wasn't she looking worried? he wondered. Did I just imagine everything? "Guess what?" she told Orbits, who was now propped on a lounge chair. "The entire stay here is free. The hotel apologized for not having a lifeguard at the pool and waived all the expenses. Are you okay?"

He could not share her enthusiasm, and he felt slightly offended that she had recovered so quickly. Just like old times, he thought. Belly filled to bursting and everyone laughing. He saw one of the men who had helped him up whispering to a friend. They glanced at Orbits and his wife suspiciously as they walked to the bar. They possibly thought it had all been a scam to get a free vacation, he thought, and some of his gloom faded. "Never felt better," he told his wife in a loud voice. "Ready for a next swim."

But the shame returned in their room, in the dark. After half an hour or so his wife gave up and asked, "Are you sure you are okay, Orbits? Maybe it was something in the water. The chlorine or something."

"Maybe."

"Don't worry," she said as she snuggled against him. "If it doesn't work by the morning, I know some other tricks. Besides there is an old superstition in the island that no one should do this" — she squeezed him, pulling gently — "before going in a boat."

"Boat?" he asked. "More water to swallow?"

"No, silly. It's a lagoon with shallow water that looks like nylon."

Lagoon, he thought. Rice and mud and miserable things biting the toes.

Soon she fell asleep, and Orbits felt her heart beating against his chest. She felt warm and cozy against his body, her leg draped across his groin, her head on his shoulder. Her snores sounded like a whimpering bird, yet she was so strong. So strong and resourceful. Just before he fell asleep, he wondered what tricks she had in mind. And where she had learned them.

He dreamed he was in an ocean floating on his back. The clouds were low and seemed to form an archway. He tried to paddle through the entrance, but his body felt thick and heavy. A current was pulling him under. He was unable to resist because the riptide was too strong. He awoke gasping. His wife was still asleep, making her whimpering sounds. It was close to dawn when he finally fell asleep once more.

The next day they visited a grave, the tombstone of which said enigmatically that the woman was both a wife and a mother without being aware of both situations. Miss Teapot seemed intrigued by the cryptic epitaph. She remarked that it reminded her of her father's Russian stories, but Orbits, who preferred plain and simple explanations, reflected whether the mortician or whoever wrote these words had not been drunk.

For the remainder of the honeymoon, not wanting to unnecessarily bother his wife, he pretended he was enjoying himself; and when on the last night, she told him how happy she was, he tried to understand her patience, or pity or delusion or whatever it was. On the plane journey back to her parents' place, where they had decided to stay until they could move out, she placed her hands on his and leaned over to follow his view. "The clouds look so real," she said and quickly corrected herself. "I mean they look as if they contain more than just water. It's no wonder people looked up and believed the gods lived there." He was on the verge of revealing his childhood fixation of floating through the clouds when she added, "So silly. When we get back you will have to gaze at the clouds all day like a crazy person." She looked at his face and said, "For your new job, silly."

✥

THE SITE FROM WHICH Mr. Rabbit conducted his operation was once owned by a local bus entrepreneur. It was a huge roundabout surrounding a triangular shed, and Orbits was disappointed to note its resemblance to a big, bustling warehouse. It was managed by Baby Rabbit, the son of Mr. Rabbit. The elder Rabbit had gotten his nickname because of his protruding front teeth, and while he was fine with the name, the son, whose mouth was covered by a bushy moustache and who looked more like an otter than a rabbit, was enraged whenever a maxi driver referred to him by his nickname. He was always busy and irritated as he walked around the place with a clipboard in his hand. Surprisingly, he had a high-pitched, girlish voice.

When Orbits asked him about his office and equipment, he said, "Equipment? What equipment you talking about? Your job is to watch up in the air and tell me if it going to rain or not. That way we will know if to send people to the swamp and the beach or to some old church or mashup building. How difficult is that? What is your name?"

"Orbits."

"What sort of name is that? Over here we don't use nicknames, you understand?"

Orbits was so intimidated by his brusque manner that he said, "Yes, sir. Yes, Mr. Rabbit junior."

"You meet Lilboy already?" He called and a skinny old man with bright eyes in a bony face appeared. "Lilboy is the coordinator here, you understand?"

36

Toronto Public Library
Gerrard/Ashdale
1432 Gerrard St E
416-393-7717

- Checkout Receipt -

Sep 02, 2021 01:46 PM

Library Card: **********6394

Number of items: 1

Item ID: 37131202638102
Title: ADULT FICTION
Date Due: Sep 23, 2021

Telephone Renewal 416-395-5505
tpl.ca

"You understand?" the other man rose on his toes and screamed. Lilboy, apart from being a coordinator, was a janitor, traffic operator and messenger. He was perpetually in motion, and because of his bright eyes and the ragged clothes on his tiny frame, Orbits was slightly afraid of him. Every morning, Lilboy collected the weather report from Orbits, ran to Baby Rabbit's office next door, and when both men emerged, Lilboy would repeat each name and location his boss had called from a clipboard and walk up along the line of vehicles, gesturing with his hands and chin.

The maxi taxis that gathered around the building were dispatched to various schools, hotels and transit points in the island. Orbits had expected a quiet little office with hydrometers and thermometers and maybe a wind vane outside instead of a small cubicle built with wayward cedar planks. He felt encircled by commotion: the noise of the vehicles, the arguments of the drivers, the shouting of Baby Rabbit, the screaming of Lilboy, the diesel fumes that seeped through the window. His job was the furthest thing from his tour guide periods. Each morning, for half an hour, he had to look at the clouds and determine whether they were dark and threatening or white and harmless. He wrote his prediction on a sheet, which he passed on to Lilboy, who rolled it in a cylinder and, holding it aloft like a relay runner, sprinted to Baby Rabbit's office, just a few yards away. "Coming through, coming through," he bawled, though there was no one blocking him.

There were just two seasons and they never varied in duration on the island. Rainy season from June to December and dry season from January to May. Although there were frequent thunderstorms, these were brief, and the damage was always attributed to "the hand of god." Orbits' work was finished by eleven in the morning, by which time the last vehicle had left the lot.

There were a few initial misses in his forecast from swift moving "passing clouds," but he soon learned to predict the weather from looking at the sky and observing the colour, height and spatial arrangement of the clouds. Baby Rabbit occasionally made a little fuss about his forecast, which always included the addendum, "The possibility of isolated showers." Orbits had stolen the phrase from the radio meteorologist to whose forecast he listened each morning in the taxi. He typically repeated these with little variations.

After the last vehicle had left the lot, he turned to his meteorological course. He tried to make sense of vertical distribution and diurnal cycles and equilibrium levels, and he struggled with the equations and calculations and all the hardened definitions. He resented the manner in which the course had transformed something as fragile and subtle as clouds into unassailable phenomena. He recalled the Christmas Eve that his brother had caught his father pushing toys in an old pillowcase and his resentment in the days following at the end of that fantasy. His brother, six at the time, had said, "I never ever going to believe anything anybody say again." It was the only time Orbits felt a vague sympathy towards him.

Increasingly, he pushed aside the course material and returned to his old fantasies about floating through the air, the cool puffs brushing his cheeks. He wondered how the warehouse and the parked vehicles would look from the air, and intermittently he imagined floating above his parents' house and listening to their bantering and observing the silence in his brother's room. Maybe he was studying for his exams. For sure he would pass and then he would get a good job and become more pleasant to everyone.

He never mentioned any of this in the little bedroom he shared with his wife in her parents' house. When he got home in the afternoon, his father-in-law would be at his desk in the living room, reading the newspaper or a magazine, and his mother-in-law would be either in the kitchen or on the couch with a book. They rarely spoke to him other than to ask, "So how was the day?" But that question seemed loaded. Did they suspect that the extent of his work was a one-line forecast? Or that he had spent the rest of the day in childish daydreams rather than on his online course?

"Not too bad," he always said as he rushed into the room to await his wife's arrival two hours later. His mood brightened as she walked through the door and later as she spoke about her day and related little incidents involving some other teacher or one of her students. She continued this during dinner, which was mostly a dialogue between mother and daughter. For this, Orbits was thankful because he was usually concentrating on eating like the rest of the family: chewing slowly, using the cutlery properly and apportioning the condiments. At his parents' home, the entire meal was ladled into one plate, but here there were little bottles, gold-rimmed bowls, vials and decanters from which he had to choose. The plates were smaller, and everything was arranged in such a way that it was possible to know when the meal was finished and it was time to stop eating. At his parents' home, his father sometimes poured everything into a basin which he shook, mixing the sauce and rice and meat and vegetables into a swirling mass that he brought to his mouth, lapping noisily. When he was finished, he would say, "My belly full now, Mamoose. The world could turn over and I wouldn't care."

"Careful it really turn over," his mother would reply with a smile.

After his meal, Orbits waited on the bed while his wife marked her papers on her bedroom desk. Frequently he fell asleep before she was finished. But on occasion he was struck by her discipline, marking papers and preparing work late in the night. And he marvelled that he was married to a teacher, a profession he had always hated and feared. Sometimes she would say, "Hey sleepyhead, come and keep me company." He would pretend to be snoring and would hear her giggling.

One night while he was waiting on the bed, he recalled a swift drizzle earlier in the day that had annoyed Baby Rabbit and Lilboy before it was established it was simply a passing cloud. This is how my job is, too, he thought. Insubstantial and shifting and temporary. He tried to laugh it off, but the comparison stuck. He was getting paid for doing nothing. It was a scam that would be discovered shortly by Baby Rabbit or Lilboy. How could they not notice this? Any fool could do his job. Maybe they wanted someone to blame in case a vehicle filled with dazed tourists overturned in a flooded river. He knew from the movies that in some countries bad luck was blamed not on spirits or the hand of god, but on real people who had fallen asleep on their jobs. So every day he approached the compound with the fear that it would be his last and that Baby Rabbit would pull him aside and point his finger like in the *Apprentice* television show and say, "You are fired." Occasionally this fear would be displaced by the greater panic that something would go wrong, and he would be led off in chains.

He tried to immunize himself by sprucing up his forecasts with little bits about the possibility of fog and mist and flash flooding, or with terms he got from his studies and which he never really understood. Baby Rabbit was not impressed. "You have the possibility of everything except snow happening here." He glanced at the sheet. "And what is this nonsense about cumulus and citrus clouds?"

"Cirrus," Orbits said weakly.

"Citrus!" Lilboy shouted.

"Look man, don't harass my ass with this nonsense. Just tell me if rain going to fall or the sun going to shine." He walked away with Lilboy in tow, and Orbits' fear deepened. He has seen through the forecasting scam, he thought. He knows it is so simple a child could look up in the sky and say sun today or rain. But in the evening when he related Baby Rabbit's mixing of cirrus with citrus, his wife laughed and said in a pouting manner that she was so sorry he had to work "with such stupidees."

The next day in the compound, the fear returned. I am going to be fired soon. It will be back to the swamp and the caves for me. This stretch of good luck, marrying an attractive and intelligent woman, employed at a place where he finished before noon and where his job description was simply looking up at the sky, had to be an anomaly. Something would snatch it all away. But what? He began to refocus on his online course; and in the nights while his wife was marking her papers at her desk, he would be on his bed struggling with some description, trying to keep his eyes open.

During a dinner, she said to her parents, "We are like two scholars every night with all our reading and preparations." Her father glanced over his spectacles and Orbits thought: He knows. He has seen through everything. He began to dread these family dinners, expecting at any moment an unanswerable question from one of the parents. He soon realized that he hated the clean house, passing both parents on his way in, the predictability of the evening scenes, the formality of the dinners, struggling to be smart and cultured. One morning he heard his father-in-law reading aloud from a thick novel: "Deprived of meaningful work, men and women lose their reason for existence; they go stark, raving mad." He began to hate these Russian novelists, feeling they were complicit in the other man's sly accusation.

One afternoon he went from his work to his parents' place. It had been six months since his marriage, and he had never visited. His father, who was on the porch patching a pair of shoes with a strip of bicycle tube, spotted him and shouted, "Mamoose, come fast. It have a stranger walking down the street."

Both seemed genuinely happy to see him. His father asked about his work with Baby Rabbit, and his mother commented on how skinny he had gotten. "This girl not feeding you or what? Or is all the hifalutin food they giving you?" She pinched the skin on his wrist and he yelped.

"Where is Starboy?" he asked, rubbing his hand.

"Come inside," the father said. "And let your mother cook some good healthy food for you." While his mother was in the kitchen, his father told him that Starboy had taken up with the wrong crowd, and he came home each night smelling of ganja. He had passed one subject, failed another and had not turned up for the third. "Boy, I thought he would be the one to make us . . . to take his studies further, but all that finish now."

"I doing a course in meteorology," Orbits said.

His father continued as if he had not heard. "The boy get so ungrateful. He say that all me and his mother did was bring him in the world and that was a big mistake as far as he concerned. After all the care and attention. Your mother breastfeed him till he was nearly four, you know."

"I know."

His mother pushed her head out of the kitchen. "Who you all talking about? Starboy? He just passing through a phase. Give him some time. All bright children like that. The brightness does make them nervous."

The talk of Starboy continued during dinner.

"He was doing so well at school. First in everything." The father put on his dessert dentures.

"The boy never wanted to leave my breast. And now . . ." She sighed loudly. "What about you? When you going to give us a grandchild?"

"You making the boy blush, Mamoose," the father said, stretching his lips and adjusting his dentures with his tongue.

Although he knew he would be sick afterwards, Orbits ate most of the oily food heaped onto his plate. Fried eggplant, curried mango and *paratha* roti, soya textured and flavoured to resemble chicken, a thick broth of split peas, sweetmeats simmering in oil. During dinner their mood lightened. His father made his old comments about teeth, remarking that a client's mouth was so deformed with thick brown teeth, it seemed as if it were stacked with toes instead. His mother said, "You remember when you apprentice with Papoose, boy? We

42

had a nice sign ready for the two of you. Swallows and Son." Orbits remembered and was surprised that the uncomfortable period seemed remotely pleasant, even funny.

He left the house soon after dinner. When he got to his room, his wife was already there. She was looking worried. "Where were you? I had to return to school to . . . to get some papers. I called your workplace from there and they said you had already left."

"What time you called?"

"Well, it was after work."

"Oh," he said relieved. "I too got a call at work. From my parents. They were worried about my brother, so I decided to pay them a visit." He was surprised at the swiftness and fluidity of the lie. His parents' village did not have phone lines, and he hoped she would not ask.

"What's the matter with him?" He repeated what his parents had mentioned, and she told him, "I suspected that during my visit there. You remember how he was bad-talking school and education and all that? I knew at once he had a serious chip on his shoulder. Maybe your mother showered all her affections on you and neglected the poor boy."

Orbits remembered the visit. He also remembered how much he had resented his brother for the misappropriated affection. Yet he told her, "He was so bright at school. First in everything."

His wife came over to him and unbuttoned his shirt. "That's why you are not looking so well. It must be so hard on you."

"Yes, it hard," he said.

"Poor baby. I believe you."

"Ouch."

From then he visited his parents each Friday. He chose that day because he had heard from his parents that Starboy always disappeared until Saturday morning, and also because the Friday dinners at his wife's place were more prolonged. The time alone with

43

his parents recalled the few years before the arrival of his brother. Maybe if he had had a little sister instead it would have been different, with the parental attention equally shared. He liked the mingled odours coming from the kitchen, his parents' nonsensical bantering, even the way his father casually replaced one denture with another. There were no rules here: dinner was served at arbitrary times and because the food was constantly replenished, it was done only when his mother or father had run out of things to talk about.

In time, he realized that what he really enjoyed about his parents' place was the lack of predictability and structure, the disorder and the chaos. All their questions were posed in the form of jokes, even their most frequent about the arrival of a grandchild. "You noticing any morning sickness?" the mother asked. "She asking only for sour things to eat? She spitting all the time? You remember how it was with me, Papoose?"

"You eat out four mango tree clean before Starboy born."

Orbits always shifted the talk to Starboy or to his father's lab, but eleven months after his marriage, he was finally able to give them an answer. His wife had displayed none of his mother's stated symptoms, and he was startled at the casual manner in which she broke the news. "Guess what?" she asked him one evening after she returned from work.

"You got promoted?"

She shook her head.

"A student got expelled? A teacher was fired?"

"No, silly." She raised her bodice and told him, "Feel here. No, not there! Here."

"What is it?"

"A baby. A little baby."

"When did that happen?"

She laughed and pushed him playfully. "I took the afternoon off and went to see the doctor to be sure. Mom and Dad don't know as yet."

When his wife broke the news, her mother hugged her and launched into a long lecture about pregnancy and about child-rearing. The father glanced sternly over his spectacles at Orbits during his wife's speech.

The reaction of Orbits' parents was more predictable. "A baby!" his mother shrieked.

His father said, "I always know you had it in you. Your mother thought the jaundice you had as a child damaged some of your inside apparatus, but I never believed that."

"Is true," the mother said. "You was a sickly little child. Not like Starboy."

"Who the hell using my name?" In his haste to share the news, Orbits had visited on a Saturday. When his brother emerged from his room, Orbits was surprised at how much he had changed. He had developed a slouch, and his sunken eyes seemed wary and suspicious. His long hair was tied in a ponytail and he had a straggly beard. When he saw Orbits, he said, "So, Mr. Married Man finally decide to pay a visit?"

"Hush, Starboy," his mother chided. "He came every Friday but you never around."

"You will be a uncle soon, boy," the father said.

"Another parasite," Starboy said. "As if the world didn't have enough already."

Orbits tried to change the topic. "How everything with you?"

"How everything with me? Let me see. I high from morning to noon. I wish I wasn't born. I hate everybody in my sight. I—"

"Boy!" Orbits had never heard his father raising his voice. "If that is all you have to say then leave now. Go back to your drug-pushing friends."

"No, Papoose, don't say that. He don't mean anything. Starboy, go back to your room, son."

"Fuck everybody! And these weed-pushing friends you talking

about smarter than the three of you put together. At least I could talk to them. At least they fucking understand what—"

"Boy! That language."

"Language? The problem with all of you is that you have no imagination. Today just like yesterday and yesterday just like all the days before. None of you could see further than you big toe. Peasant mentality. Spinning top in mud."

The quarrel continued and Orbits was forgotten. They barely noticed his departure.

His wife, too, shifted her attention. She spent most evenings talking with her mother in the living room. One night a thought hit Orbits: Was this his only purpose? He knew it was mean-spirited to be thinking in this way, but he missed the attention and the little flirtations and even the recounting of the school day. She also grew slightly irritated with him, especially when she had to explain a symptom of her pregnancy he could not fully grasp.

Yet there were benefits: no one seemed to notice his presence at the dinner table or if he left early to the bedroom. No one would notice, too, if I were not here, he thought. He briefly considered and discarded the idea of daily visits to his parents' place. One rainy morning, he hopped on a maxi taxi that was always the last to leave the compound.

"You going to the museum today with we, brother?"

"Yeah," Orbits told the skullcap-wearing driver. With his headgear and yellowish colour, it was impossible to guess the man's ethnicity.

"You is the weatherman, not so? You fellas have to have plenty brains to study all this weather business. Where your parrot?" He didn't wait for an answer but continued, "Me, I just happy to drive this maxi and do me little prayers and keep out of trouble. Used to sell drugs at one time, you know. Then one night I see a bright light coming from the sky and a voice telling me that the devil, *shaitaan*, fixing up a room for me. I thought it was the coke talking but for one week, I keep getting the same message. Shaitaan waiting. Shaitaan waiting. From dog and cyat and once a goat. Stop eating goat after that. So this is the story of my life. What about you?"

Orbits did not have a similarly dramatic story to share. He told the driver, "Wife pregnant."

"She full!" He laughed scandalously. "Don't take it the wrong way, eh brother. I have nine myself. Four with the madam and five outside. Children is the salt, brother. The salt." He continued chatting until they picked up a few disgruntled-looking tourists from a hotel's lobby. His tone and his accent changed whenever he responded to a question about the destination or some other local point of interest.

The museum, which Orbits had never visited, was a disappointment. There were a few cannonballs, a rusty anchor, and some knives in a glass case. Many of the cases were empty. The tourists seemed interested, though, and Orbits felt it was because they were so wet and miserable. After Skullcap had dropped off the last tourist, he told Orbits, "You see how these people making fuss about all these museum things? What you think?"

"I really can't say."

"Is because they does see far. We does only see the piece of ground we stepping over, but they does see miles ahead." Orbits recalled his brother's observation, and he wondered if Starboy would have been happier if he had grown up in some distant country where people could properly imagine things.

The next day, Orbits went to a mud volcano and the following day, to a heritage site. Over the following weeks, he visited with Skullcap a monastery in the mountains built by St. Benedictine monks more than a century earlier, a zoo with curious, bright-eyed monkeys and a temple that had been built somehow in the ocean. He heard Skullcap telling the tourists, "The man who build this temple, a *sadhu* we call him, do everything by hand. Brick by brick, he alone. He had to understand the drift of the waves and the tides otherwise everything would have washed away. It take him his entire life to build it. Brick by brick." While the tourists were taking photographs, Orbits asked the driver, "One person alone build the temple?"

"Is true. But we lose all that now."

"What you mean?"

"Everybody living for themselves, brother. Living for today. Tomorrow dead and gone. People here only concern about they little plot of land. They does talk as if a nearby village is on another continent. Who is not friend is enemy."

The next week, they went to the bird sanctuary. Orbits decided to wait in the maxi with Skullcap because he did not want to meet the boatman who had been so mean to him. He expected the tourists would return miserable and itchy, but two hours later when the boat swung into view, they all seemed happy, and Orbits wondered if the spectacle of flamingoes and ibises had been saved only for foreigners. The boatman didn't recognize Orbits and he told Skullcap, "Bring back these tourists any time you want. Is flamingo season now."

"Not mosquito and sandfly season then?" Orbits blurted out.

In the vehicle, Skullcap told him, "That was a good one, brother. I didn't read you to be funny. Next week we going to a Amerindian grave site. You know a couple hundred years aback, these Spanish fellas force a group of native Indians to build a church, and when the Indians couldn't take the jamming any more, they rebel. Slice up all these fellas who was whipping them. Well, when word get back to the capital, the soldiers hunt down these Indians one by one and dim they lights. We need people like that now."

"The soldiers or the Indians?"

"That is a good one. You does be funny sometimes."

EACH DAY ORBITS WENT somewhere new, and as his wife's pregnancy progressed, he felt that even as she was becoming a stranger, he was growing to know the island better. He enjoyed all the stretches in remote villages shaded by teak and immortelle and those bordered by coconut trees on the coasts. Intermittently, little villages appeared out of nowhere and disappeared just as quickly, swallowed by a forest of immortelle and cedar and hardwood. There were areas of cocoa, the polished pods looking metallic in the sun, and of cashew and tangerine he could smell from the vehicle. He passed ancient towns with Spanish-style stone buildings hugging the narrow roads and little enclaves that led to fields of waving heliconia and ginger lily. Spanish street names gave way to French and French to English and English to Amerindian and Amerindian to East Indian. He couldn't believe there were all these points of connection, and he felt that if he had remained in his village, never venturing out, he would never have suspected there were all these convergences right on this little island.

He knew this was not the true extent of the island. There were shanty towns and settlements of squatters from other islands, places that were dirty and filled with vagrants and drug dealers talking in the slang of religious men, but travelling in the maxis and seeing everything through the eyes of the tourists, hearing it being described in such an unfamiliar — and unexpected — manner, gave him a new appreciation of the place. The foreigners were always saying things like, "Wow, the ocean is so green," or "The light adds so many different shades to the forest." He had actually passed some of these places before and had noticed nothing. He began to view villages like the one in which he grew up, with their old, crumbling houses renovated so erratically that the parts never matched, as romantic and the confusion of flowers and shrubs that surrounded these houses as exotic.

One day the vehicle passed his old house. The front door was shut, as were all the windows. In the evening when he got home, he saw his wife on the couch and her mother sitting next to her. "Your wife needs you," the older woman said sternly and disappeared into the kitchen.

He sat and asked, in what he hoped was a concerned voice, "What happened?"

"You are never here again."

"It's my work and—"

"Now I need you more than ever."

"I thought you wanted to spend more time with your mother." He knew this sounded silly, and he glanced up to see his father-in-law glaring at him. Old man, what the ass you looking at? he thought. You have nothing better to do all day than sit by that desk with a newspaper or a book you pretending to read? "Is everything ok?"

She began to cry, small sobs that sounded like breathless chuckles. He wasn't sure about the protocol for comforting a crying person, so he wiped his own eyes and issued a few sniffles. He thought of how often he had cried at school after being bullied. The memory shattered his decision to never show this weakness again, to withhold all his tears, and he broke down and began to sob louder than his wife.

In the end, it was she who had to comfort him. "Don't worry," she told him in the bedroom. "Just now the baby will arrive and it all be over. Hush, hush."

But the tears wouldn't stop. "I will make sure I here when the baby come," he promised.

But he missed everything.

Two weeks after his breakdown, Baby Rabbit came to his office and told him, "Your father called from the station and left a message. Is better you go now." On his way there, he debated whether his mother had fallen ill or word had gotten around of his malingering all across the country while his pregnant wife was alone at home. It was neither: when he got there, he saw a crowd gathered on the porch. He heard a sound, a low wailing ululation that sounded at once like a plea and a curse. He rushed inside. The sound had come from his mother, who was surrounded by other women. She was screaming, "Why this had to happen? Why he had to go? Why they had to go and do that to him? Oh god, why?"

He felt a hand on his shoulder and saw his father's red eyes. "Starboy," his father said, leading him to his brother's bedroom.

He seemed to be asleep with the blanket pulled over his body as he had done as a child during rainy nights. "What happened?" he asked his father. He was aware that a group had gathered at the doorway to peep.

"We don't know. They find him in the abandoned community centre up on the hill. He was gone by then." His father began to cry but soundlessly, his face hidden by his hand. He seemed like someone shielding his eyes from the sun, his body ruffling so gently it was hardly noticeable. "He was gone . . ."

"Hug your father, boy," someone shouted from the doorway. "Don't be selfish. Hug the man. He alone know what he going through."

He was so enraged by the intrusion that he wanted to say, Why the hell you don't come and hug him? Instead, he rushed to the door and pulled it shut. Someone outside sucked their teeth. He saw his father now at the body, rubbing the feet. "I could look at him?" he asked.

When his father remained silent, he raised the sheet and saw his brother's face looking more peaceful than he could recall. Robbed of his scowl and frown, he looked handsome in a way that Orbits had not seen over the last years. There was a tiny bruise on his lower lip, like a wire drawn over the flesh, and a blue welt above one closed eye. His eyelashes were long, almost feminine. In death, he appeared frail and imaginative and beautiful. Maybe like one of the Russian novelists. No, like a poet who daily gazed at the sinking of the day. Each day with more apprehension. Orbits pulled the sheet lower and saw bruises around his brother's neck and on his shoulder. He replaced

51

the sheet and asked his father once more, "What happened?" He could hear bawling outside, and he tried to differentiate how many bawlers there were. In the room, it was difficult to tell.

A man knocked and entered the room. Orbits recognized him as the sergeant who conducted most of his investigations propped on a stool in the rumshop. He pulled down the sheet to expose the entire body. "It look like a suicide. You want an autopsy done or not?"

When his father said nothing, Orbits told the sergeant, "Do what you have to do."

"No! No! Nobody going to cut up my baby. Somebody do this to him and you have to find that person." His mother rushed to the body and had to be restrained by some other women. Once more, she began her horrible low moan, and Orbits felt as if her life were climbing onto the prolonged sound and slipping out of her body. He left the room and felt hands patting his shoulders as he walked out of the house.

He continued to walk until he reached the junction. He was not thinking; he watched his feet moving forward and he felt as helpless as when he was a child. With each step, his brother's face appeared, younger each time until he was just four years old, clinging to his mother's breast. God is paying me back for hating my brother, he thought. He tried to shift his thoughts from what he had just witnessed; he didn't want to know if his brother was murdered or had committed suicide. He recalled taking this route a year and a half earlier. It was with his wife-to-be, and he had been startled at how quickly his marriage had been settled. He had felt trapped that night. But now he wanted to be with his wife; he wanted to be far away from the chaos he had actively sought out over the last two months. He broke into a run and pushed out his hand at the first taxi he saw. The branches streaming outside the car's window seemed to be alive with fingers; another passenger was whistling a song from a Hindi movie.

When he got to his in-laws' place, the lights were off and the house was empty. Already wrought by the death of his brother, he rushed through the house calling his wife's name. He walked around the house and looked into the drain at the back and at the branches of the trees before he returned inside. He sat on his mother-in-law's couch, leaning forward, his head on his knees, tired and drained. He did not hear the car arriving or the door opening. "You finally decided to show yourself." He could see his mother-in-law was seething with rage, and he waited for some equivalent emotion. "Well, congratulation."

"Where Teepee?"

"She in the hospital, but I wonder why you asking."

"I really wonder," the father repeated.

"I have to go now," he said. "I could get a lift?" He asked again, louder.

"Find your own way," his mother-in-law said. "We waited long enough."

"We don't have time for this," the father added. "For this damn foolishness."

The closest hospital was three miles away and he ran, recklessly at times, not diverting to the pavement when a car approached or avoiding the broken bottles on the road. Midway there, he stopped to catch his breath. He bent over and saw the clasp of a sandal had come undone. He took both off and prepared for the rest of the journey. Why am I doing this? The voice seemed to have come from somewhere close by, and he glanced around. Again, he heard the voice as he sped off.

He arrived at the hospital two hours later. He mentioned his wife's name to a nurse. She looked at the sandals in his hand and the sweat running down his shirt and pointed to the front desk. No one was there. He walked up the stairway and saw men in pyjamas walking about. On another floor, he saw patients dragging their IV poles. An old man with unruly grey hair that gave him a clownish look seemed to smile, but it was just his lips flapping, trying to find words. The nurses seemed hoggish and the white-clad doctors indifferent, so he climbed another flight of stairs. At the end of the floor, he saw his wife on a cot, her head turned to the window. He walked in and called her name softly. She opened her eyes and when she tried to sit up, he put his hand on her shoulder and sat on the bed. He asked if she was okay and she smiled weakly. "Where is the baby?"

"In the respirator," a sturdy-looking black woman in the adjoining bed said. The woman glanced past him and added, "Don't worry, dearie, is just a precaution. They will bring her out as soon as she strong enough. Look, she coming now."

A nurse walked in with a bundle. "You is the father?"

He nodded and she passed the bundle to him. The woman on the nearby bed walked over. "Is a pretty little baby girl. I could see you will have trouble on you hands when she grow up."

Orbits placed the bundle on his wife's chest.

"What happened to your foot?"

He looked down and saw blood. "Nothing. Is nothing." But the blood reminded him of his brother; and in the years to come, he always connected these three: blood, birth and death.

He was not there when his wife went into the hospital nor was he there when she was released the following day. His in-laws blamed him for his absence, and his parents blamed him for not showing up at the wake. Yet he told neither of his reasons. He wanted to tell his mother, but it seemed inappropriate in this moment of grief; and it was only during the ceremony preceding the cremation when she was sitting, wasted and numb, that he whispered, "My wife had a baby."

She grasped his hand tightly. "Tell me again."

"My wife had a baby."

She offered a sickly smile, and he felt it was a kind of madness caused by grief. But later as the priest was talking about reincarnation and the soul limping from one vessel to the next and death as just a stepping stone, he saw her looking at him and nodding. When it was time to take the coffin into the hearse, the women who had been eyeing her warily came up, but she waved them away. She maintained this strength during the cremation and while the body was burning, she told Orbits, "You and Starboy never get along and yet you find a way to bring him back. You find a way." She held his hand, squeezing with unexpected vigour.

Eventually, word got around to his in-laws about his brother's death, and they tried to make amends not through direct apologies but by skidding out of their stiffness. When he returned after work, the mother said, "Look, the new father reach."

Yes, you old bitch, the father reach.

"Mr. Meteorologist, I wonder what the weather going to be today?"

I wish it was a flood that would drown you old ass.

"Listen to how the baby crying as if it know the father arrive."

It crying because it surrounded by bloodsucking parasites.

He began to hate them not only for their earlier treatment of him but also because of their assumption he could be so easily fooled. He stopped bothering to acknowledge them, not answering their questions or engaging in any conversation, and whereas before he had made an effort at etiquette, now he ate noisily, dipping into his food with his hands, piling everything into one plate.

"Moms," the father said one evening. "Look how the boy invent a new convenient way to mix everything together."

I wish I could invent a way for all you bitches to be a thousand miles from me.

That night he told his wife, "We should find a little place."

She was not aware of the situation with her parents — he never mentioned it — and she remarked she would want to be close to her mother during this period as the older woman knew so much about babies and child-rearing. Child-rearing, he thought. Just like rearing an animal. Rearing a goat or a sheep. Animal husbandry. Sometimes he was surprised at the extent of his anger, and during a moment of unusual clarity in his office, he considered whether he was trying to displace guilt with hatred. For as long as he could remember, he had resented his brother, and every single day he went over how he could have adjusted their relationship, how he might have pre-empted his brother's death. He was older by almost four years, and yet he had simmered in resentment at Starboy's favoured status.

He began spending more time at his parents' place, going there straight from his work. They had both handled the death of their son in different and unexpected ways. His father, the former joker, grew withdrawn, betraying no emotion as his wife talked in a nonsensical way about gods, spirits and alien beings, placing these entities along-side each other as she did the deities from different religions. She visited pundits and priests and once a local seerwoman, who assured her that her dead son was now happier than he had ever been, and he was grieving to see her.

During every visit, she asked Orbits about his daughter, whether she had taken her first step or uttered a word. Orbits invented little things, but the truth was he had no idea. During his wife's leave from school, he would lay next to her in the bed, hold the baby above him and marvel that he'd had a hand in the creation of this complete little thing. He was stunned by her growing recognition of her mother, gurgling in delight and pushing out her little hand, or the way she crept around like a morrocoy. At his primary school eighteen years earlier, the teacher had displayed some little black tadpoles in a bottle, and Orbits had been intrigued by the way their tails had dropped out so they gradually began to resemble frogs. He had wanted the project to continue — maybe they would become something more than frogs — but the teacher had emptied the aquarium at the back of the school, close to the latrines.

Each week it seemed his daughter was doing something new,

showing some unexpected sign of intelligence or familiarity with her mother and grandmother. When his wife returned to school, his daughter was transferred to the care of his mother-in-law. During the first year or so, she would tell the child, "Look, your daddy get back from work, Chickadee" or "Ask your daddy what the weather is going to be tomorrow because I taking you to the mall." He never responded to these provocations, and soon the indirect repartee stopped.

By then he no longer bothered to ask his wife about moving out, but the idea was never out of his mind. In his tiny office, he tried to imagine himself living in one of the little villages he had passed in a maxi taxi earlier in the week. On occasion, he hit on a particular house, a little flat far from the road and hidden by shrubs. He imagined quiet weekends with his family and a return of the affection that once existed between himself and his wife. He missed the light jokes, the tenderness, the mischievousness, the attention. He feared that his wife was becoming a version of her mother even though he understood that her new hardness was because she was balancing the responsibilities of motherhood with those of her profession. He, on the other hand, did nothing but write a single prediction on a sheet of paper. He had always known she was far more realistic than him, and one day while he was in a maxi taxi, looking at the old but well-kept houses in a coastal village, he had the sudden fear that she would come to her senses and leave him. She has her parents, her job, her child, he thought. What use I am to her?

He tried to come up with ways he could reignite some of the lost affection, but all these measures involved him interacting with her parents. In the maxi, he watched the foreign couples' public displays of affection, and although he knew the island viewed this behaviour as inconsiderate and lewd, he sometimes closed his eyes and imagined it was him and his wife. One evening after the skullcap-wearing driver had returned the last of his passengers to a hotel, he told Orbits, "I want to make a little detour to check out one of the outsides. You could remain in the van if you want." He pulled into a dirt trace and stopped before a shack. A mixed-race girl of about six or so saw the vehicle and ran out from the porch, which was covered with *carat*, a palm thatch. "A outside child," he told Orbits and stepped out.

He disappeared into the shack, and when he returned a few minutes later, the girl was with him, holding his hand and skipping along. "Bye, Daddy," she said.

He stooped to kiss her and said, "Till next week then, Cherry."

"So your wife know about all of this?" Orbits asked him in the vehicle.

"Yeah. The girl spend a few weekends with us. Together with the other outsides. I want them to know each other."

"And the mothers?"

He chuckled. "That is a different story. I had to part a few fights in the beginning. One of them nearly knife the other. They settle down now. Everything does settle down if you give it time." He began to talk of growing up not knowing his father and of his early troubles. "Had a time when I used to work just to save money to buy a gun. I do a little robbery here and there, and the gun was just to scare people. A little prop. But that is the past tense now. As you see, nowadays I moving different. Try to talk to some of these young fellas too. Try to put some sense in their heads. Put some god in their heart. But they not ready. When the time reach, it reach. God pull me out in the nick of time."

He spoke in this manner, not making much sense, frequently contradicting himself, but Orbits felt he was happy in a sort of delusional way. He had worked out a philosophy that forgave his mistakes and allowed him to be contented. "You know sometimes I does look at the sky and even though I can't see the big man I know he there. When you look at the sky what you does see?"

"Clouds."

"And what you think it have behind the clouds?"

"More clouds. And space."

The driver laughed. "I forget I talking to a matter-rologist. Alright brother, this is your stop here."

Later that evening, Orbits listened to his mother talking about rituals she had gleaned from a pundit to guarantee Starboy's happiness in his new incarnation. He felt this was a phase she would soon slip out of, but one year passed, then two, and Orbits saw her settling into a kind of cold, erratic jubilance, a dead joy; so he was not surprised to learn of her visits to one of the evangelical churches that was springing up in all the small villages and that had happily incorporated many of the local superstitions into their doctrines. His father meanwhile receded even further into his silence, and frequently Orbits saw him alone at home, staring into the distance. Every so often, he had to repeat his questions to get a response. Orbits wondered how his father was able to manage in his dental lab, and if perhaps it was only there he found solace and there he sprang to life.

>⋒⋒⋒

THE NOTION OF THE uselessness of his own job never left, and daily there was the concern he would be found out and fired by Baby Rabbit. His meteorology courses had long lapsed, and he wrote the school requesting an extension. He was surprised to receive a response three months later encouraging him to continue and mentioning all the benefits from a career in this field. He folded the letter, and in his little cubicle of an office, he fantasized about chasing storms and riding into the eyes of hurricanes and reading weather reports about impending tsunamis.

He brought the course material to the bedroom, hoping the sight of his wife marking her papers in the nights would anchor his mind. And so each night while his wife was seated at her desk and their three-year-old daughter in her crib, he would be on the bed, sitting, his back against the wall, reading his material. On the surface, it seemed a perfect little family, diligent and ambitious. And some of his wife's affection returned too. Frequently she glanced across and asked, "How is the studies coming along, Orbs?"

"It coming to come," he would reply. As the tornado tore through the town and everyone was cowering in their basements, meteorologist Orbits followed the whirling mass, getting as close as he could.

"I am glad you decided to continue with the course."

"Me too." As the monster hurricane barrelled through the ocean, Orbits and his team plunged deep into its eye. He tried to calm their fears by telling them—

"Is it difficult?" she asked.

"It's a joyride." He caught himself and giggled as if he had spoken jokingly.

Eight months later, he wrote an exam and miraculously, he passed. He had answered half the multiple-choice questions and had guessed most of those. Some of his satisfaction faded when he noticed "Stage One" on the certificate. What the hell is this? he fumed. A hurricane or something? Stage One, everything okay. Stage Two, it getting a little serious. Stage Three, get you ass away as fast as you could. Stage Four, you dogs dead. But his wife was pleased. She framed the certificate and told him to hang it in his office. "Is just a small office," he told her. "And with all the vehicles shaking up the place, it will fall down every morning. Better we keep it here."

She hung it in the living room, close to her father's desk and beneath a dozen other certificates. Orbits felt pleased that it was in the line of vision of the older man and that he had no choice but to see it whenever he looked up from his magazine.

As the months passed, his wife asked him about completing his course, and he always replied, "In time." He saw her frustration returning, and one night he told her, "Stage One was pure theory but Stage Two is plenty practical work." Finally, he got an excuse for travelling about each day with the skullcap driver. "Today I noticed a nice little landspout," he told her in the evenings, or "I wish you could have seen these rope clouds today." He barely understood the terms and she asked for no clarification.

He continued to visit his parents each week and was disappointed by their response to his little successes that he garnished with random prevarications. Most of the times his father was alone. Orbits sat next to him and mentioned some of the places he had visited, but the old man just swished around his dentures, not saying anything. One evening out of the blue, he said, "I never see my grandchild." He was slightly more animated that day, reaching for and rearranging the plastic flowers in a nearby vase, straightening the doily, passing his fingers along the undersides of the table as if testing for nail dents.

"That's true," Orbits said, guessing the old man would soon relapse into his regular stupor, but he asked how old the girl was. "She is four," he said after a while. "In less than a year she will be in primary school."

"Primary school," he said and resumed his touching and rearranging the flowers. He began to sing in a stuttering way a nursery rhyme. "I had a little nut tree / Nothing would it bear / But a silver nutmeg / And a golden pear."

Two days later during a trip with Skullcap, they passed a small primary school on a hill. This was in a village nestled in a valley and formed around an abandoned cocoa plantation. Most of the buildings were old cocoa houses with sliding roofs or Spanish-style flats of crumbling concrete. There were just four other passengers in the vehicle, two couples who, even though they were in khaki shorts and light cotton shirts, were sweating profusely. But as the maxi weaved through a little valley and up a slight incline, the shade from the interlocked bamboo and the arching immortelle cooled the air. Orbits heard one of the foreigners saying, "This is quite nice. You can smell the cocoa. And the fruits look so polished. Is that a lilac or violet shade?" The shaded road was gloomy, this gloom enhanced by the epiphytes that seemed to be crawling along the trees and the creaking of the bamboo and the stale, sugary aroma of rotting fruits. A pair of squirrels were fluffing their bushy tails as if they were preparing for a show. From a distance came a warble so cheerful and melodious, it seemed to be mocking the mournful solitude. "That is a *chichichong*," Skullcap said, and when a tourist asked him to spell the word, he added instead, "I was using the local term. It is really a bullfinch." He mentioned another bird, a *pawi*, which he said was a kind of wild turkey. "Just a few left in the world. Maybe fifty." Orbits could see the tourists were impressed.

As they drove on, a woman wondered aloud why there weren't houses here. "So idyllic. It's perfect."

Orbits had passed places like these hundreds of times, and he always felt they seemed both sad and treacherous. Yet these foreigners, dressed more suitably for the heat than people who were born here, were noticing some hidden beauty. He wondered if they were crazy or seeing some aspect he and everyone else had grown numb to. Soon they came to a stretch of teak and poui, the slim, straight trunks creating the effect of swaying bars. A little later, the teak and poui gave way to cocoa sheltering beneath immortelle and mahogany. Epiphytes, clinging to thick vines, seemed to be leaping from one tree to the other, and beneath the pine cones were daubs of wild orchids. There were a couple ravines bordered by little thickets of balisier. On the road, there was a carpet of yellow bird-shaped flowers

"Stop here," a foreigner said as they finally came upon a building in this desolate place. "Is that a school?" a woman asked, pointing to an L-shaped structure on a hill. The path from the road to the building was lined with palmiste.

"It look so," Skullcap said. "A well-known school." He winked at Orbits in the rear-view mirror. Orbits understood his pretense, but as he listened to the foreigners, he began to see the scene through their eyes. Opposite the school was a bungalow painted entirely in dark green, which gave it the illusion of merging with the bamboo at the back and the lemon trees at the sides, from which vines stalked the eaves and jalousies. Because of this, the house appeared bigger than it was, and Orbits imagined a concrete pond at the back and some sort of greenhouse that attracted hummingbirds and parrots and bullfinches and maybe a pawi, too. This is the place, Orbits thought. This is where my daughter will attend school and where we will live.

On the way back, after they had dropped off the foreigners, Skullcap asked, "You notice we only had four people today? Most of the maxis and buses nearly empty these days."

"Rainy season," Orbits told him.

"Is more than that. The tourists going elsewhere. To other islands. Just the other day I hear two of them talking about how people here don't have a service mentality. That was the words she used. To tell you the truth I wanted to lean over and say, 'Madam, that is because we are no longer slaves.' But she was talking about something else. Rudeness. Laziness. The dontcaredamn attitude. Anyways, what I getting at is the talk I hear that Baby Rabbit intend to close down the depot. If that happen it will be back to hustling for me. What about you?"

"I doing these courses. Should manage to pick up a job with the government."

"That is the value of proper schooling, brother. I always try to pound that in the head of all the outsides. I tell them that they mother and father will be gone one day, but the education will always remain."

"Very true," Orbits said. But all his old fears resurfaced. He had neither the skills nor the confidence to find another job. At home, with his daughter as usual in her grandmother's room, he told his wife, "Getting fed up of this job. Is the same thing day after day."

"Lucky you," she said.

"Lucky? You know that in some countries boredom is the leading cause of death."

"Really? Which countries?"

"Sweden or Denmark. Maybe Finland." He tried to recall the names of smaller European nations. "I think Bulgaria too."

"I wish I could buy some of the boredom from them. With all the work I have to do at school."

"Maybe I should start helping you."

"You! Thanks. I will manage," she said chuckling. The little girl entered the room and she scooped her up. "Little Miss Smarty. What did grandma teach you today? Did she teach you about Bulgaria and all the boring people there? Eh, Chickadee?" she asked, using the grandmother's designation.

"Chickadee is not a good nickname," he told her. "Twenty years from now when she is a big woman, people will still call her that."

"Okay, Mr. Orbits."

"Thank you, Miss Teapot."

These moments with his wife displaced some of Orbits' apprehension, but they returned the minute he got to the depot. Ever since working at Baby Rabbit's place, he knew that the stretch of good luck would not last. The death of his brother had confirmed the treacherous nature of contentment; bad luck was always around the corner, sometimes out of view but always waiting patiently. In the nights he frequently imagined calamity as an actual figure, ragged but graceful. Now and again, just before he drifted off to sleep, he would see a tall man with edges so sharp he could slice a victim simply by dancing with his arms spread. He tried to fight these horrific images by creating a counterpoint. He began to think of the school in the old cocoa plantation village more and more, imagining an idealized future rather than one filled with uncertainty. He felt that if his wife could just see the place, the roads with their canopy of bamboo, the stretches of teak, the small, neat school on the hill, she would know at once why he had been so smitten. In the evenings, he tried to convey its unique appeal to her, but found that he could not properly communicate its exoticness in the manner the foreigners had done.

"A broken-down school in a haunted little village," she said one day. "Thank you, but I prefer to remain right where I am."

He continued to plead his case in this half-hearted manner right up to the moment his daughter began to attend the school in which his wife taught. Each morning he waved to both as they made their way to school. He then walked to the junction for a taxi. One day a new fear positioned itself alongside the anxiety about losing his job; he was watching both walk away and he felt: I may never see them again. He tried to examine this dread on his way to work, trying to convince himself it was nonsense, but the fear remained. What if a car knocked them down? There were always drunk drivers slipping into ditches. What if a snake was hiding in the grass, waiting patiently? What if they were kidnapped? What if his wife decided she would not return?

He grew obsessed with the thought of an accident, and every morning he reminded his wife to stop and watch whenever she heard an approaching vehicle. He used the company's phone each morning to call the school to ask if his wife had arrived safely. She requested him to put a stop to that, explaining that in the mornings the other teachers were busy with the assembly. Cell phones had recently been introduced to the island, and he badgered her to purchase one. After a few months of this, she told him, "I have a better idea."

The following week he saw a used Nissan Bluebird parked in the yard, and each evening his in-laws took his wife to practise her driving. He was put in charge of his daughter during that period, and whenever she asked about her mother, Orbits would say, "Your mummy gone to knock about with her mother and father." On occasion, he would add, "By now she knocked down two dogs, three cats and a goat. How much animals your mummy killed?"

His daughter would count on her fingers. "Six."

"Very good. You could count. Thank god you didn't take after me in brains. And don't let anybody call you Chickadee. Tell them to call you Chick. No, you better tell them to call you Dee. And make sure none of them ever call you Pusskins. You ever hear that story about the gnome that resemble your grandfather? What was his name again? Rumpeltilskinskin?" At other times, he would point to the sky and say, "How many clouds you see there?" One evening he told her, "Once upon a time, it had a little bear that used to climb on the moonbeams straight to the sky. And there he used to float on the clouds, happy as was possible." He enjoyed this time alone with his daughter, and he began to see that she had a personality of her own. She was serious and persistent but would giggle whenever he said anything funny.

One midday as he was leaving his office for Skullcap's maxi, Baby Rabbit handed him the phone. "Hurry up. This is a business phone."

He took a deep breath before he placed the receiver to his ear, but he heard his wife's voice. "Guess what? I got my license this morning. I took the day off and now I have nothing to do, so I am coming to your work."

"Here?" He glanced at his little cubicle and he recalled telling her that his office was stocked with all kinds of equipment. He tried to make excuses, but Baby Rabbit was glaring at him, so he said in a whisper, "Will meet you at the front gate."

She arrived half an hour later. "Hop in. Where you want to go?"

"I know exactly where," he told her. And even though they got lost a couple times, eventually they arrived at the old cocoa village. "Drive a little farther," he said. "Okay, stop here. What you think?" He pointed to the house opposite and added, "And look at that cottage there. Just a tiny walk across the road to the school. It look abandoned so it wouldn't cost much. We could fix it up and—"

"Are you serious? That house is probably filled with snakes and bats, and the school was closed more than ten years ago."

"I didn't know that."

She drove off and he said nothing as they passed the fruit vendors on the road, the stalls with breadfruit and purple pommerac and the little parlour with bottles of sauce and spices on the front ledge and the old shop from which he had smelled molasses and sugar during a previous trip. Now he saw just poverty and neglect. When they emerged from the village into the main road, she said, "Thank god."

Something in him broke during that trip. He realized how much his wife was different from him, how much he had been pretending. Just before they arrived at her parents' place, he asked her quietly, "How long we going to live here?"

"I have been paying them a rent ever since. They didn't want to accept it but I insisted."

For the second time that day, he told her, "I didn't know."

He grew more quiet and moody at home, deferring the trips in the Bluebird to the groceries or the malls, and frequently he was left alone in the house. At times, they returned late in the night, his daughter, Dee, already asleep. He, too, pretended to be asleep, and he would hear his wife humming a song as she changed her clothes or sat at her desk.

He tried to compensate at the depot. He showed off with technical terms he barely understood from his courses, and the drivers glanced impatiently from him to their watches. One day he told Skullcap, "I thinking of applying for a job with the television station. Or maybe with the government. I fed up doing the same thing day after day here."

"I know how it is, brother. If I had your brains I would have done the same thing. To tell you the truth, I happy with this job here."

These conversations temporarily displaced Orbits' disquiet, and in their immediate aftermaths, he returned to his old fantasies of riding a storm somewhere in the ocean or forecasting a hurricane that everyone else, all the real meteorologists on radio and television, had missed. He imagined being interviewed by grateful government ministers who testified he had saved the island from certain ruin. He was gracious in this fantasy, explaining that it was simply a matter of observing the unusual cloud formations and the velocity of the wind. Who would ever imagine that a simple thing like the clouds could tell us so much, the prime minister would say admiringly. You deserve a medal of valour for identifying what all these glorified meteorologists missed. In his fantasy, he made an earnest and stirring speech about unsung meteorologists like himself. We never expect praises even though the island rests on our shoulders. We, my friends, are all that stand between catastrophe and progress.

FIVE YEARS AFTER HE began working at Baby Rabbit's place, there was an actual storm, and just as in Orbits' fantasy, its approach was missed by all the television meteorologists. Orbits was in his cubicle at the time when the rain began. He grumbled about the water trickling between all the spaces in the cedar planks and the jailhouse slit that served as a window. He put his hands against his ears so he didn't hear the tinkling growing into a rumble or the shouting of Lilboy outside. It was only when he heard a crash and felt the water raining down and looked up and saw an aluminium sheet flapping as if it were a child holding on to the edge of a cliff that he realized what was happening. He tried to open the door, but it felt like someone was pushing on the other side. He stepped back, kicked it open and rushed outside. The sky, which an hour earlier had been grey and relatively peaceful, was black and angry. Rain was beating down from the left and then from the right. On the periphery of the roundabout, the trees were swaying this way and that, the branches combed by the wind and the leaves flying around like frenzied locusts. An aluminium sheet flew through the air and Orbits wondered where it had come from. There were a few vehicles parked in the yard, but with the torrential downpour, he couldn't tell if the drivers were inside. Only Lilboy was about, running here and there, and Orbits expected a draft to suddenly pitch him in the air. Orbits hustled back to his cubicle.

Then, just as suddenly as it had appeared, the storm ended. The drivers emerged from their maxis, Baby Rabbit came out of his office, and Orbits peeped from his cubicle. He spotted the owner with Lilboy in tow, inspecting the damage, conferring with the drivers, glancing in his direction. He saw Lilboy jumping up and down and gesturing to him. He briefly considered returning to his desk and pretending he had not noticed anything unusual. Too late. Baby Rabbit and Lilboy were walking in his direction. "You remember the prediction you make this morning?" Baby Rabbit asked.

"You remember?" Lilboy shrieked.

"A average day with temperatures around thirty degrees. That is what you say. Average."

"*And* the possibility of isolated showers," Orbits said timidly. "I believe I also said that."

"Showers? That was a shower?"

"Shower!" Lilboy echoed.

"Isolated," Orbits said weakly, wondering how he would get through this.

"Don't talk up in you ass, man. Look around you."

Orbits obeyed, and he saw Skullcap approaching. "Even the hifa-lutin radio weatherman didn't say anything about it. I always tune my radio to the station every morning," the maxi driver said. "Not a single word. This storm come like a thief in the night."

"Matter-ologist." Baby Rabbit seemed so annoyed that he fumbled with the pronunciation of the word. "Matter-ologist, fatter-ologist."

Then he said something that Orbits had suspected ever since he began working there. "Is a blasted fake profession if you ask me. More bogus than Humphrey Bogus."

"Humphrey!"

When the pair departed, Skullcap told Orbits, "Well brother, that is it for the day. You want a lift to the taxi stand?"

In the vehicle, Orbits told him, "Thanks, man."

A few minutes later the driver said, "I didn't lie. And is no wonder. Look how dry all over here is. Is like the storm only affect a little portion of the place."

He was right, and Orbits couldn't decide whether he was relieved that his wife and daughter would not have been in any danger, or disappointed that he was denied a dramatic story of being trapped heroically in a storm. At his in-laws' place, no one seemed aware of the isolated storm. His father-in-law was reading one of his thick novels at his desk, and he briefly glanced up to notice Orbits' dripping clothes. His glance travelled down to the mat and back to Orbits. *What the ass you looking at?* Orbits thought. *You never see a make-believe meteorologist who spend his last day in his job? Why you don't go back to you Pusskins book and stop* macoing *me?*

Orbits turned out for work the next day fully expecting to be summoned to Baby Rabbit's office and handed his papers. But the boss was not in his office that day, and by the end of the week, he assumed he had been forgiven and the storm forgotten. Still, he worried, and just as he had missed the storm's approach, he did not see the changes around him and all over the island that would eventually lead to the end of his job.

A month after the storm, he noticed Skullcap driving a new vehicle. "Where you get this from?" he asked.

"A loan, brother. Banks start giving loan from Sarran to Barran. That is why it have so much new vehicles in the places. Foreign used."

Orbits, caught in his own distress, hadn't noticed that the roads were now filled with strange new models of cars and vans — sleek, sporty Japanese and American vehicles. He hadn't noticed, too, that there were fewer maxis parked in the compound each morning. One morning he heard Baby Rabbit grumbling. "Is this blasted oil boom. The government getting all this money and they don't know what the hell to do with it. But don't worry about me because I thinking of building a hotel right on this spot."

Later in the week, Skullcap said, "The government build something call a priority bus route for east-west maxis. I thinking of moving down that side. Some of the other drivers already leave. It will good to be my own boss for a change. What about you?"

And Orbits, who had boasted about applying for jobs with the television station or with the government, was finally honest. "I don't know. I really don't know."

The business closed at the end of the month, and for an equal period, Orbits left the house each morning, not telling his wife he was unemployed. He took the government bus to all the towns he had visited with Skullcap and now, sitting with disgruntled passengers rather than with awed tourists, he saw confusion everywhere. Piles of rubble and asphalt and bricks were jammed halfway into the road so he could not determine whether the materials were for the houses or for the road. The newer, faster cars crashed against these barriers and every so often, the bus was caught in traffic because of an accident or a backhoe destroying or building something. Some days, vehicles were diverted because a newly installed telephone pole or cable had been ripped by machinery on its way to an offshore oil rig. The other passengers always seemed irritated with these delays, and Orbits wondered if this sudden wealth had also introduced a new level of impatience in their lives.

Every mile or so he saw little groups of men and women dressed in green, staring solemnly against their forks or spades at a drain or a culvert. When rain fell, the material was washed away, the drains overflowed, and the place was covered with mud. This scene was repeated every week. Everywhere there was dust and mud.

One day on the bus, a man with an explosion of moles on his face, said, "You see all this money? It will run through this country like diarrhoea."

And in the meantime, Orbits thought, it's like I have constipation.

"You know how you could tell if somebody working on a road project?" the man across the aisle asked. "Look for the print of the hoe handle on they face or neck. Look! Just as I say." The bus passed a group resting against the handles of their implements. "You know if I wasn't so old and so qualified, I would apply for the job myself. Get to work at seven and finish by eight."

Orbits tried to picture himself in one of the gangs. He imagined the blazing morning sun beating down his back while he walked through broken bottles and all the litter thrown out by passing vehicles. He imagined snakes and scorpions hiding in the grass, watching his approaching feet. The next day he took the bus to the capital. The frames and foundations of the burgeoning office buildings looked like skeletons hovering over the old stone cottages constructed a century ago. Trees had been cut down to make way for pavements, and there were concrete culverts crushing little rows of shrubs. As he walked along the street, he stopped to gaze at men on scaffolds heaving bricks and buckets and at the vendors directly beneath. He stood there waiting for an accident, and when it began to drizzle, he moved on. Soon he came to a street of dilapidated two-storey offices. The sign on one of the buildings said Ministry of Agriculture. He entered the building and saw piles of cardboard boxes on the desk but no people. "Hello," he shouted.

A man rose from behind a stack of boxes. "What you want? We moving next month. Come back then."

Orbits noticed — and was reassured by — the man's fatness. "Where everybody else?"

"Is two o'clock. Everybody went home."

"But you still here."

"Yes, I still here. What is it you want?"

"I am a meteorologist."

"That nice. It raining outside?"

"I believe so."

"How long the rain will last?"

It was just a light drizzle, so Orbits said, "An hour for the most."

"Okay. Come and sit on that empty chair, and if the rain stop before an hour you will get a job."

Orbits guessed the man was joking but as he was tired from walking around the city, he laughed and sat. Half an hour later, he felt that he had been tricked into listening to the man complain about the other workers, the disruption of the move to a newer building and the relocation of some of his favourite eating places. "By the way, my name is Wally. Short for Walrus. What is yours?"

"Orbits."

"Short for what?"

"Nothing. Because of my job."

"Orbits. I like the ring of that. So you really is a meteorologist? What you think of the man with the parrot on his back?"

"I think they use the same film every day."

"What! You joking right?" Orbits admitted he was, and the man said, "Go to the window of the next room and check if the rain still falling."

It was still drizzling lightly, but Orbits said, "It stopped."

"Okay, you just get hired."

Although Orbits wasn't sure if the man was serious, he asked, "Field work or office work?"

Wally chuckled and his belly jiggled. He had a big round nose and curly hair that covered his ears. "You see that pile of applications on that box? I want you to file it according to date. And if you see anything more than five years old, pitch it in the dustbin." While Orbits was completing this task, Wally walked over. "Don't be surprised if that little drizzle cause a big flood."

"So you is a meteorologist too?" Orbits asked lightly. Wally pulled a chair next to him and said that the original planners of the city had designed a network of culverts and drains to cater for the water rushing down from the mountain, but all those had been neglected and were now filled with garbage and mud. Orbits was surprised by Wally's knowledge and planned to casually mention this bit of information to his wife.

When he got home, he told her, "I finally left the job for a position with the government. More security."

"What is it you have to do?"

He recalled the time when she would have been thrilled with the news. "The Ministry of Agriculture," he said, not mentioning that he had spent much of his first day listening to Wally and filing papers.

"Did you sign a contract? What's the salary?"

"No contract as yet. Salary to be negotiated," he said uneasily. He noticed that his wife had not looked up from her papers, and he turned to his daughter, who was bent over a book. "Hello, Dee. You could tell me if it raining outside? When this rain going to stop? Now? Okay, you hired."

When he arrived the next morning at the ministry, he walked through the corridor to the row of boxes. Wally was not there, and a thin man with thin lips and a high nose that emphasized his nostrils and revealed the lush growth inside coughed into a kerchief and asked, "Who you is?"

"The new employee. The meteorologist?"

Now a woman who seemed to be in her forties, wearing huge stylish glasses that seemed mismatched with her old jacket and bruised shoes and grey hair, said, "The what?"

"Mr. Wally hired me yesterday."

"I see," the man said. His thin, rubbery lips gave him the look of a raconteur, but when he spoke his eyes grew weak and treacherous. "You just walk in and he hired you off the bat."

Orbits didn't like his sarcastic trembling nostrils and unstable lips and he said, "That is exactly what happened."

Just then, Wally walked in. He was sweating and breathing heavily, and his shirt was stained yellow. "I see everybody meet Orbits already. Okay, back to work." Orbits resumed the task he had been given the previous day, and the two other employees settled behind their own boxes. After an hour, the man disappeared and soon after, the woman.

"Lunch break already?" Orbits asked confused.

"They finish for the day. But is *my* lunch break." He took out a bucket of chicken from his knapsack and walked to an adjoining room. The barrack-shaped building had once housed several ministries according to Wally, and all but this had been relocated to newer structures. So that there were abandoned and unlit rooms leaking from the roof and smelling of damp cardboard and rotting paper. In one of these rooms, Wally and Orbits ate.

As Wally tore into and gnawed at the chicken, he kept up a stream of chatter. The Ministry of Agriculture was a neglected department because of the association of fieldwork with the island's past. This section of the ministry had been tasked with the granting of subsidies to farmers, but there was too much *bobol* he said, using the local term for corruption. "People who know nothing about farming get acres of land and money to open pig farms. And guess what? Pigs start running wild all over the place." He related other stories of corruption and mismanagement, about officials requesting hunting permits and of a government minister who had developed a taste for the scarlet ibis, a protected bird. No wonder we couldn't see any in the swamp, Orbits thought. "These people, the minute they get any power they begin to act like they own the government," Wally said. "I used to like to hear them talk though. Plenty rhyme but no reason. People don't care if you making sense or not once you could flap your gum and don't allow anybody to interrupt you."

Another day Wally told him that the political leader of one party was reputed to lock herself in her mansion watching Bollywood movies, emerging periodically draped in saris and with a martyred, manic expression, while the leader of the other party, who revelled in his reputation as a bad-john, took his inspiration from Blaxploitation movies. Orbits enjoyed talking with Wally. The other man revealed that he was the only one in his family who had not migrated, and he infused his stories of corruption with snippets of his relatives and of the history of Portuguese people in the island. Orbits, not familiar with the mix of town people and their range of colours, hadn't even known of his ethnicity when he first met him.

He guessed that Wally did not get along with the two other employees because he waited until they had left at about 11:00 before he pulled out his bucket of chicken. He felt a kinship with the older man, a fat boy again but without the fat or the shame. Wally never seemed unduly angry, impatient, reproachful or petulant. Even his criticisms of the government and the sagaboys had the feeling of distance, as if all of this was to be expected and life would go on and he would live as he always had. His comments could have been directed at some other island and to complete strangers. Orbits could not understand how someone of Wally's weight carried no discernible baggage. Or, if he did, how he managed to hide it so skilfully. Orbits was unaware of the complexities of town life, so he did not suspect that Wally's colour, even though it was just a shade lighter than his dead brother's, had put him a step higher and immunized him from the usual bacchanal, all the rivalries and racial distress. He surmised instead that Wally was wealthy, and he was in the job just because he could roam about the town and into the restaurants and rumshops he talked about.

HE GOT HIS FIRST paycheque six weeks after he had stepped into the building and he was disappointed at the paltry sum even though it was about the same at the depot. He had always heard that government employees got hefty salaries for doing nothing. More than the salary, he was disappointed at the title on the pay stub. Clerk 1. Wally had given him the envelope and at noon he said, "We have to celebrate."

They went into a little Chinese restaurant where the customers called out to Wally. During the meal, while Wally ploughed through the plates of stewed chicken and roast pork and the bowls of wontons and *brûle gueule* on bake, Orbits was wondering who would pay for everything. He himself had ordered just a plate of shrimp and chow mein. When the bill came, Wally said, "Big celebration. First paycheque."

On his way back, Orbits tried to calculate the percentage of his salary he had spent on a single meal. "The big ravenous beast," he grumbled to himself. "It look like he hire me just to eat me out." But he found himself going out more frequently with Wally, to a breakfast shed next to the wharf where there were huge plates of baked kingfish and plantain and dasheen, to the street vendors around the Savannah who sold boiled corn and pudding and *souse*, pickled pig trotters in lime and cucumber from pitch-oil tins, to a host of little parlours that displayed their coconut and cassava cakes behind an array of high stools.

Wally didn't just eat; he commented on taste and texture and speculated knowledgeably on the ingredients and the types of preparation. He considered himself a gourmet, and gradually Orbits felt the appetite he had tamped down for a third of his life returning. He started off by sampling the fare from the pitch-oil tins, tiny bits that he felt would be harmless, before he graduated to the greasy sandwiches. He came into his own at the breakfast shed, where he discovered that the baked fish and the boiled tubers and fresh vegetables did not bring on the queasiness he recalled so well. He had forgotten the satisfying glow of fullness and solidity that an overloaded belly would bring. One day Wally told him, "Orbits, boy, you becoming a real gourmet. Just like me." They began to include nips of rum with the meals. "The first one is for the digestion," Wally explained. "The second one is for pleasure. And any that follow is for vice."

Orbits appreciated the fact that Wally treated him as an equal, but more than this, he had opened a window into town life. He spoke about the time when the Americans had a military base in the island, and he pointed out the roads built by the soldiers who had visited whorehouses that were still in operation. "The things the people build here tell we what they intentions was. The French and Spanish build with wood but the British use stone and concrete. They was here to stay." Another day he said, "The British people build roads to avoid the mountain but the Americans cut through everything *toute baghai*. That is they style." He had the habit of talking about events in the island's past, when it was controlled by the French or the Spanish, as if these had happened just as recently as the battle between two women to lead the opposition party or the comment from the prime minister that who didn't like what he was doing should leave for some other island. In this way, the history of the place, stirred with current rumours and *commesse*, seemed alive and completely the opposite of the lessons Orbits had done at school. And Wally spoke to him as a confidante, revealing information that was transformed by the rum and the smoky rooms into secrets that went beyond their jobs, beyond the island, beyond the century even. One afternoon, Orbits told Wally, "You know, if these miserable teachers didn't only expect us to remember dates and names, maybe I would have passed my history exam."

"Believe it or not, it was my favourite subject. I was always interested in how my people manage to come down here. People from
every corner of the earth land in this little place. Some with chains,
some with guns and all with ghosts. What about you?"

Not knowing how to respond, not wanting to reveal thoughts
like these had never entered his mind, Orbits said, "I have enough
trouble with my own parents to go so far back."

Wally, sensing his awkwardness, said in a boisterous voice, "The
War of Captain Jenkins' Ear. You ever hear about that one?"

"A war about somebody ears? You joking."

Frequently Wally's conversations shifted to even more impen-
etrable topics, about books he had read in his youth, the music he
had compiled, the films he had seen. When he drifted to these topics,
Orbits imagined he was taking a crash course in everything that was
foreign to him. From time to time, he thought back to his teenage
years, to the time when all he could think of was surviving.

In the evenings when he got home, his head still spinning from
the rum and the stories, he would tell his wife, "You ever listen to this
fella Mussolini? I looking for his album all over the city." Or, "The
problem with this place is everybody listening to one kind of music.
What kind of culture is that?" His wife listened quietly to Wally's
recycled comments, she smelled the rum and noticed Orbits' red
eyes, but she said nothing even when her husband mispronounced a
name or mistook Mussolini for Mantovani or talked about a singing
quartet he called the Beatlejuices. If Orbits had been sober during
these periods, he would have noticed, over the months, the shift in
his wife's reactions from minor amusement to a frayed patience that
gradually gave way to outright frustration. Finally, there was just
indifference. But denied any kind of friendship for so long, he revelled in the conspiratorial tones that Wally used in the smoky rumshops surrounded by strangers. Once, while he was listening to Wally
explain the differences between town and country politicians, both

equally corrupt — the former looking only for solid cash and the latter for favours for his family — Orbits wondered once more if Wally had also been bullied at school. Yet he showed no scars, no signs of ever having been humiliated, no self-consciousness about his appetite. He wished he could be like that. Every once in a while, on his way home, his tipsiness giving him a languid optimism, he felt as if Wally's confidence had wiped away some of the shame that had marked most of his youth. Maybe the teachers had not been as oppressive as he recalled, or the other students as cruel. Perhaps, too, he had misjudged his mother's affection only for his younger brother. In this way, he felt that his association with Wally was helping him to reassess and readjust his life. The visits to the rumshops grew from weekly to every other day.

One evening, a little over a year after he began the job, Orbits' daughter said, "Daddy belly looking big."

"That is because I working with the government, Dee. All government workers have big bellies. It's the law."

"Why mummy belly not big then?"

"Because . . . you better ask her yourself."

The mother told the girl, "If you go to sleep early tonight, me and you and grandma will go to the mall tomorrow. Okay?"

But Orbits persisted. "Ask your mummy, Dee. Ask her."

She slammed shut her book and took the girl's hand. "Because I don't come home every evening smelling of rum and pork and nasty food and talking nonsense about things I don't understand." She turned to her daughter. "Do you want to go to grandma? She will read you a story."

Orbits felt his wife was pushing him aside. He asked her, "That is true, girl? I does really be talking nonsense about things I don't understand?"

He had asked the question in a jocular manner that at one time would have provoked some amusing rejoinder from his wife, but she remained serious. "Look, Orbits, you have your life to live and I have mine."

"What you mean by that?" he asked, sitting on the end of the bed

"Nothing. Don't bother."

He asked the question louder, his jocular tone gone. She got up from her desk and stood over him. "Everything I do is with my parents and my child. You are always missing. I might as well be a single mother."

"That is what you want?" he asked quietly.

"Never mind."

"Never mind?" He felt his temper, roused by the rum he had consumed a few hours earlier, rising and he tried to adopt a joking tone so she would not suspect. "I going to get send to detention now? Or penance on the blackboard? Eh, Dee? Ask your mother."

Now his wife turned from her folders. "Ask him, Dee . . . ask him what is his intention."

"Ask her what she mean by intention, Dee. Intention about what?"

Now she faced him directly. "About everything. What is it you want from your family? From yourself?"

He began to lose control. It sounded like one of her lesson plans. This is what I have become, he thought. A part of her syllabus. A hollow thing with no life. He told her, "I happy with anything that fall in my lap."

"And that is it?"

"What the hell you expect me to say?" He was startled by his voice and the fright in his daughter's eyes. She began to cry. "I can't predict the future," he said softly.

The next day at work, chatting with Wally, sipping rum in a restaurant, the light low and the fan creaking steadily, the aroma of meaty soups wafting from the kitchen, his argument with his wife seemed removed; it could have happened to some other person, maybe one of the other customers or a passenger, a man or woman on the bus who discussed marital problems with no inhibitions. Yet, the moment he got home and saw his wife, distant, her shoulders hunched, her head over her books, her annoyance visible only from her measured breathing, his own defences went up.

In the nights after the drunkenness had gone and he was awake on the bed, turned away from the desk, he felt like an appendage, like the tadpole tails that had dropped off in the teacher's experiment. In the mornings, he left before his wife, no goodbye kisses now, no little flirtations. He tried to stabilize himself by counting his footsteps to the bus stop, but the minute he got on board and noticed the always-inquisitive faces of the other passengers, he felt they knew that he had been rushed, tricked and trapped into marriage. "I didn't know I got married until after the wedding."

The man sitting next to him nodded his head sadly, and Orbits realized he had spoken aloud. "I see something on a gravestone just like that," the man said. "About a woman." Orbits guessed the man was referring to the epitaph he had seen on his honeymoon. Yet at intervals, he saw himself more clearly, and he would wonder if the other passengers were also noticing this man who, always expecting rejection, was forever preparing for it. Then the blame shifted from his wife and her parents to his mother, his teachers, his taunting schoolmates, to himself.

In the afternoons and evenings, when Wally spoke of important government officials and the transfer of funds between permanent secretaries and of his family who had fled to Canada, Orbits saw his own problems as inconsequential and temporary, but his wife's question remained with him, resurrected the minute his tipsiness shifted into a dull reflectiveness. During one session, Wally mentioned his relatives' idea that he should migrate to Canada. "What I will do in that cold place?" Wally asked. "With nobody understanding my accent I will be roaming from one end to the next like a madman." Orbits had laughed at Wally's lugubrious description, but on the bus, he tried to imagine his own future and could think of nothing specific. When Starboy was about fourteen or so he had announced he was going to build a raft to sail around the world. "Kon-tiki-tiki-tiki," their mother had said as if his brother were still a baby. Orbits' fantasies were punctured more disdainfully. He recalled an essay his teacher had given the class when he was in primary school. The students were asked to write about their imagined lives as adults. Orbits had written about a thin and successful man who had dedicated his life to helping poor people.

He had been surprised when the teacher asked him to read the essay before the class. But two paragraphs down, he heard the snickers of the boys in the front row. He stopped and looked at the teacher, who had a meditative look, before he continued. The laughter grew louder. At the final paragraph, Orbits felt like crying, but he continued to read. "In conclusion, I will help everyone who come to me for help. All the chimney sweepers and orphans and children with leper."

The teacher had scrambled him. "You will help the chimney sweepers, Mr. Dickens?" Slap. "How much you see around here?" Slap. "Orphan, Mr. Mark Twain? And children with lepers?" All of them in Chacachacare. How much lepery children you see here?" Slap. The teacher had stopped only when a girl pointed at Orbits' pants and held her hand against her mouth. "Go and clean yourself, Mr. Tommy Lee Jones," he shouted, using the name Orbits had adopted in the essay.

Orbits was humiliated by the memory, and he looked around the bus nervously. He tried to recall if he had cried during the episode. "I never cry," he muttered to himself, and suddenly he saw the abuse as funny. "Fatboy fall down but he didn't shed a single tear." He decided he would relate the episode to his wife. Let her know what he had had to undergo. He had survived and now he had a wife, a daughter, and a respectable job. He had answered her question almost two decades earlier in an essay. But by the time he dropped off, the tipsy notion of redemption had begun to fade. He walked quickly to his wife's house. He related the episode to her. He made the teacher more tyrannical and his own stoicism more heroic. He omitted the shame of peeing his pants. He added breezy dialogue; he made himself Tommy Lee Jones. His wife was not impressed. She continued marking her papers. "Hello. You didn't hear what I just say?" he asked her.

"And I am supposed to be impressed? How long ago was that? And what happened in the interim?"

"Interim? A big word. A very big word." Dee was asleep, so he had to speak to her directly. "Almost as big as . . ." He tried to think of a word. "As petty. No, that too small. As malcontent." His mood began to shift as he sensed the ridiculousness of his behaviour; the word he had picked up from Wally and was not even sure of its meaning.

Her eyes were flashing, so Orbits was surprised when she began to sniffle. He rose from the bed and hugged her. He took her to the bed and there they made love for the last time. In the years to come, he invented more amenable versions of this final bit of intimacy, but for a long time, he only recalled her unmoving body beneath his and her eyes cold and unblinking.

The following day he told Wally, "Me and the madam going through a rough patch."

"Well, boy, I always say that love is like a nice peaceful sleep and that marriage is the alarm clock." Orbits laughed, and he noticed the other male employee listening in an irritated manner. Later in a restaurant, Wally divided the nip of rum into two glasses and said, "They say marriage is a process of discovery, but the real discovery is about the kind of man or woman the other party would have preferred."

Wally, speaking like this, trivialized the issue, and Orbits felt his domestic situation was just a temporary rift that would in time set itself right, but at home, the breach seemed to widen each day. On his way from work, tipsy from the rum, he considered ways he could ameliorate the situation, but by the time he had arrived at the house, he felt that apologizing would be an admission of wrongdoing. As far as he was concerned, the fault lay elsewhere. It was his wife who had refused to move out, who ganged up with her parents, who cut him out of her life. So he walked into the house shackled with an undefinable rage. Sometimes he imagined he was living several lives at once, and he wondered whether jumping from dread to anger to guilt to a pinprick of pleasure was normal. Yet at other times, he felt he was a bystander helplessly watching events unfold. He began to be plagued by dreams of his brother flailing in a pond, trapped on the upper floor of a burning building, bleeding from bullet wounds. And always he was on the sideline watching. Paralyzed.

AS HE HAD DONE in the past, he sought comfort from food, and by the time he moved out, after nearly eight months of silence between him and his wife, he was close to Wally's size. He had never expected to return to his parents' place, and apart from his last years, when he moved to a place about which he had always fantasized, he spent the rest of his life in the house where he had grown up. During those eight months of silence, he knew it was just weakness that was keeping him in place. Weakness and the frail hope that magically he and his wife would remember what they had liked about each other. To this end, he summoned images like those of the night he had run all the way to the hospital, but that memory came hitched to the recollection of his in-laws' impatience and intransigence. Every single memory was burdened with another, and one day at work he told Wally he was leaving early. "A little emergency," he told his boss, who spread his hands and crossed his legs tragically like a fat Charlie Chaplin. That afternoon, he travelled around for three hours, perhaps hoping he would have a moment of lucidity when everything would make sense and the world would right itself. By the time he arrived at his in-laws' place, he had resigned himself to the only option available.

In the village, a husband's abandonment of his wife, or, more commonly, a wife's hasty departure, was always a scene of bacchanal. There were curses, threats, recriminations, and unabashed crying. Neighbours came out and took sides. Intermittently, there were open scuffles. Orbits' departure had none of this drama: while he was packing his clothes into two suitcases, his wife was at her desk, papers before her, a red marker in her hand. When he walked out of the room with the suitcases, his father-in-law did not look up from his book, nor did his mother-in-law emerge from the kitchen. He felt a faint hope when, on the porch, he heard his wife saying, "Dee, go and tell your daddy goodbye."

His daughter had been in the yard, under a cherry tree, pretending to have a picnic with her dolls. He scooped up his daughter. "What you have inside there?" she asked, pointing to the suitcases on the ground.

"Nothing much. Just some old clothes."

"Mummy buy new clothes. For me too. You want to see them?"

"No, Dee. Some other time. Daddy have to go now."

"To work? But it getting dark."

"Yes, it getting dark." He put down his daughter and glanced at the bedroom to see if the curtain had shifted. Instead he heard a low humming, one of his wife's favourite songs. As he walked away from the house, with each step he felt the lifelessness of the last hours falling away, so that by the time he reached the junction he had to compose himself before he opened the taxi's door. Instinctively he looked up at the sky. In the twilight, the wavy clouds appeared iridescent, and he imagined that if he were twenty years younger, he would pretend there was a big fete somewhere beyond with firecrackers and strobe lights and women with gauzy tinsel dresses dancing with men who grew transparent the further away they moved from their partners. A term from his meteorological course came to him: polar stratospheric clouds, a phenomenon that only occurred thousands of miles away. In the car, he continued gazing up until the sun sank and the sky went pitch black. He thought of the composed wife and the innocent child and the impassive in-laws he had left behind, and one clear thought burst through his despair: how do these people manage to live such orderly lives?

>~~

ALL HIS OLD FEARS resurfaced when he moved back. On the first night, sleeping in his old room, he thought: Nothing has changed. I am back where I began. Fat and useless. Chimney sweep. Slap. Lepers. Slap. Fatboy fall down. Hahaha. This is my life. I was a fool to expect anything more. But this self-pity melted over the following weeks as he realized it was not the same; he now had a job, a friend, and his mother's attention was not directed elsewhere. Her fascination with the evangelical churches had come to an end — the pastor accused of molestation, beaten and duly driven out to another village — and now she was home or in her backyard garden, her new project, for most of the day. But she still spoke in the slightly demented manner of someone clinging to a shifting and insubstantial optimism. She was overjoyed that Orbits had returned, and she claimed that she had anticipated this event down to the date. She brought out vegetables from her garden and packed containers of chicken and rice for his work each morning. In the nights when he returned, his parents would be asleep and the table laden with covered dishes.

His father, too, gradually seemed slightly more interested in what was happening around him. Orbits' mother revealed that his father had sold the dental lab because everyone was now going to licensed dentists. "Is a good thing too," she said. "Because he was making the wrong size teeth and sometimes forgetting appointments. "For some, he make little pointed rat teeth and for others, long teeth like that man . . . what is his name again?"

"Mr. Rabbit."

She chuckled. "Is a good thing Papoose home now. You too." Her eyes clouded for a moment and she added, "He don't talk much again. You remember when he used to describe all the dentures he make for his customers? None of that again. Something eating him up from the inside."

On weekends, Orbits tried to engage his father in conversations about his old job and his former clients, and the older man nodded and rubbed his fingers along a nearby object; during one conversation, Orbits felt his father was trying to assure himself he could still touch and feel. One weekend he brought out his father's shoes from beneath his bed. "We going for a little walk."

Throughout the walk to the junction, his father's steps short and faltering, Orbits pointed out all the familiar buildings: the wooden house hidden by bougainvillaea in which a beekeeper lived by himself, the old concrete flat owned by a retired surveyor and next to that an oil-stained yard littered with vehicle parts. "That is where Joe the mechanic and his madam live," he said. "And look at the parlour where Miss Bango used to sell her sugar cakes and tamarind balls. You remember when people use to say she would grind up the sugar cake with her teeth? Over there is the rumshop where the sergeant spend most of his time. Maybe he retired now." They walked past the junction where his father usually got his taxi to a stretch of cane land. "The cane growing wild now. The sugar factory closed a little while ago."

His father asked in a distressed voice, "It closed? Why it closed?"

He recalled a conversation with Wally and said, "Everybody connect cane with slavery and bondage. Sugar have a bad name."

His father giggled, and Orbits remembered that Sugars was the name of his father's former client. "Sugars don't pay."

"Yes, yes, that is true." Orbits smiled, thinking it funny.

On the way back, he told his father, "The money didn't reach this village as yet. Everything is the same. But all over the island people building big houses right on top their old ones and all kind of new cars making accidents every day. Everything topsy-turvy."

"Really?" His father stopped.

"Yes, is true. All over mud and concrete and steel beams scatter about like if is a war zone."

"A war zone?"

"And workers going around in a circle like crazy ants."

His father giggled.

When they returned, Orbits' mother told him, "It look like Papoose enjoy the walk. He perk up a little bit. He need to go outside more often instead of chook up in the house all day interfering with everything in sight."

That week at work, Orbits told Wally, "I thinking of buying a little jalopy."

Wally responded immediately as if he had been waiting for this revelation. "I know just the place." The taxi drove out of the capital and into a street where every house had been converted into a car business depot. The yards were packed with cars, and from the porches and upper windows, bumpers, fenders, rims and windscreens were suspended from cables. An hour later, both men sat at a nearby shop, waiting for their order of chicken roti to be brought over. "One year ago, all the houses on this street were shacks. Then one fella get into this foreign-used business and he tell his cousin next door and his cousin tell his uncle and so it spread. Muslim people. They help out each other like that. So you see anything you like?"

"I have to see some more to make a comparison."

"That make sense, yes."

But the prices of the cars were far more than Orbits had expected. Each place they visited, Wally asked him, "So you see anything that you like?"

And Orbits' reply always was, "I want to make a comparison." This went on for close to half a year, and Wally never seemed displeased or disappointed. During each trip, they visited some nearby restaurant or a little shop serving Indian food, and after the initial conversation about the suitability of a vehicle had been put aside, they chatted about the job and the oil boom and about Wally's family in Canada.

One afternoon while they were in a rumshop munching on cutters — gizzard and cracker — Wally told him, "The family up in the cold always telling me I should forget this place and join them, and I always say that I happy here and I will die here. But you notice how much crime it have now? This is what money does do. Criminals from near and far flooding to this place. Once, you could have recognized a criminal from a distance because he was always weighed down with gold chains and had a scar across half his face. Now it could be the little *nashy* boy with a gun hiding in his pocket. Coward tax. That is what all these big people paying the elders to safeguard they businesses and children." Orbits was surprised; he had assumed that these community elders were wise old men with flowing beards and gentle eyes, but Wally explained they were gang leaders given respectability because of their access to politicians. Both men finished the nip and ordered another. "Is four years now they planning to move us to the new building and we didn't move an inch. Still operating from cardboard boxes. This place going downhill and uphill at the same time. Spinning top in mud."

Orbits was dismayed, but he guessed that Wally's talk of leaving was simply a way of continuing the conversation, of matching Orbits' complaints about the brief and curt telephone conversations he had

had with his wife. "You believe that is months since I didn't see the daughter face?" he asked.

That was a lie because he had not visited since he had moved out. During those initial months, he considered dropping by but was always stopped by the image of his reproachful in-laws and by the memory of his wife that last night looking up at him with a focused hatred. He had called a few times, hoping he would hear something in his wife's voice that suggested longing or guilt or even pity, but each time he heard on the receiver, "Dee, that man want to talk to you. You want to talk to *that* man?" His last call had been about three months earlier, and his mother-in-law had answered. "The girl is busy with her common entrance." Then she had hung up.

The day of the examination, he hovered around the phone in the office, and he even dialled his wife's number before he hung up. At midday, he called the school and a teacher told him that the students were still writing the exam and he should not call again. "Sure, sure. I understand," he said, but when he got home, he told his mother, "These blasted people don't want me to talk to my own daughter."

"I never trusted them," his mother replied, misunderstanding whom he was referring to. "I never trust anybody who eat with knife and fork." He didn't bother to correct her, and he was pleased when she continued about how all their ambitiousness had dried them out into thin *marasme* people. "Thank god you escape," she said. "Look how nice and plump you get back."

But my daughter didn't escape, he thought. Maybe I should go to the school and ask her to come with me. But what if the mother already turned her mind against me? In that case, I could prove that everything the mother said was a lie. But will she believe me? In that mood of indecision, Orbits finally bought a vehicle. Not a foreign-used, but an old Kingswood from Joe the mechanic just six houses away. He had seen Joe halfway inside the hood during a walk with his father. The mechanic, a black, bald man with a protruding belly that looked hard as rock came to the road to chat with his father, who asked about the car he was repairing. "Australian brand," Joe said. "Build for the outbacks." He led them to the car, and Orbits' father walked around trailing his finger along the hood and the trunk and the shiny chrome bumpers. "Nice eh? Once I get the alternator running I will have she purring like a cyat." His father stepped inside and ran his palms on the dashboard. "A fella give me to fix it up and like he forget about it. I sure he already buy some foreign-used that will break down in one year time."

"So these new imported vehicles not good?" Orbits asked.

"Don't talk to me about them cars," Joe said. "They good for nothing. Nice and pretty and well behaved like a girlfriend before you put ring on finger. But after that . . ."

"Yes, yes," Orbits said.

"But not this Kingswood here. The more you run, the tougher she will get. She build for durability. This is wife material."

At the end of the conversation, an agreement was reached: Orbits would buy the vehicle for twelve thousand, five hundred dollars. "We could drive it home now?" the father asked.

"No, Uncle, not yet. I have to repair the alternator and clean the brake lines and the plugs. Might have to get another battery too."

"All that?" Orbits asked anxiously.

"Listen man, the strongest mule wouldn't go anywhere unless you feed it properly. Is just some minor preps."

The next day Orbits withdrew five thousand, the extent of his savings, from the bank and made a down payment. Joe counted the money slowly and told him, "Man, is a good thing you make this payment because a fella was passing on the road and he see the car and decide there and then it was for him. He beg me not to sell she to anybody else, but as they say in primary school, the early bird get the car."

"So when I will get she?"

"Just some minor preps, man."

It was five weeks before Orbits was able to collect the car. He out-lined his frustrations to Wally, who, initially disappointed that Orbits had made a decision on his own and had bought an old model instead of a foreign-used, recovered to lament the profusion of small-time schemers in the island. "This place have more smartmen per square inch than any other place in the world. The only difference between a sagaboy and a thief is that a sagaboy didn't get catch as yet. Thank god you didn't make a down payment."

"That is the thing. I make a little one. A small tiny deposit," he lied. "But is the principle of the thing that have me upset."

As they grew tipsier, Wally told him, "Let me tell *you* what does upset me. Everybody have a nice plaster for this skulduggery busi-ness. If you ask me, it started way back with slavery. Small man against big man and everybody rightfully supporting small man."

"So far back?"

"It had a purpose then, but the thing is it never stop! So now, every manjack have some scheme in they back pocket. If I was you I would forget the deposit and move on."

In his drunken bravado, Orbits told him, "Never happen! Is the principle of the thing. I will haul his mangy ass straight to the court-house. He don't know who he playing with."

The next morning, sobered up and on his way to the junction, Orbits would ask Joe, "So when I getting the car, Joe?"

"Don't rush the brush, man. How you will feel if I give you a defective car?"

"I will feel bad."

"Exactly."

And that afternoon, Orbits would continue his tirade, "He get-ting frighten. I could see it in his eyes. He didn't know who he was messing with. Ay-ay-yai."

His bravado lasted as long as his tipsiness. He was embarrassed by his weakness and frightened by Joe's growing insolence. One evening Wally was called to a meeting and Orbits returned from work early. He noticed that the mechanic was now working on another car and that the Kingswood was covered with a tarpaulin. "I notice you hiding the car," he told Joe.

"From the dew. Dew does look like a little simple thing, but it could destroy a piece of metal in no time. Worse than acid, if you ask me."

"So when I getting the car?"

Joe looked up and wiped a spanner against his dirty pants. "I tell you already, man, that I don't want to give you a defective car. We is neighbours so how it will look?" He resumed his knocking at an engine block.

"Listen, Joe, I have a friend who giving me some strange advice. A lawyer fella. Portagee. High-class Portagee from the town. He saying I should bring you up."

The knocking stopped. "Tell that high-class Portagee he could kiss my oily ass. Bring me up! When next you meet him tell him that Mister Joe fight his way out of all kind of battle." He knocked the spanner against his solid belly. "Tell him that Mister Joe nearly kill a man for spoiling his good name."

Orbits, thoroughly frightened by then, regretted his provocation of the mechanic. He eyed the distance to the road. He would have to jump over a drain and run for five minutes before he got to the junction. By then Joe would be bludgeoning him with his spanner.

Then the mechanic began to cry. "Poor people have no place in this world. Corbeau pee on we head. We worse than dog. Worse even than cyat." At the end of the episode, an agreement was reached: Orbits would pay the balance by the weekend and collect the car. He took a loan from the bank, and Wally agreed to stand as security.

"So when you getting the vehicle?" his friend asked over a meal.

"This weekend."

"You will drive it home? You know with all the crime in the place nowadays, it make sense getting a vehicle, never mind the type and the age."

"These newer models like a high-maintenance girlfriend."

"I not living too far from this work here, so I never see the need for a car or a driving license. But for a country boy like you it make plenty sense." As Wally continued in his optimistic manner about restaurants in remote areas they could now visit in the vehicle, Orbits was reminded that he had never driven a car and had no idea how to operate a vehicle. Also, he did not have a driving permit.

That weekend the car had to be pushed onto the road from the mechanic's place to Orbits' yard. "I tell you that she needed some prepping. This is what happen to people who harden and don't listen."

"I don't know what my Portagee lawyer friend will say about this," Orbits replied, wiping the sweat from his face.

"I think is the battery. I will take one out from another car and drop it this evening." He kept his word and for three months, every morning Orbits drove the car from the yard to the road and back into the yard. His parents watched expectantly from the porch. One day he told Wally, "You know in the excitement about buying a car, I clean forget about driving permit."

"I know somebody," Wally told him.

The somebody was a businessman who, tired of being robbed, had applied for a gun license. He had been told he needed to be registered as a farmer before one could be issued, and Wally had facilitated his registration. Wally and Orbits met the man in a rumshop not far from the street of foreign-used vehicles. The businessman boasted openly about getting most of those vehicles licensed by substituting their registration numbers with crashed and written-off vehicles. Orbits paid the man two hundred dollars, and the following week, the two met at a licensing office, where his photograph was taken and a license issued.

AT THE AGE OF thirty-three, Orbits began to drive. During his first few trips to the grocery just half a mile away, he recalled his journey along that route on his way to primary school, when he had emphasized his new nickname by pointing to and gazing at the sky. Those daily trips had been agonizing, and after a while, he stopped telling his parents he no longer wanted to go to school because of the bullying. They had laughed away his complaints because like everyone else on the island, they could not understand the idea of abuse. Children were either strong and resilient or weak and disappointing. He hoped his daughter took after her mother instead of him. Off and on, he took his mother to the local market, but he never ventured out of the village. During these trips she was thrilled and talked about visiting relatives he had never heard about and who lived in the opposite ends of the island.

Every morning while he was on the bus, he would look at the cars speeding by, cutting in and out of the traffic recklessly. And each evening his mother reminded him about the journeys he had promised her. "It will be good for Papoose too. Whole day he chook up in the house."

Ever since he got the vehicle, Orbits had fantasized about paying an unexpected visit to his daughter and taking her in his Kingswood to ice cream parlours and fast food outlets and to the cinema. But his first trip out of the village was with his parents. He drove through backtraces and dirt roads to avoid the highway, but his parents did not seem to mind. His mother in the back seat commented on the fruit trees, the bridges and the newly paved roads. Eventually they came to the primary school on the hill and the green bungalow opposite. Orbits stopped and parked the car. "What you think?"

"I think I went to that school."

"Hush you mouth, Papoose. That was never your school." She chuckled and added, "You Papoose always making up things. This is where your daughter going, boy?"

"No. That is about half an hour away. She write her exam and waiting for the result. It will get published in the papers any day now."

Orbits' second trip out of the village was to his daughter's school. Two weeks after his trip with his parents, he saw her name listed in the newspapers; she had passed for one of the prestige colleges in the town. He felt a surge of pride and called the school. His daughter was in a class, he was told, but there would be a farewell function for the successful students on Friday. He told Wally he would be away and mentioned the reason. In the evening, he went to a department store. The clerk pushed aside the trousers and shirt he had chosen and brought over another pair. "The biggest mistake fat people make is to buy tight-tight clothes," the clerk explained. "And stop pulling in your belly. Is nothing to be ashamed about. Is your genes."

"That is true. Is genes." But for the first time since his childhood, Orbits felt anxious about his weight. What would his daughter think? What would the teachers? And his former wife?

"I don't care one shit about that," he muttered the following morning as he put on the new shirt and pants. He glanced at himself in the mirror. His belly was hidden by the oversized clothes, but he saw a round stuffed animal wrapped in a blanket. "That blasted, scheming no-good clerk," he grumbled all the way to the car. "He add a good hundred pounds to me."

By the time he got to the school, he was sweating from the thick fabric, and the shirt, drenched with sweat, followed all the contours of his belly. The place was already filled with parents, and he sat at the back looking for a sign of his wife and his daughter. He saw his daughter first, sitting on the stage, and she seemed so pretty and poised he wanted to get up and call out to her so that everyone would know he was the father. He noticed his daughter waving and he did the same, but she was looking elsewhere. He followed her gaze and saw his wife. She was in the front row sitting next to another teacher. He couldn't see her face, but he noticed all the familiar gestures: twirling her hair, leaning as the teacher whispered into her ear, her shoulder shaking with suppressed laughter. She had done all of this during their courtship and the first few years of their marriage. He wished he could see the face of the teacher, and he hoped that he was pock-faced and ugly.

The principal got on the stage and spoke about the sacrifices the students and their parents had made, and he saw Dee looking at her mother and nodding. When it was Dee's turn to receive her congratulatory handshake, her mother and the other teacher got up to applaud and Orbits saw his face. He resembled Starboy, in a way, with the same insolent expression and long hair, but he was well-dressed and appeared confident. At the end of the ceremony, they both walked to the front, and as he bent forward to pat Dee, her mother brushed his shoulder lightly.

Orbits left without meeting his daughter. When he reached home, he flung away his soaking shirt and pants. "Terylene, my ass."

The next day Wally asked him, "How was the function with the family?"

"Good, good, man. The daughter get a nice certificate. Real proud of her."

"You know, Orbits, it good to have a family around. I know that you and the wife working out your problems, but the important thing is that you could just drop in or phone if you want. With me, it's different. The last of a dying breed."

"Which breed?" He tried to make it a joke. "Alsatian or pothound?"

"What I mean is that I am the only one still here. What if something happen to me? Besides, this job is a dead end. It look we will never move to that other building. This government more interested in relocating their big-pappy friends from the cocktail circuits and putting party supporters in jobs they know nothing about. This oil boom is just like scattering money before a group of children."

Orbits had heard this sort of talk before, but Wally returned to it almost daily. He was softened by Wally's references to family, and he called the school several times to talk to his daughter. One day his wife answered. He was so startled, he immediately identified himself. There was a pause before she said she had heard of his calls and wanted to do the same. She wished to discuss a matter and wanted to know if he could arrive at 3:00 when the school day ended. He left immediately, his mind a whirl.

He arrived at 3:30. She was sitting on a bench close to the assembly area, shaded by a spreading samaan tree. He wished the schoolyard were not so big because she would have the opportunity to get a long look at his approach. But when he sat on an adjoining bench, her expression was neutral, as if she did not notice his weight. "Your daughter passed her exams for a very good school," she told him. "Just a few weeks ago there was a ceremony at the school. It's going to be expensive sending her to high school. Travel and uniform and books and clubs and everything."

Orbits noticed a man getting out of a parked car. He was walking towards them with long athletic strides, and Orbits felt he was a PE teacher. Then he saw that it was the teacher who had been sitting with his wife during the ceremony. He heard his wife saying that she wanted him to contribute a monthly sum for his daughter's maintenance. The sum would be determined by the same lawyer who was handling the divorce. Perhaps it was the presence of the other teacher standing at his side and then sitting next to his wife, holding her hand for support, that made Orbits agree with all the terms.

"I am glad you understand," his wife said. She got up and walked away with the other teacher. Orbits was relieved they had left before him. He sat on the bench after they drove off. Divorce. He had never thought of this even though they had been living apart for so long.

The word sounded so potent and empty at the same time. *Dee-vorce*. No, it sounded like one of the processes he had studied in the meteorological courses his wife had encouraged him into. Like evaporation or distillation.

He didn't want to get up. He watched the clouds floating above the samaan, broken into fragments by the leaves so that they looked like a child's puzzle. Someone was saying something to him. He looked downwards and saw the janitor. "We have to close the gate soon," the man said.

"That is a good idea. You see those dark clouds in the distance . . . it mean that a storm is on the way."

Orbits kept his word. Each month he allocated five hundred dollars, a quarter of his salary, to his daughter. Another five hundred went into the payment of the car loan. He went to work, filed the papers in the cardboard boxes, spent an hour or so with Wally in a restaurant and ate alone in the night in the same mood, neither bitter nor relieved. He convinced himself that the distress of one burden was always displaced by the pleasures of some other obligation. He didn't arrive at this philosophy entirely on his own because each weekend he watched his parents together.

Everything balances out, he told himself. There is no need to struggle. He was thankful that as part of the divorce settlement, he got the opportunity once a month to see his daughter. He met her on the lower floor of the library opposite her high school, and whenever he climbed the front stairs and saw her, he was struck at how different she was from him. She was unmoved by his attempts at bantering, at his childish jokes, and once, she told him in a stern voice, "I am twelve, you know. Next year I will be thirteen."

He had been trying to perk her attention by talking of clouds and their shifting shapes that could be an animal one minute and the face of a departed person the next. "When I was your age I couldn't get enough of clouds. How you think I become a top-notch meteorologist?"

"Mom said you are a clerk at the Ministry of Agriculture."

"Just a temporary measure." He recalled one of Wally's statements. "In this country, you have to bend your ambition if you want to survive. Bend it and twist it and roll it in a little ball."

She tapped her pencil against her chin and said, "I have to leave now. Mom and her boyfriend are taking me to the movies."

"Really? What movie?"

"Something." She gathered her books.

Orbits wondered if they were going to the cinema he had visited with his former wife during their courtship. "Bye, Dee." She waved without looking back, stylishly, as if unscrewing a slack bulb.

During another meeting, she asked why he never came with his car, and he didn't say that he was afraid to drive in the busy towns and, after a year, still chose the back roads to his destinations. Instead, he blamed the car. "The car have a will of its own. Sometimes I turn the steering wheel left and the car decide to go right." She mentioned that she would miss the next meeting because her mother was taking her to another island during the Easter vacation. "It's my gift for coming out second in my last test."

"Only second?" he joked, and when he saw her annoyance he added, "But it's still better than me. The last place was always reserved for me. So just you and your mummy going?"

She rolled her eyes, a gesture he could not interpret.

During that Easter, Orbits drove to his work for the first time. It took him twice as long as his regular journey on the bus, and because he drove slowly, almost at a crawl, he had to put up with the curses of other drivers.

"You think this is a blasted funeral?" one driver shouted.

Another pushed his head through the window. "Carry that thing to the scrapyard."

Yet he was relieved and proud when he parked on an empty street not far from the office, and as he headed there, his briefcase stuffed with food his mother had packed, he tried to imagine Wally's reaction to his conquest of the car and of the roads. Later they drove to a rumshop close to the Savannah, and on the way, Wally mentioned the spaciousness of the vehicle and Orbits told him he could fit an entire cricket team in the back seat. But once in the rumshop, some of their exuberance faded. As usual, Wally brought up his frustration with his job and the entreaties of his family abroad and his loneliness at being the one left behind. "You know, Orbits, I used to tell them they were like rats leaving a ship. Colonials who had no use for the place once it started to treat them just like everybody else. Transients." As Orbits pondered the meaning of the word, Wally spoke about his relatives' disillusionment with and desertion of the island and his slow realization that he was no different. "I used to think that all these upper-class people was no better than these long-time absentee plantation owners living high and mighty in France and England while the overseers managed the business. Running away at the first sign of trouble as if this place don't mean anything to them, but maybe I misjudged them. All this money that flowing through the country will run out one day, and we will have nothing to show for it besides a few stadiums and fancy buildings. Pappyshow only." As Wally spoke about all the things that had been dismantled in the island, the tramcars in the capital, the trains that once criss-crossed the place, the castles at the Savannah, the century-old buildings, the heritage sites, the samaan-lined promenades, Orbits felt that this new side to his friend was really a conversation with himself, trying to convince himself that he possessed no choice in the matter. "But I try, man. I really try."

He had always assumed that Wally's despondent sermonizing was connected with the frustration of his job and — as he knew so well — with the recurring bouts of dissatisfaction associated more with his weight than anything else. Once he had thought of a term — "Fatman Blues" — and he couldn't recall if it was the name of a song or if he had invented it. But as he listened to Wally talking about neglect and disdain and ingratitude, some of the other man's mood latched on to him. He thought of his former wife taking her boyfriend to all of the places they had once visited; he thought of his daughter, who seemed so remote during their meetings and who always seemed in a hurry to leave. He revealed for the first time his troubles with Joe the mechanic. Wally countered with the revelation of a robbery across the road from where he lived, a widow living by herself, beaten and tied up. "This could still be a nice place if you look at it, but the people spoil it."

They drank in this manner, their mood darkening with each new revelation, each feeling the other's pain; and when they stumbled out of the rumshop, it was already dark and Orbits, realizing he was too drunk to drive to his place, was forced to take a taxi.

The next morning, the car was gone, and when he learned from the rumshop's proprietor that it had been towed away, he seriously contemplated leaving it there. "I could help you out." The proprietor was a stout mixed-race man with a hanging lower lip that gave him a both critical and gluttonous look.

"How?" Orbits asked.

"I know somebody." Orbits, unaware of the little subtleties of bribing, could not understand at first, but the man told him that for ten dollars he would get the car from the police yard. He paid the money and walked to the office. Wally was not there that day, and Orbits guessed he was nursing his hangover. In the evening, he walked across to the rumshop, expecting to see the car parked, but the owner told him, "I had a little problem."

"So you didn't get the car?"

"That is the thing. The fella I know wasn't there and his replacement playing tough. He know full well that the longer a vehicle remain in the yard the more parts that get removed. A man I know once, a country boy like you, collect his car after a week, and when he was driving it home he had a flat. And guess what? When he open the trunk, jack gone, spanner gone, spare tire gone. Speakers too. I tried to talk to him about getting out his car, but he didn't listen. Country boy. Didn't know the ropes."

Orbits gave the man another ten dollars. In the bus, he cursed Joe the mechanic, the driver of the wrecking vehicle, the proprietor of the rumshop and the thieves at the police yard. The following day he dropped in at the rumshop before he got to his work. The proprietor began making excuses. The replacement was acting up. He was asking for additional money because of the size and age of the Kingswood. He believed an attempt had been made to steal the battery. Orbits noticed how his lip dropped with each excuse. "The man playing the fool. He asking for ten more just because he know that it better to get a whole car than a shell. I wouldn't say he is a scamp but . . ."

He wiped his lips with the back of his palm. The gesture infuriated Orbits. "You wouldn't say he is a scamp? I wonder why? Is because you is a bigger scamp. A blasted rogue and vagabond. A damn malcontent."

The proprietor sucked in his lower lip and his mouth bunched into an apelike expression. Then he spat out his lip. "Look man, who you calling a malcontent? I try to help you out and that is how you behaving. This is not the country, you know. It have rules and regulations here."

"Rules and regulations, my ass. This not finish, you hear me. It not finish at all. I going to write the commissioner of police."

Suddenly the man began to laugh. "Oh lord. The commissioner? I frighten too bad." Just as suddenly his laughter stopped. "Look, man, haul you ass from my place, you hear me. And don't let me see you here again."

As Orbits rushed away, he stopped in the gap to shout, "And I writing the health inspector too about them gizzard you does be selling that hard like rock. Kidney stones gizzard." From inside the shop came a burst of rolling laughter. Later in the day, while Orbits and Wally were walking to the police yard, Wally said, "You must be the only person in town who wasn't aware that the rumshop fella and the owner of the wrecker real tight. They running this scheme for years now. The two of them like Simon and Garfunkel."

Orbits didn't understand the reference, but he recalled a teacher from primary school asking him to spell carbuncle, and he sputtered, "A damn sore in truth. A nasty boil. Selling bad gizzard. I already plan the letter." At the yard he was further infuriated to learn that the cost of releasing the vehicle was just twenty dollars; he had assumed it would have been many times the sum. "Money gone down the drain," he told Wally. "This car only bring trouble on my head."

Wally responded with a phrase he had been using recently: "The place not bad. Is just the people."

From then the car remained parked at his home and he resumed his normal means of transportation. He still took his parents on weekend trips to small villages, mostly places that had been denied the money flowing through the rest of the island. But while his mother commented on the fruit trees and the flower gardens, Orbits began to see something entirely different. Once, while they were driving through a dirt road, Orbits, as was his habit, glanced up at the sky. His mother was saying something about a perfect picture and he told her, "Only the top half."

His father giggled, and Orbits didn't bother to explain that if the scene was viewed as a photograph, the top would display a perfect tropical paradise with lazy clouds in a blue sky and palm trees waving next to poui covered with striking orange colours. But beneath would be a street of houses built from galvanize and boxing board laid erratically so that there were gaps in the walls from which the children, if they watched outside, would see the stagnant drain, yellow and oily looking.

"So nice," his mother said.

But the people spoil it, he thought. People always spoil everything. "Bring your daughter next time."

Orbits glanced at his father in the rear-view mirror. He rarely spoke, and Orbits was surprised that he even remembered Dee. "She studying for her exams," he told the older man. His mother sighed loudly.

His monthly visits with his daughter continued, but now he matched her disinterest and both seemed relieved when the visits came to an end. It was only with Wally that Orbits relaxed and revealed the blankness that seemed to be chipping away at everything. He revealed all that he had formerly kept to himself: his umbrage at his mother's treatment of his brother and the guilt following his death; the deterioration of his marriage that was so gradual that he could not pick out the defining moment it was dead; his daughter who seemed more a stranger during every visit. One evening he told the other man, "Up until I was an adult, I used to be gazing at the clouds and wishing I could be there instead of down here. I used to imagine that I was floating above everyone. It seemed so peaceful. You know, I try to make everything so unreal that I never name anything. This island, teachers at school, everybody. I always believe that the minute I give something or someone a name, it will make it more real. Was nicknames from a side." He felt he had gone too far, revealed too much, and added, "That was until I start doing meteorology."

Wally said in an amused way, "Is a good thing I have a nickname, or you would have written me off too."

FOR HALF A YEAR they spoke in this manner, moving between comedy and farce and genuine sadness. Wally revealed a visit to a nursing home where he had seen an old Englishman who was the only patient not surrounded by friends or family. "It looked like he was the last one in town. He died not too long after according to the nurse. I imagine it was a very small funeral. If they didn't chuck him in the crematorium." On occasion, his confessions were more personal. "When I was in high school, I was popular because I was jokey. You could count on me to come up with some odd way of describing things. The class clown. That way I could make jokes about myself before anybody else. Oops, he fall down. Oops, he get up. Oops, he fall down again. But the funny thing is that even though I was popular, I tried to avoid everybody. Even at home. If we had visitors at home, I used the back step to get away. Everybody wanted a performance."

On another evening, at another rumshop, Orbits told him, "One recess, I notice a commotion in the field at the back of the school. It was my brother in a fight with another boy bigger than him. My brother begin primary school just when I was about to leave. I wanted to go and part the fight and save my brother from the licking, but I was too afraid so I just stand there watching until the teachers come. You know, while he was on the ground, I noticed him looking around. He spotted me. He spotted me in the crowd. But he never mention a word to anybody or to me."

There were long periods of silence after these confessions, and they drank slowly, shaking the glasses, staring at the ice cubes, dusting the table, each respectful of the other's pain. But in the late evenings, just before they were about to leave the rumshops, they made self-deprecating jokes about themselves and each other, almost as if the weight of the rum had, just for a while, pried loose slivers of honesty. Once Wally told Orbits in a half-drunken manner that he would have left years ago, but he felt a sense of duty to the department. "Every man have a task to perform and I thought this was mine."

Wally was the sole friend Orbits had ever had, and on the bus back to his parents' place, he felt that this friendship was the only bright spot in a life that seemed to limp in spurts, where his happiness was constantly interrupted by the unexpected. Death, abandonment, betrayal; only Wally was dependable. One evening, Wally told him,

"It look like I will be passing through your clouds soon." He revealed that he had finally given in to his relatives' entreaties and had decided to join them in Canada. Orbits was shocked into speechlessness even when Wally said that he had recommended him as his replacement. When he recovered he asked in a stunned manner, "But what about your duty to the department?"

"That is your job now," he said.

In the three months prior to his departure, Wally recovered some of his old sanguinity as he spoke about Toronto, to which he was headed, and the nieces and nephews who lived there. He brought blurry photographs of his family posing against the CN Tower and Niagara Falls that he showed to Orbits in the restaurants and rum-shops. "My sister tell me that couples could walk alone in the nights in the loneliest spots without any harassment." Orbits pretended he was amazed. But as Wally, on subsequent days, mentioned all that he had gleaned from his relatives about the place, Orbits felt increasingly despondent. Once Wally said in a joking manner, "You should consider the move yourself, boy. Imagine living in a place where everything runs on time and in every street, it have a park just like the botanic gardens. Every street with its own buffet restaurant too."

Orbits had actually imagined this during each of Wally's descriptions. "If it was possible, I would leave tomorrow. But I have my parents here. And the daughter . . ."

Wally was a little surprised as he had spoken in a joking manner. He told Orbits, "I recommended you highly for my old job. I hope you get it. Remember the day you walked in the office? Rain was falling and I asked you to tell when it was going to stop. Who would have figured out that little shower of rain would have made us such friends?" Because Wally had spoken in a joking manner, Orbits turned away so his friend would not see his sadness.

On the day of Wally's departure, Orbits hired a taxi to take him to the airport. As the driver passed the mountain range, which was perpetually shrouded with clouds and trails of mist, Orbits wondered if this was how a snowy vista looked from a distance. Soon Wally would be in a place like that, with a family and, shortly, with new friends. He felt like asking the driver to turn around; Wally was moving towards a new life; he had no use for debris from his old. As they passed stretches of vacant lots and others filled with warehouses that reminded him of Baby Rabbit's place, he felt he would embarrass himself before his friend. It would not be a fitting finale to all the expansive limes they'd had. Without thinking, he asked the driver to stop at a rumshop. It was an old, dusty building, but it was crowded with students from the nearby university. They were all dressed in loose clothing that made them seem carefree and nonchalant and stylish. Orbits ordered a beer and sipped slowly. Then he ordered another.

When he got to the airport, he asked the driver to wait in the parking lot. Wally's plane was already speeding from the tarmac. He walked around the airport as if the plane had not left, as if Wally were somewhere among the families and groups walking to and from the departure gates. When he stood at the gate, a small hunched man who looked like a turtle in his brown coat asked him to read the sign above the gate. Orbits told him it was the departure gate, and the man, as if he didn't believe, asked him to spell the word. When he did, the man said in a voice that seemed to be bouncing around his tongue, "My son and his wife. I am waiting for them, you see. It's a bloody bother." When Orbits moved away, the man followed him. "Can you read the flights on that board? I am seventy-five percent blind, you know. Just last year I was fifty percent. Next year will be one hundred percent. So it goes. I am not complaining. Nothing much to see. Are you waiting on someone too?"

The man seemed in a mood to chat, and Orbits felt he had lived alone and was impatient for the arrival of his family, who would soon grow fed up of him if the visit was longer than a week. "A good friend just left. I think I miss him."

"Do you mean to say that you were late or that you regret his departure?" He spoke in the manner of a retired teacher, and some of Orbits' sympathy evaporated.

"I have to leave now myself," he said suddenly. When he got to the taxi, he saw the driver slouched on the seat, one foot outside the open door, the other on the dashboard. He threw away his cigarette when he saw Orbits. "I thought you and all had gone to Cyanada. I nearly smoke a half pack waiting here for you."

"My friend was very emotional. I had to cheer him up."

"Yeah, some people like that, but the majority does be acting as if they leaving a refugee camp. Happy like pappy and mouthing off about all the fancy thing they going to do and how they new life will be so rosy as if the pope going to meet them in Cyanada or America. Some of these people wipe they hand clean and you does only see them when they come back for some visit looking like if a steamroller pass over them, but still they insisting in they new brogue that life real sweet in the cold and this place going down in a hole. I drive plenty of them. Families with miserable complaining children. Dengue and malaria, my ass."

The driver spoke in this manner for the entire trip, and with each new outburst, Orbits' melancholic mood lengthened.

Wally had hinted that his job might be given to Orbits, but it went instead to the worker with the quivering nostril. Orbits had never interacted either with him or with the woman because they both left after a few hours, during which time he was busy at work. A week following Wally's departure, the new boss, who had never hidden his dislike of Orbits, summoned him and the other worker, the woman who wore the same old suit each day, for a meeting. "Change is in the air," the boss said in a high-pitched voice. "I am not Wally," he repeated several times. "I intend to whip this department into shape." He spoke as if he were addressing a huge audience, walking around the table, leaning onto his knuckles on the desk, standing upright with his hands folded against his back. The woman applauded after each of his pronouncements. And Orbits asked him a question that was not provocative but really to clear up his genuine confusion. He asked how the new boss was going to accomplish these things when he disappeared for three hours each day. "I will brook no insubordination. Meeting finished!" he screamed. The woman got up in a huff, her chair scraping the floor.

The next morning, Orbits saw several handwritten signs on all the walls. *Think outside the box. Hit the floor running.* On the wall facing his desk he read another saying *A glutton lives to eat, a wise man eats to live.* Whenever the woman passed the sign, she chortled, a low jumbled jangle that sounded to Orbits like a huge bird trapped inside an accordion. The boss and the woman left at 11:00 but returned at 2:00, when Orbits was about to leave for home. He began to suspect they were conducting an affair, but it was hard to tell because they rarely spoke to each other at work.

He missed Wally more with the passing of each month; he missed his friendship and the daily sojourns to the restaurants and rumshops where they had sampled almost every type of food the city had to offer. Wally had no real drive, but he was straightforward in the manner that few people were. Orbits went to some of these places after his work, but sitting by himself the rum and the food didn't taste the same. Besides, he was now forced to remain at his job until 4:00 in the evening.

A few times, he got out a sheet of paper from the Xerox machine and began, "Dear Wally. It's more than half a year since you left and I have been thinking every single day of moving to Toronto. There we will resume our gourmet meals and our sparkling conversations."

He always threw these into the dustbin. One morning, just after his arrival, he heard laughter from the desks of the two workers. They were at the opposite end of the room and the view was obscured by a filing cabinet. The words sounded familiar, so he paid more attention.

He heard the woman saying, "The food has lost its taste without you. In Toronto, I imagine us sampling pizza and poutine and other exotic fares." She stopped to chortle before she continued. "And listen to this one. 'I believe you were wrong to say the island was going both uphill and downhill at the same time. Now it's heading in just one direction.'"

Orbits felt his rage boiling. He began to sweat. When the woman began reading again, he got up and rushed past the filing cabinet. He saw her and the boss with several crumpled sheets on the table. "Allyou two *macos*! Who give you permission to read my private correspondence?"

"People don't put their private correspondence in the dustbin," the woman said, her stern look now reappearing.

"And I won't tolerate that tone from a junior officer," the boss added.

"I see! I see!" he sputtered. But he could think of nothing else to say. He stormed back to his desk, and he heard the pair laughing derisively, a sound that sent him straight back to his childhood. He felt like pushing over the filing cabinet onto the pair. When they left at 11:00, he got a sheet of carbon paper, placed it between two pages, and began to write. "Dear Wally. You have left me here with the two most disgusting individuals it has been my misfortune to know. I believe you know who I am talking about. A hard-faced old fowl and a man who looks like a mongoose. They should be natural enemies, but each day they leave at the same time and return at the same time. I believe you always knew about their nasty illicit affair but you was too polite to mention it. I am different from you because I am already drafting letters to the permanent secretary and the minister of agriculture."

He walked across with the original and threw it into the woman's table and the other he flung into the man's. When the pair returned at 2:00, he told them, "I have worked four hours. The same as both of you will do today." And he walked out of the office. His rage weakened by the time he got into the taxi, and even though it returned in spurts each time he listened to a piece of *mauvais langue*, idle gossip, from the other passengers, by the time he arrived home it was gone altogether.

His mother told him, "You get home early today, Orbits. Everything okay?" He nodded and she continued. "You sure? I don't like how you losing so much weight these days."

He realized that following Wally's departure and the end of the daily feasting, his pants were slacker around the waist, but he did not think it was noticeable to anyone other than himself. He was in a good mood that evening not only because of his mother's observation but because for the first time in his life, he had taken a stand. "Let's go for a drive," he said.

"Is weekend already?"

"Hush, Papoose. Is not weekend but who say we can't go on a weekday."

In this mood of self-satisfaction, Orbits ventured into the small town where his father's old lab was located rather than to a village. His mother kept up a stream of commentary about all the construction taking place. When they got to the location of her husband's old lab, she said, "Oh gosh, Papoose, what happen to your place?"

Orbits glanced at the spot. "It look like they pulled it down to make way for a new building."

Unexpectedly, his father began to cry. He repeated several times, "They pull it down? It not there again? Why they do that?"

Orbits' mother said, "Boy, I don't know what happening to your Papoose. A few days aback he asked me why he not seeing Starboy again."

"Me?" his father asked. "Not me. Starboy kill himself."

By the time Orbits returned home, both parents were sniffling in the back seat. In his room, he calculated that his father was seventy

— exactly twice his age — and his mother was sixty-four. They had both changed following the death of his brother, but while his mother, who he assumed would be permanently inconsolable, had recovered in most ways, his father had remained stuck inside a foggy prison from which he occasionally peered out. He knew that his father believed his brother's death was due to suicide, and he wondered if it was that burden that had so afflicted him. Perhaps the silent guilt, the self-reproach associated with the contemplation of a self-inflicted death, was even worse than the horrors of a murder.

That night he forgot about what had transpired at his workplace and for the first time he tried to think of his brother's passing in a rational manner. What had driven him to drugs and to suicide if that were the case? Was it a rebellion against the suffocating tenderness imposed upon him by their mother? Was it the company he kept? Did it have anything to do with the imagination he always boasted of? Something that he alone was able to see? Orbits realized he had no clear idea because at that time he had already moved out. But his brother had always been a stranger, and Orbits couldn't tell who had shut out whom. He remembered the day of his brother's death, the scene at his former in-laws' place and his marathon to the hospital to see his former wife and their newborn. So many things had happened all at once, and he reflected as to whether the absence of one could have pre-empted the arrival of another. Before he fell asleep, he contemplated the purpose of his marriage. The last time he had seen his daughter was three months earlier, their visits curtailed to the beginning of each school vacation.

He carried this mood with him the following day to his work. He saw another poster on his wall and without reading it, he tore it down. His boss was saying something to him, and he was aware the woman was listening, but Orbits was thinking: what is the purpose of my life and why am I struggling? At 2:00, he gathered his container and his file, placed both into his briefcase, and walked out. The next day he came to work, filed his papers and left at the same time. A dispassionate observer would have seen him as a diligent employee of the ministry because during his time at the office he busied himself with his work, rarely looking up.

Yet the daily grind of his job, the numbing efficiency, could not remove the notion that he was on borrowed time; when his boss asked for copies of his diploma for record-keeping, Orbits remembered the day Wally had hired him without any vetting of his qualifications. Perhaps his boss knew, he thought. He sank deeper into his work, began to pay more careful attention to all the applications for grants and subsidies. He saw how the sums had expanded over the years, and he knew that while many of the submissions were genuine, most were either inflated or bogus.

The final approval had to be authorized at another department, but he knew from his conversations with Wally that most were approved. So much money was changing hands in the island while he, one of the overseers of the transaction, had almost nothing. Perhaps, he felt, it was this unfairness that had driven away Wally, all the talk of his relatives begging him to leave just a sham. His old romance about leaving was rekindled, the flames nourished by his boss, who each week reminded him that he could be fired if he refused to provide the appropriate certificates. Orbits did not know that in the civil service, still operating on antiquated legislation, it was almost impossible to fire an employee, and so he prepared himself for the worst.

He continued to work at the ministry for another three years. Before Wally had departed, he had spoken about duty as if it were a solid thing that could be hefted and weighed, and Orbits had not completely believed him, but as the months went by he found that this reflexive completion of his tasks — the depletion of the stacks of files on his desk, the addition and subtraction of numbers, the careful vetting of applications for fraudulent claims, the letters that offered bribes, written with ink pens on the pages of copy books — tore away at his sadness. One midday he felt that barricading himself with his daily tasks could be considered an approximation of Wally's duty.

When he was transferred to an agricultural station at the opposite end of the island — for while it was impossible to fire, it was still possible to transfer — his boss felt that he had finally won. On Orbits' final day, he told him that his demotion was well earned. "This is what happens when you are insubordinate," he said. After so many years of working with the other man, Orbits realized that apart from his quivering nostrils and rubbery lips, he had never observed him properly. Now he saw that his pants were hitched high, almost to his shallow chest. He saw the callouses, black and spreading, on his elbows and the acne marks, so deep they were like scars from an icepick, on his cheeks. Up close, he noticed, too, that he was older than his full head of hair had suggested and that the corners of his eyelids had already begun to sag.

He felt no pleasure in noticing this and would have been rueful if the other man had recalled the threats to report him and the woman to the minister. Orbits thanked him for bringing the letter of transfer personally and he meant it. The other man saw sarcasm and told Orbits he had gotten what he deserved. Orbits took this as a kind of sensible fatalism and nodded. The woman began to sniffle, and Orbits wanted to tell her everything was alright, but at that moment, the boss walked to her side and said, "Is back to the fields for you. That is where you belong."

～⌒～

HIS NEW JOB WAS at a field station about fifteen miles from the coast, the opposite end of the island from his former job. It was in a concrete building with three rooms and a large waiting area where the visiting farmers and fishermen came for price listings, hunters for seasonal permits, and the general public for one of the colourful brochures on horticulture and home gardening. The rooms, one of which was assigned to Orbits, were shabby and dusty, the concrete fallen away to expose the red bricks beneath, and there was the perpetual odour of guano that seeped from the leaking Celotex ceiling and which reminded Orbits of his stint in the caves. His room had two small windows: from one, sitting before his table, he could see the tractors and pickup vans of the visitors arriving through the dirt track that led to the main road; from the other, standing close to the door, he could see the trees at the back, mango and cashew and pommecythere and avocado and broad-leaf breadfruit, in the distance. The windows of the agricultural department in the capital had opened to a high brick wall beyond which he could see the poui and samaan planted generations earlier now wilting from exhaust fumes and smoke blown from the burning garbage dumps in the shanty town at the edge of the city. The windows there had to be kept open, so he had grown used to the sound of cars and hammering of construction vehicles. At the field station, the noise was less abrasive, and he felt it was because the breeze here scattered the fragrance of ripe tonkobeans and cashews into his small office.

He could smell the alcohol, too, on many of the farmers and fishermen who sat on the chair opposite him, and he guessed it was their tipsiness rather than his position that made them so deferential. When Wally had spoken about the differences between country and town people, Orbits had assumed it was simply to *mamaguy* him, a country bookie, but the men and women he saw each day fitted his friend's descriptions: they were simple, excessively deferential and perpetually grateful though Orbits suspected there was more to their silence than they were letting on. At the ministry, he had overseen huge sums, but he had been an anonymous figure, unknown to the people who may have benefitted from his diligence; at the field station, he was the man in an office who stamped permits and handed out official forms. He could facilitate or withhold permits if he chose.

He worked at the field station for much of the remainder of his life, and his first years there were among his happiest. Each evening his mother expressed her relief that he was working closer to home, the distance to the field station was less than a third than to his former place of employment. When he began to bring home hands of plantain or parcels of plums and cherries and mangoes or muddy yam wrapped in newspaper, all bribes and tokens of appreciation from those he had granted permits, his mother said, "Orbits, you giving my backyard garden real completion." She said this even though the garden had dwindled to a few string beans that grew wild and seemed to resist every type of weed or vine.

At first, Orbits did not pay much attention to these comments or even to the sight of his father, his dentures all broken, chewing toothlessly at some pulpy fruit. But daily the inertia that had gripped him since the departure of Wally fell away. Since Wally's departure from the ministry, he neither spoke to nor interacted with anyone, but the field station was always a buzz of noise and activity. Vehicles grinding, fishermen joking, a drunken disputation renewed in the compound. The people who came to him were, at first, more reserved than the men he had met in the capital city, but with familiarity, they became regular oletalkers. The fishermen described their trips to catch cavalli, carite and grouper and the frequent mishaps — running out of fuel, drifting for hours in the Bocas, caught in storms — in a colourful way that matched the accounts of the hunters who got lost in the forests, were injured by trap-guns and claimed to regularly spot entities like Papa Bois, the reputed protector of animals. Orbits was never sure where fantasy began or ended with these men. Each Friday afternoon there was a cook-up, either a fish broth with tubers and vegetables and kingfish simmering in a massive pot on a single burner or all three burners fired up and the aroma of curried duck or goat or wild meat and rice and a peppery sauce filling the compound.

The cooking was always done by one of the employees of the

field station, an old wiry *cocoa-pañol* everyone called Spanish. The two men who peeled and washed were the other employees: Gums, a perpetually smiling man, and Doraymay, his opposite, always serious even when he drunkenly whipped out a mouth organ and played the only song he knew, a country and western sung by Jim Reeves. *This world is not my home / I'm just a-passing through.* Orbits, who knew nothing about cooking, was nevertheless invited, and to his relief, the hefty appetite that had been stoked during his regular sessions with Wally did not resurface, the food, both blazing hot and extremely spicy, a real deterrent.

Spanish, pointing with his pot spoon, gave a running commentary on the ingredients. "A proper cook is like a scientist. He have to know how much and in what order. One little mistake and everything *kilketay.* For instance, you throw in the seasoning with the oil first and when it begin to sizzle, then and only then you toss in the plantain, dasheen and yam." About ten minutes later, after he had taken a couple drinks of rum, he added, "Okay, now for the grouper. The best fish for broff." A few more drinks later, he would ask, "How it smelling? You getting the taste of the lime and the pepper in the air? Eh?" He would then peel a block of salted butter. "Now for the finishing touch. Golden Ray." He would lever the entire block into the pot, stirring until the liquid was golden yellow.

"The best thing to increase cholesterol," Gums said, and Orbits wasn't sure if he was joking. "You finish with the mother-in-law?" he would ask Doraymay, referring to a bitter melange of cucumber, pepper and eggplant.

At times, while he was looking on and listening to the commentary, Orbits wondered what Wally, with his gourmet sensibilities, would have made of this scene. His friend had a good sense of town people, but Orbits sensed that, apart from the farmers who came to visit, he had little contact with men like these. But he would fit in for sure. He had that way about him. Orbits liked the simple conversations of the men, but he could feel no connection apart from the duties they shared at the field station. He never moved beyond a single drink and once, while he was listening to the trio knocking the pots and singing a parang tune, he wondered whether in his mind these sessions were different from his limes with his old friend because the cook-ups represented the uncontrolled and unpredictable life — the swift descent from jokiness to indignation, the reflexive gossiping, the casual retreat into fantasy — from which he was trying to escape.

Once, while he was caught in this reflection, Gums told him, "I know you grow up in a place just ten miles from here but you is a hard fella to read."

"Eat some more, Orbits," Spanish encouraged. "This is real healthy food. No chemicals and preservatives. Blue food. Eddoes, dasheen and tannia."

The following Friday, Gums said to Orbits, "The way Spanish does be mouthing off while he cooking you must be know all these recipes by heart now."

"Leave the man alone. He is the book man not the cook man. Always dress up in stiff long sleeve and pants with seam. Not like the rest of we with muddy clothes." Sometimes Orbits felt there was some bitterness in Doraymay's bland observations, but the other workers did not seem to notice, and Orbits let it pass.

But Doraymay was right; once it was established that Orbits was efficient with paperwork and filing, that area of the job was left to him. So he was usually in the station while the three other workers tramped about in the field. There was no real competitiveness; all were in the same pay grade and the supervisor never visited from his office in the capital. Within three months, Orbits felt he had gauged the culture of the place — the drinking, the liming, the penchant for ignoring particular laws, the little outbursts that seemed to hide deeper pockets of violence — and in six months, he had settled completely in his job, his time at the ministry a distant memory. He continued calling his daughter once a month, and he no longer felt awkward when her mother or stepfather answered. Their conversations were brief, and it was usually Orbits himself who terminated them, having nothing to say other than his inquiries about her school and her exams. Her responses, also brief, never varied: she was doing well. Once, when he called, she mentioned she was in form six, and he was surprised at how many years had passed. He told her, "Just now you will be independent." He heard some of her old irritation when she said she had been so for a long time.

Following the conversation, Gums, who had been listening in the next room, asked him, "So you and the madam separate, boy?"

When he nodded, Gums began to talk in a general way about the ways of modern women, and Orbits felt obligated to defend her. He told the other man that his former wife was smart and practical and had, until recently, been single-handedly raising their daughter. Their marriage had failed not because she was modern or he old-fashioned or anything like that, but only because she always knew what she wanted. He may have phrased it wrongly because Gums began to make sympathetic noises, beating his tongue against the roof of his mouth. Orbits tried to joke it off by saying, "She had her foot on the ground and my head was always in the cloud."

"That is why you do weather studies?"

"Exactly."

Following the conversation, Orbits considered his neutral responses. On his way home, he knew his defence of his wife was partly because of the dim local view of a divorced man, but he also felt during the brief conversation he had been describing a stranger he once met fleetingly. When he tried to recall their intimate moments, these had the vague familiarity of a scene from a movie or a conversation he had overheard — familiarity, but no real connection. As the months passed, he had to actually remind himself that he had once been married for seven years.

He was surprised that he wished nothing of his former wife nor anything from her.

He felt at peace: not the dull stupor that had enveloped him following Wally's departure but something close to satisfaction. Yet there were moments, in the evenings while the other workers were out in the field or at a rumshop and he was alone at the station, when he would hold in his hands one of the booklets describing organic farming or instructions on rearing tilapia and feel a slight unease at his sense of comfort, which he knew never lasted and always presaged some disaster. He also reflected as to whether the startling distance from reality that he saw everywhere — the belief in spirits and unlikely conspiracies and crazy rumours — was beginning to also infect him.

ONE EVENING WHILE HE was reading one of these booklets, a woman appeared before him. She was tall, dark-brown and alluring in a robust way. She sat on the chair at the other side of the table and began to talk. Orbits was lost in her monologue not only because she spoke breathlessly, without pauses, but because of the way she was constantly leaning forward and fanning her chest with a brochure. He tried to look away from her unbuttoned blouse. Eventually he had to interrupt her. "So what is it exactly that you want, madam?"

"Madam? Madam is only for old people. I look old to you?"

"No, you don't look old."

"Thank you! Now tell my husband that." As she went on, he gathered that her husband, a teacher, drank heavily and spent more time with his friends than with her. Orbits felt uneasy at this recollection, and his mind drifted to his own marriage. "The only thing that would change him is if I put a good horn on him." She laughed, loudly and scandalously. "Look how you blushing, mister. You never hear that a horn is the best tune-up for a marriage?"

"No, I never hear that."

"Then why you was staring at my tot-tots the minute I enter your office?"

Orbits heard a low giggling from the office next to his and he asked once more, "So how I could help you?"

"I nearly say something else but let we say that I interested in planting some flowers. Not the common kind like daisy and zinnia, but these kind that you could export." She unrolled the brochure and read. "Heliconia. Ginger lily. Hawaiian torch. Anthurium."

He tried to muster some kind of formality and he asked her, "You have any prior experience in horticulture?"

"No, but I need to find some hobby, something to do real fast, otherwise . . ."

Once more, Orbits heard giggling from the other office. "Well, we have these brochures here that can give you a start."

"I need something else to give me a start."

"What?" he asked uneasily.

"I want someone to come and tell me if the land is fertile and if it suitable for planting anything." She leaned forward, her hands on the table, wrists to elbows, and her breasts were pushed upwards. Orbits tried to distract himself by focusing on a tiny skin tag beneath her left ear. "I need proper guidance from a professional."

"We have other officers here who are more experienced in field-work."

"Who? These three others? They must be in a rumshop right now drinking with some fisherman—"

"Hello. I right here." That was Gums from the adjoining room.

In the end, Orbits agreed to visit her place on the weekend. She wrote her address with much flourish in Orbits' appointment book, circled it inside a heart, and left with several brochures. She returned almost immediately and said, "I didn't get your name."

"Orbits!" Gums shouted.

He decided to accompany the woman to her car. She walked close to him, brushing his shoulder. "Orbits. In that case you better call me Moon."

"Why?" Orbits asked uneasily.

"You figure it out," she said a little angrily. "According to what I hear, your head always bury in files and folders."

When Orbits returned to his office, Gums pushed his head into the doorway. "You make a real pick up, Orbits."

"Just doing my job."

"I think that woman have a different job in mind."

"Is just flowers—"

"I think she want you to plant something else." He smiled and his upper lip rose to touch his nose, giving him the appearance of an amused horse. "Why you think she didn't bother to come to me or Doraymay or Spanish? We too old to satisfy she."

"You shouldn't be saying that about an innocent woman."

"What! If she innocent, then I is the best-looking man in town."

Orbits felt awkward with these little taunts, but at home he looked at himself in the mirror. Once his wife had complimented him on his nice body. That body had been cloaked a few years later in blubber. He had lost much of that, and he now saw himself as an average-looking man, slightly heavy but not buttery looking as he had once been. He was not handsome — his lower lip from his days of gluttony still hanging out, his smallish eyes sloping down at the sides, the skin on his neck loose and tinged with the dark-brown spots that he now noticed were on both sides of his cheeks — but neither was he spectacularly ugly. He wondered what the woman — if Gums was right — saw in him. At forty, he was younger than the other workers, he dressed neatly and disguised his shyness with an air of formality. Perhaps he looked respectable, and he wondered if he should get a pair of spectacles to complete the look. He circled an eye with his thumb and index finger and felt a thick-rimmed frame would suit him.

He had not been with another woman since his breakup. For a short while, he suspected that Wally, who knew so much about the city and its inhabitants, had been seeing a prostitute, but he never asked directly, and Wally never actually confirmed his suspicions. He thought of the woman during dinner, and his mother, who noticed his mood, asked, "So you and all worrying? He becoming a new man in his old age." She spoke in a fatigued manner with the trace of amusement she used whenever she was concerned. "I used to think it was joke he was making. Tying to provoke me like when . . . like before, but I beginning to feel something seriously wrong with your Papoose."

Orbits glanced at his father on the sofa, a bowl of soup in his hand, staring at the space between him and the small black-and-white television. Orbits had bought the set with the first pay cheque he got at the field station, and now his father rarely moved from the spot. "He just getting old," he told his mother in a low voice.

"Sometimes he get vex and quarrel with the people in television." She pressed her hands to her lips and laughed, but she soon regained her distressed look. "From the minute Starboy die your Papoose change. I thought it would be me who would never recover, but something inside your Papoose break that day. Something that could never join back." She cast her gaze in Orbits' direction, but he couldn't tell if she was looking at him or at some object beyond. "The worse thing that could ever happen to a mother or a father is to lose a child. It not suppose to be that way. Not suppose to be . . ." Orbits thought of his daughter and how they had lost whatever minor connection they had possessed. He heard his mother saying, "He still enjoy the little drives though."

The bowl clattered on the floor, and Orbits' father said sulkily, "The last supper."

"Oh god, Papoose. Look at the mess you gone and make." In spite of what she had just revealed, her tone was one of annoyance. A few minutes later, she turned to Orbits. "Every time he make a mistake while eating he mention the last supper."

From then Orbits resolved to take his father every weekend to some new spot. That weekend, they visited a pitch lake, where his father ventured close to the oily crater, alarming both Orbits and his mother. But his father was enjoying himself, shouting, "Ten blackbird dead."

"What he mean by that?" Orbits asked on his way back.

"Boy, your father alone know what going through his head. Look at him digging out the pitch from his sandals and putting them on the seat like if is insects."

The following day they drove around the village choosing some of the backtraces. His father was mumbling in the rear seat and his mother said, "Well, I never! You know what your father saying, boy? He calling the names of all the owners of these abandoned estates. How he could remember something so when he can't even remember that his son not here again?" In a playful voice, she asked him, "Papoose, is trick you playing on we or what?"

He clapped his hands and laughed. Orbits' mother smiled but in a worrying way. She looked out the window and said, almost as if she were talking to herself, "We never know what going to happen. All these tricks that get play on we." Orbits imagined she was referring to her husband, but she added, "You could never see what coming. All the preparations you make, all that you plan for . . ." She returned her attention to her husband and, in an unexpectedly affectionate act, placed her hand on his leg. "But we have to see it out to the end, not so Papoose? That is we duty. Everybody have a cross to bear."

Orbits always arrived to work an hour before everyone else

showed up. That Monday, immediately after he opened his office's door, the phone rang. "Hello. You forget our date or what? All weekend I in the gallery watching out for your Kingswood." Orbits tried to recall if he had mentioned his vehicle. Over the phone, Moon's voice sounded singsong and a bit pouty, the way a mother would cajole a child.

"I'm sorry. My father not well and I had to . . . to take him out."

"What wrong with him?"

"He having trouble remembering."

"Remembering what?"

"Small things. Names and people and places."

"And you call that small? You realize somebody gone and put a light on his head?"

"A what? Where?"

"Put a light. On his head. I see it happen before. With my own father, believe it or not. The minute my mother pass on, he started to drink. At first, we thought it was Ma spirit taking revenge, but she would never do that. It was her nasty sister. She and Ma never get along."

"So why she decide to choose your father instead?"

She sighed over the phone. "That is another story. One minute Ma strong as ever, and the next minute she start getting pain in her chest. And guess who name she was calling out? Not Pa or me or anybody else but that wicked sister of hers. *Mal yeux*."

"Bad eye? I don't believe in all—"

"Then you is a fool." He was taken aback by her candour, but she laughed and added, "How your mother?"

"Healthy so far."

"Any family you all don't get along with?"

If Doraymay or Gums had been in the adjoining offices, Orbits would have hurried along the conversation, but he was a little intrigued as to where this was going. So he told her, "Not really. As far as I know they never keep close contact."

"What about daughter-in-law? That is a big one. Always cat and mouse between the two until one gone"

"Is only me and I divorce a long time now."

She paused and Orbits, in an uncharacteristic moment of confidence, wondered whether the entire crazy conversation had been to determine his marital status. Orbits imagined Moon moving her hand up and down, tracing the fabric of her shirt. But she asked him, "Your old madam leave anything in the house? Clothes? Perfume? Comb?"

"She never visited."

"Not once self?"

"Not after our marriage."

"I never hear anything like that." She sighed once more, so prolonged that before she was finished, Orbits knew what he would say next. He told her that he would call her later in the week and confirm a suitable day and time.

He didn't get the opportunity because each morning he entered his office to the sound of his phone ringing. And with each call he received, some of the attraction or lust or excitement he had felt during her brief visit weakened. One day she asked if pieces of cloth had been found in the driveway — she was specific about colour and fabric — and the next day she wanted to know if during the nights, he smelled a mixture of clotted blood and sweet oil. Before the week was over, she had touched on almost every silly bit of nonsense that Orbits had overheard on the buses and taxis. Did he hear the sound of a chain dragging in the night? A dog howling for no apparent reason? A strange bird circling the house? Blue marks on his parents' legs? A black handkerchief on the porch?

She was angered, though only briefly, by his scepticism, but one Friday while she was remarking on some businessman from her village who had suddenly built a big house, his sudden prosperity due to a little spirit he kept and fed in a bottle, Orbits told her abruptly,

"My father is much better." He then said that someone was waiting outside his door and he had to hang up.

But the damage was done. Gums had arrived early that morning and had been listening intently in his office. "Like you and this woman working *obeah*, boy?"

Orbits, who never liked revealing too much of his private life, told the other man, "Obeah? You too believe in that nonsense?"

"Nonsense, you say. If nonsense does make a big man behave like a dog or cyat, then is really nonsense."

Later in the evening during the cook-up, Spanish, who was stirring the pot, said, "I hope you know what you getting into. These people from all these backtrace don't bite easy, you know." He tossed in two whole peppers and added, "They don't make a move until they check all the signs and say all the prayers. They know things that even I don't know. Be careful she don't feed you with sweat rice."

Gums laughed scandalously, puzzling Orbits. "Sweet rice?" he asked, drawing more laughter. In the corner, Doraymay took a deep drink but said nothing.

During his conversations with Moon, Orbits had imagined what his wife and her parents, what Wally would have made of her silliness, but an hour into the cook-up, listening to Spanish and the other workers, he wondered, in an amused way, how he had spent forty years in the island with no knowledge there were spirits hiding beneath every rock. As the first bottle of rum was emptied and another opened, they seemed to attribute every disease, every type of misfortune, all that was unexpected and distressing to *mal yeux*, prates, bad eye, spirits, *jaaduu*, potions and chants. Gums spoke of an uncle who was afflicted with "goat mouth" because every negative thing he forecasted came to pass while Spanish revealed that stick fighters came to him to bless their weapons with secret prayers. They described ominous coughs, sneezes, sniffles and other flu-related symptoms. "The only thing worse than a dog howling is a goat sneezing," Gums said.

"What about you?" Spanish asked Orbits. But before he could answer, Doraymay took out his mouth organ and blew his mournful country and western.

Orbits typically took a drink or two with the other workers and left at dusk with the pretense that his headlights were not working properly. Now he delayed a little longer, trapped by the desolateness of the station in the fading light and by the fully formed stories they each related of their encounters with spirits and prates. He had no doubt they believed all they were relating, their voices hushed as if there were spirits about listening to them. They claimed to have each seen animals with human features, children appearing and disappearing at will, balls of fire over the ocean. The fire from the three-burner dully illuminated their faces, hardening the shadows and accentuating all the hollows and curvatures. In the distance, the broad leaves of the breadfruit seemed to be dancing and nudging each other; beneath the trees, the fan-shaped dasheen appeared sinuous and silky like the skin of some sleeping animal. In spite of himself, Orbits was captured by the mood. He recalled his childish fascination with clouds, and he felt that the world of spirits and unseen things these men were conjuring was simply an attempt to bend and shape the world into something they understood. Perhaps, in the manner of children or Skullcap the driver or Baby Rabbit, they could only understand the world if it were presented in a few simple brush strokes. That would explain their belief in conspiracies or the urgency they gave to signs and coincidences. Maybe their refusal to believe the world operated in random patterns had led them to create their own shapes, linking and joining as a child might.

It was a romantic view, and the woman who had instigated this topic became tied in Orbits' mind to this fanciful, shape-shifting world. That night, almost as tipsy as he had been with Wally, he began to see her as unreal and temporary as his co-workers' *mama diglous* or *la diablesses*. The image, which he assumed would disappear with the sobriety of the following morning, held, and during that weekend's trip with his parents, he imagined he beheld her skittering through the dark cocoa fields or trailing the Kingswood along the forests of poui and bamboo, leaping and floating over ravines and bridges. It was frightening and alluring at the same time.

On Monday when Moon called to ask about his parents, he cut her off and said he would visit her field in the afternoon. He left soon after twelve, carefully following the directions she had given him and trying not to think of why he was going there. It was not too far from the field station, five or six miles at most, but to get there he had to divert to roads that had partially caved and into traces where the boulders had washed away and the surface had been reformed by tractors into thick, muddy ridges. He was pleased that the Kingswood handled the bumps so well, and he recalled Joe the mechanic talking years ago about the soft new plastic cars.

Moon's house was on a hill, and he drove up and parked next to a wooden stairway. The house, standing on ten-foot teak posts, was well maintained. The wooden walls were unpainted but the windows and doors were uniform. He saw a hammock between the posts, and on the concrete ground, a pair of slippers. The woman appeared by the stairway and held open the wrought-iron gate that led to the porch. There were three high-back rattan chairs, painted white, on the porch, but she walked inside. Orbits, not knowing what to expect, was nevertheless surprised by the articles of domesticity scattered around: the baby crib, a repository now for stacks of newspaper, the photograph of Moon with two children and a man standing against a beach, the safe with decorative china plates, the cabinet stereo set and the almanac with a picture of a lone cactus in some type of desert. Because of her superstitions, he had expected a jumbled house.

He was staring at the photograph when Moon came and sat next to him on a sofa. She was saying something about her plants, and after a while, he was aware that her hands were on him, idly at first, then unbuttoning his pants. Then she stopped talking, but he continued to gaze at the almanac's picture. How did a single plant manage to live in that hot, forlorn place? And why weren't there any clouds in the sky? Afterwards, they walked down the stairs and to the back, where he saw an acre of para grass on the incline leading to a ravine and, beyond, a forest of bamboo. She resumed the talk of her flowers, demonstrating the sandy loam in the area by circling with a bare foot the ground close to the post. As she did so, he noticed her thigh exposed, unshaven yet glistening, and the serious way she was talking of her plants and of the soil, as if nothing had happened and the memory of her mouth on him was fake.

She had been tinged the previous night with the drunken, fanciful talk of spirits, but seeing her now in this way, in her home clothes, beneath her house, sharing her concerns about cuttings and insects, reassured Orbits and lessened his guilt about the act. And he carried this feeling during each of their subsequent encounters, always at the same time, always on the couch as if her bedroom was out of bounds. Afterwards, they spoke of her proposed field of flowers and discussed technical details about moisture and sunlight and properly tilling the soil. This had all happened so fast that Orbits, unprepared and so unsuited to recklessness, began to believe he was helping Moon. Beyond this view, he never stepped back to consider why this attractive and unsatisfied woman had chosen him for her affair, or why he had fallen so quickly into it. Afterwards, driving along the abraded road, avoiding the potholes and the landslips, he did not feel as if he had just done something illicit or even reckless. He was a field officer assisting a client; following their moments of intimacy, they spoke only of her plan to grow flowers. And it was this belief that encouraged him to ask of her husband, whose photograph hung on the wall, and about her two daughters, who were in primary school. He offered advice for which, too, he was unsuited. But he was sincere when he told Moon she should work out her problems with her husband and should consider the effect of a separation on her daughters. In the photograph, the husband, though standing at a distance from the photographer, seemed well built and the children smiling and happy.

She revealed that she had no intention of leaving her husband and would kill anyone who stood in the way of her children's happiness. She said this in the same brazen manner as when she talked about her spirits, and this, too, reassured Orbits. As his visits continued, she stopped phoning, and because Orbits never mentioned anything to the other workers, they moved on to other little scandals involving policemen and politicians and a crooked but powerful businessman everyone called Halligator, who was involved with both groups. "Everything tangle up in this place," Gums said.

But Orbits tried to keep his domestic life separate from his work. Each weekend he took his parents on a trip, venturing farther with each visit, exploring some new village detached from the others by miles of forests or acres of sugar cane and bramble. These trips with his parents had a somewhat similar tenor to the half-hour or so he spent with Moon each week: in both situations, he was performing a task that seemed prescribed and which brought a temporary pleasure. His only moments of unease were when they were driving through some small town, and his mother asked about his daughter. Then he would be reminded of Moon's daughters, whom he only knew from the photograph on the wall. He always told his mother that his daughter was studying for her A-levels, which he had discovered not through one of their infrequent telephone conversations but through the assumption that, at eighteen, she was close to finishing her high school. In fact, she was nineteen, had already written her exams and was awaiting her results. From time to time, too, he thought of Skullcap, the maxi-taxi driver who had such easy access to his outsides, as he had termed them, that he was free to drop in whenever he pleased. Orbits had never mentioned his former wife's remarriage to his parents, nor her move with her daughter to one of the enclaves, vacated decades ago by expatriates and now bearing all the signs of new wealth: elaborate extensions to every house so that small, cottage-like flats were converted into two-storey mansions that seemed to overlap each other, the stone elephants and lions on the gates warily eyeing each other.

During a weekend trip, his father mentioned a name to which his mother answered with the usual rejoinder: "Stop talking nonsense, Papoose." But a few minutes later, she told Orbits, "You know I think your Papoose talking about one of his family. The last time we see them was when Starboy born, so I wonder how he pull out this name from his head all of a sudden." She began to question her husband about his reason for exclaiming the name, but he resumed his pointing to street signs and billboard advertisements in a childish manner. "Look, look." He pointed to a billboard where a Bollywood actor was touting some sort of skin-whitening cream. "Just like Starboy."

Orbits knew what would follow and he quickly asked his mother about the relatives' location. She mentioned a little coastal town.

"Okay, that is where we heading." He was also trying to rid his mind of his last encounter with Moon, who had asked if she could meet his parents and who was mentioning her spirits and her malicious aunt even more frequently. The town was close to two hours away, and they had to stop once for gas.

Just after the gas station, Orbits slowed by a roadside vendor and bought a soursop. His father turned the fruit in his hand, examining the spiky skin.

"No, Papoose, don't dig it like that. Look how you mess up you hand."

"The last supper," his father said, sniffing his finger.

A few minutes later she told Orbits, "Who would ever think this is the same Papoose who a few days aback I see writing down names on a copy book. And you wouldn't believe who names he was writing. It take me a while to figure it out, but it was people who still owe him money for dentures."

"Maybe we should try to collect the money."

"How, boy? The only proof we have lockup in Papoose head and he alone have the key."

Soon they came to a steep incline that led to a Bailey bridge, and his father looked out anxiously, pointing to the spindly mangrove roots. The town itself was filled with steep little hills, and Orbits worried that his Kingswood wouldn't handle some of these. He stopped at an old grocery built with unpainted wood under a concrete house and asked for directions. The young cashier called out to someone and an oldish man appeared. Orbits mentioned the name and the man told him to look for a big yard with two trucks.

"Hello, hello." He turned and saw his father out of the car, in the gap. "You remember me?" The man shook his head. Orbits' father seemed disappointed, and when they returned to the Kingswood, he hunched himself in a corner in an almost petulant fashion. Five minutes later, they came to the yard with the trucks.

The yard was huge and the trucks, newly bought, seemed expensive, but the house by comparison seemed tiny and rundown. He honked his horn and a woman watched angrily through a side door. "I tired tell you people not to park in the way of the truck," she said, wiping her hand on a towel. "It have a big public road for you to park." She stepped back inside and shouted, "Some customers here to see you."

Now a man appeared in a sleeveless vest and a khaki pants that was muddy and cut off at the knees. The clothes did not suit him with his grey hair and sagging belly. He threw away a cigarette. "Come back on Monday. I don't work on weekends."

"Hello, hello." Again, his father had stepped out. "We come visiting."

The man frowned and scratched his stubbles. "Wait a minute . . ."

The inside of the house was jam-packed with tools and cables on every surface. There was a huge television set, and around it was arrayed more junk. During the half-hour visit, the man described his business. He had started small, bought one used truck, traded it for a newer model, bought another, and had made a down payment on a backhoe. It sounded as if he was complaining. "Now I making more money in one month than it used to take me a year to make. But what I will do with all that money? Go to trips abroad? I tired do that. Buy fancy clothes for me and the madam? We closet stocked with that. Invest? I have to hide from the banks the way they after me."

The relative displayed no interest in Orbits' father, who with each boast, clapped his hand and said, "Good, good, man." But in the vehicle, he asked, "Who was that fella?"

His mother laughed; her husband's forgetfulness on occasion had that effect on her. "That was your cousin, Papoose. Your first cousin."

"Good good man," he told her, drawing a fresh burst of laughter. "We should visit him again and carry this crazy thing for him." He held up the soursop.

Five and a half months later, he died. Two months before his death, he had been found wandering in the village and had been brought back by Joe the mechanic. "This man becoming an explorer in his old age," the mechanic said. "I don't know what Mr. Christophene Columbo expected to find in that lonely stretch of road." Then his wife confined him to his room, shutting the front door and listening for the creak of the loose boards on the porch or his footsteps on the front step. The crash she heard was from his room, and she felt he had been trying to climb through the window from the bed and had fallen backward, hitting his head on the bedpost.

She had found him sprawled on his back with his head hanging on the edge of the bed. His eyes were open and did not seem to be in pain or anything. But he grew even quieter, and frequently while he was before the television set, his body would slip sideways and she had to rush to set him upright. He was okay in the mornings, so Orbits had no real idea of his decline, and his wife, too, looked at that period of relative normalcy and believed he would improve over time as the fall's effect lessened.

During this period, he would attempt to engage his father while his mother fed him with a spoon. "You have to get better soon so we could go and collect all the money that people still owing you. Sugars. You remember him?"

His father nodded slowly, and Orbits did not notice what his mother had observed, that the outer circles of his pupils had grown lighter, each day the circles seeming to spread inwards. And she worried that when it reached the centre and her husband's eyes were completely clouded, he would be gone, so as she fed him she asked continually, "Let me see your eyes, Papoose." One morning he mumbled some words, his lips loose and his eyes vacant. "What is that you trying to say, Papoose? The last supper? You have plenty more suppers. Me and you and Orbits."

Nineteen years earlier she had been inconsolable for most of Starboy's wake, but at her husband's funeral, during all the rituals, she stood at a distance, holding on to a post, her face hard and cold. It was a small affair, and she noted that none of his relatives, not even the cousin he had visited five and a half months earlier, had showed up. Her gaze passed over the meagre crowd, neighbours and loiterers, with no acknowledgement of familiarity, no sign of recognition. But she finally got one of her wishes granted.

At the end of the cremation ceremony, when the two dozen or so villagers had already dispersed, Orbits was looking at the embers and the smoke as it curled upwards, buffeted by the trade winds. He glanced up and noticed that the clouds, at different elevations, were moving in opposite directions. He tried to recall the name of the phenomena from his course and was surprised to remember the term. Differential advection. He guessed that rain would soon fall and a few moments later, he felt a tiny droplet on his wrist.

Someone was tapping him on his shoulder. He turned and at first could not recognize the young woman in glasses nor her companion, a fair-skinned young man with features that seemed partially Chinese. "Dee?"

"Mom heard it on the radio," she said. "In the obituaries. I am so sorry."

"Sorry?" He had no idea why he asked her. She nodded, and he felt he saw concern on her face. His eyes began to water, and he turned away. She misunderstood and told him that everything would be okay. Perhaps she was speaking for the benefit of her companion or simply saying what was expected in this situation, but this expression of concern was so unexpected, her appearance so unanticipated, that Orbits could not control himself. He walked away to the post by which his mother had stood, and he felt his shoulders shuddering. He wiped his eyes suddenly and told his daughter, "Come meet your grandmother." Dee stood outside the car, her knees straight but leaning forward to talk to her grandmother, and Orbits saw the older woman pulling her closer to kiss her head, and he felt he saw a bit of impatience in his daughter's stiff posture. Her companion stood some distance away, his hands folded against his chest.

Now it began to drizzle, and his daughter took two or three steps back and walked away to join her companion. His mother's hand was still outstretched, and he wanted to go after his daughter and say something to delay her departure, but she was already in the vehicle, a new Japanese car. The drizzle strengthened into a downpour halfway to his home, and one of the wipers flapped against the windscreen with each upward swipe. He glanced at his mother in the back. She looked small and frail. He resolved he would call Dee more often, perhaps invite her to make up for the years apart and to get to know the grandmother to whom she had, at an earlier time, at another funeral, given the courage to carry on. But when he was approaching the house, he watched how the headlight was illuminating the porch with the creaky board, the drizzle transforming and smoothening the weeds, the water from the guttering spilling into the soft mud that would find its way to the yellow drain at the back; when he saw this neglect and he recalled the ordered lives of the family from whom he had separated, imagining that they had no time for grief, his resolve weakened, and by the time he shut the door after his mother, it had broken altogether. His mother told him, "Such a nice child. And I never get to know her."

It was a simple statement uttered without reproach. She walked tiredly into her room, and Orbits knew that things would carry on as they always did. Later in the night, he listened to the rain falling violently on the roof and abruptly receding to a sound that seemed to come from far away, a soft metallic chirruping, before it struck once more. It fell in that manner all night, ebbing and strengthening and ebbing once more. He felt helpless in his room, his bereft mother in another room, his father gone, his daughter gone, the storm raging outside. He considered his life from the time he had gazed at his mother fretting over his younger brother and had assumed that his life would be one struggle after another. But he had struggled for nothing, really. The early jobs, the work with Baby Rabbit, at the Ministry of Agriculture, his present job — they had all been handed to him. It was his former wife who had pressed the marriage and who had encouraged him into signing up for the courses. It was this other woman, too, who had instigated the affair. He had gone along as he had always done. Throughout his life, he had done nothing, made no effort, showed no determination. His mood matched the fickle storm: he felt within minutes guilt and relief, shame and satisfaction. He fell asleep with these conflicting feelings, but when he awoke the following morning, they had merged into something less oppositional: the idea that he had survived. Somehow, he had managed.

He arrived at his work feeling that the mood of the previous night was a normal reaction to the death of a parent and that he would soon get over it. And in a way, he did; his father had a while ago lost whatever distinctiveness he once had, and it was easy to imagine that he had died a lesser person and that, in fact, his death had rescued him from further devastation. Instead, Orbits turned his attention to his mother. When the other workers were offering their condolences, when Moon called to assure Orbits that his mother would be next as whoever had placed the light on his father would not be satisfied with a single death, when he put the phone off the hook, he was thinking of the life she had lived and what she had surrendered.

His mother had struggled with her husband's affliction over the last years, and although she showed flashes of anger at having to repeat some simple instruction or even at his blankness, those moments never stretched out. She had found a way to transform irritation into amusement, and her complaints, too, fell into this mode. At an earlier time, she would ask Orbits over and over when his daughter would visit, but abruptly she stopped as if she knew of his shame. He thought, too, of her coldness during her husband's cremation, standing apart from almost everyone, retreating into the car as if she were determined not to allow anyone a minuscule glimpse of what she was feeling.

He had never considered her a strong woman, but she had practically run the house for as long as he could remember. This was a surprise because her demeanour never suggested strength; the greater surprise, though, was the discovery that he had once hated her. He tried to push this belated acknowledgement out of his mind and when he could not, he decided he would try to make her remaining years more comfortable. Over the following weeks, he brought home fruits she liked, pulpy sweet caimite and sapodilla. He tried to engage her in conversations about her day, offered to take her to places she once spoke of, but everything she refused. Weeks passed, and months, and he saw how thin she was becoming, how drawn her face was, how slow her footsteps. He tried to get her out of the slow, dripping lifelessness by talking of his father, but all she would say was, "He with

Starboy now. He in a better place." But she spoke the words looking at the floor with so much regret that Orbits felt she believed none of it. And when he persisted, she grew annoyed, bit her lips, got up and moved away. Sometimes when he returned from work, he would see her in the backyard garden. Occasionally she would pluck a leaf from a vine or a blacksage, crush it between her fingers and taste it. She did this slowly and carefully, like the rituals of a *puja*.

One afternoon he told this to Moon, who despite all the promises to himself, he continued to see. "Your mother gone already," Moon told him. "She walking around as usual and she have the same voice but is not she. Is somebody else. Somebody gone and thief away your mother."

Orbits got angry with Moon although he did not say anything, and as she continued, he felt a welling of revulsion, a tiny tendril of disgust both at what she was saying and doing and at himself for not leaving immediately. He left eight minutes later, and on the porch, he turned back to look as if it would be the last time he would see her in that position, reclining lazily on the couch, the ankle of one leg resting on the knee of the other, her clothes hanging on a nearby chair.

He did not return to the station, and midway to his mother's place he diverted to the main road that would take him to the highway. The last time he had taken that route was more than a decade ago, but now he was too distracted to be nervous of the drivers cutting in and out. No one cursed him either because he was maintaining a steady pace. Every now and again, he glanced at his watch, and one hour and fifteen minutes after he had left Moon's place, he parked at the back of a library. Opposite the library was the slight hill that led to his daughter's school, and he went to a café that from an angle looked abandoned but opened into a spacious rectangle smelling of molasses and coconut and cinnamon. He stationed himself by the window, and when he saw the first students hurrying down the hill, he finished his mauby drink and walked outside. The students, mostly from the early forms, were walking in little groups that got bigger as the older students, their pace more languid, appeared.

Orbits walked to the edge of the curb because he did not want to miss his daughter, and once or twice, he stopped himself in the nick of time from shouting to someone who resembled her. When he saw Dee with two other girls, she was looking in his direction, so he waved. She continued walking and when she shifted her gaze, he shouted her name. "This blasted traffic," he grumbled about the rumbling of the trucks and vans. When she was almost opposite him, he called her name again and she looked past him. He wanted to leave, but he recalled the abiding hatred he had felt towards his in-laws on the day of her birth; in the face of their hostility, he had remained silent and rushed to the hospital without explaining the reason for his lateness. He would not allow this to happen again. So he pushed out a hand to signal to the incoming traffic and sprinted across the road. "Dee!" Now she turned, and he was happy that she still responded to the name he had given her. But she appeared irritated, and he wondered if there was something in his appearance that betrayed his earlier encounter with Moon. "Can I talk with you?"

"Can't you just call? I am busy." She glanced fleetingly at her companions.

"It's about your grandmother."

"Is she okay?" She asked this loudly as if she wanted her friends to hear; and Orbits felt it was an attempt to explain why this stranger, dressed in formal country clothes, white shirt with the cuffs rolled, creased khaki pants above muddy boots, was addressing her with such familiarity.

"I believe she is grieving over your grandfather."

"I am sure she will get over it," she said quickly, and Orbits felt he detected a twinge of sarcasm or perhaps bitterness. "I have to leave now."

One of her friends, a chubby girl with eyebrows that met at a point and gave her an accusatory look, said, "We are going to the library now, mister, to plan the end-of-school celebration." Dee walked to join her, and as they walked away, she waved without looking back, a habit picked up from her mother.

The gesture irritated him and he shouted after her, "I will be sure to call you when she dead and bury." He knew she would not hear above the noise of the traffic, but the statement released some of his anger. He returned to the café and told the man behind the counter, "Give me a coconut tart and a mauby drink." He tried to engage the server in the manner he and Wally had chatted with the rumshop proprietors in the capital. "First time I drive in this place. And second time I use the highway even though I driving now for eighteen-nineteen years. Came to see my daughter from the school up in the hill. She busy with some after-exam fete. I never even knew she had written her exams already. So is a good thing, when you look at it, that I come today. Just now she might go to university. Maybe I will find out that by guess too."

The server, who had an impatient and harassed-looking way of blinking quickly, said, "You want anything else to eat or not?"

Orbits patted his belly and said in a jovial manner, "That tart already playing with my stomach. How much bucket of sugar you put in it?" But he felt his annoyance returning. He drove recklessly on his way back, weaving in and out of traffic like everyone else. Once he came across an old man hunched close to the steering wheel, and when he passed him, he shouted, "You think this is a funeral?" He was about to tell the other driver to take his vehicle to a scrapyard when he noticed that it was newer than his Kingswood. The observation forced an uneasy laugh from him, but a few minutes later, he was almost pushed off the road by an overtaking van. He drove carefully to his home.

When he got there, his mother was looking out from the porch, which encouraged him as he got out of his car to ask her, "You was in the backyard garden?"

"That garden finish."

"You could bring it back and—"

"Why? Why I must bring it back? Bring it back for who?"

He was taken aback by her harsh tone as he walked up the three steps. At the doorway, he asked her, "What you looking at?" He tried to follow her gaze, to the hill opposite the house.

She followed him inside without answering, but an hour later, when the sky was getting grey, she returned to the porch. She had prepared his food as she always had since his return, and it was covered in various bowls on the table. He ate slowly and watched her standing on the porch looking out at the hill where palmiste towered over the bramble beneath, the tangerine and guava trees and blacksage stitched together by vines. He had been in that maze a few times, in primary school, during moments of bullying when he felt he could not face his parents. Sometimes he had surprised ground doves and cuckoos and dozing screech owls, and once he had stumbled over tiny frail bones that he had tried to reassemble. Starboy, too, had disappeared there when Orbits had been working in the swamp and the cave, and whenever his brother emerged, bleary-eyed, with a rolled copy book in his back pocket, his mother would say, "Why you have to go so far, child, when it have a toilet right inside the house?" Beyond the bramble was the community centre where he had been found less than ten years later.

The next day Orbits brought home a bamboo rocking chair that he placed on the porch. He watched his mother walking out of the house and settling into the chair. She didn't say anything to him or acknowledge the gift, and her dead manner reminded him of a cat claiming an empty box.

He had planned to avoid Moon, but not knowing who else with whom he could share his distress, he told her about his mother's withdrawal from everything that had once sparked her interest. It was a mistake he realized almost immediately. Over the phone, her voice sounded charged with floating specks of madness as she told him that the house had to be cleansed and that the chair's purchase was the worst thing he could have done. "You encouraging her to be alone, outside, in the dark? Exposed. What wrong with you and all?" He stopped listening when she recited a list of ingredients he needed to sprinkle around the place. He wished Wally were still around, or even Starboy, whose mere presence might have staunched his mother's depression or whatever it was.

〜

ONE MORNING WHEN HE was driving to work, he imagined himself far away, maybe in Wally's city, where everything was surely bright and predictable. He wondered how his life might have turned out if he had been born in another village, in another country, maybe another time. During his courting days, his wife had dragged him to see a movie set in Spain where a group of children looked at the trains and imagined they were carrying a monster. He had been bored of the movie, but his wife had remarked on the village and the forest and the mountains, shot always with a long-range lens so that everything looked remote but complete. She had wondered aloud what it would be like to live in such a place, and Orbits had been puzzled by the extent of her ambition.

He was imagining these scenarios later in the morning, wondering what Wally and his family were doing and the places they were visiting, when there was a knock on his office. A man entered. He was slim and seemed a bit overdressed for a farmer. Orbits pointed to a chair and waited for the man to begin. The man seemed hesitant, even embarrassed, and Orbits asked him if he had come to file a claim or was interested in a subsidy, the two most frequent requests of his office. The man looked down at the chair's leg and pulled it closer to the table. His sad, handsome face appeared familiar somehow, and

Orbits tried to place him. The man began to talk, but in a wistful, hard-to-follow manner, about religion and culture and love and fate. He seemed to be pleading for some sympathy, but Orbits still didn't understand what he wanted. "Sometimes I wonder if god really wanted us to love each other or just fall into a union. Or maybe not even that. Like an animal just to breed. I really don't know." He glanced at Orbits only briefly before his gaze returned to the ground. "You ever find yourself in a position where it have no one you could talk with? Nobody who will understand what you going through and all that on your mind? So you have no choice but to talk to yourself, but the minute the words leave your mouth, you begin to feel like is nothing and that life is nothing and everything is nothing." As he continued talking, Orbits felt that the man was reflecting his own despair, and it was through this connection that Orbits finally recognized him from the photograph taken on the beach with his wife and two children standing at his side.

The man had closed the door behind him, perhaps because of politeness, but Orbits knew of quiet men unexpectedly shrugging off their reserve and slipping into a tightly wound, dangerous temper. Perhaps he had a knife hidden in his pants. He heard the man saying, "I always believe that if you wait long enough everything balance itself out in the end, but I have to tell you that sometimes the waiting is hard. Very hard. I wouldn't lie about that." He pressed his palms on the desk and got up. "Anyways, thanks for listening."

When he walked away, Orbits looked through the window to make sure he had left in his vehicle. He had a slight stoop and seemed to walk on his toes with a springy momentum. Only when the car drove off did Orbits relax, but as the day progressed, his relief choked off and he shifted from disgust to dread to hatred and finally to impatience. So that by the day's end, he felt it would have been easier if the man had stormed into his office and made a scene. Even if he had been overcome with melancholy and self-loathing, as

Orbits imagined cuckolded men to react, it would have been tolerable. He waited for guilt and was disgusted with himself at the absence of this lacerating emotion. But he could not forget the man's calm, almost tranquilized talk of balance and waiting, and on his way home, Orbits considered once more how much the man had seemed to be reflecting — and clarifying — his own scattered anxieties.

When he got home he saw his mother on the chair. He opened his car door but stood for a while outside. He spotted a house bird flying into the eave. Overhead a scissors-tail was circling, and at a higher altitude there were three specks that seemed to be attached to the clouds like ink spots on a painting. Then the specks detached and he saw they were mile-corbeaux, which were frequently on the telephone poles. When he was a child, he would watch these birds flying upwards, getting smaller until they disappeared. He remembered how much he had wished to be like them, so free and powerful. Now the predatory scissors-tail changed its trajectory, flew higher until he could no longer see it. Little black specks seemed to be floating in the distance, and he assumed it was a delayed reaction to watching the birds. He closed the door. His mother maintained her gaze almost as if she had not noticed his entrance.

He stood by his car for close to five minutes. He felt a drop of water on his hand and when he looked up, he noticed the ribbon of grey, so far above it made the sky seem higher, the world bigger. People are linked more by sorrow than by anything else, he thought. Betrayal, disease, other diseases, death. No one sees the chain. They treat these tragedies as separate. This is the normal state of the world. The man with whose wife he was having the affair was wrong. Nothing balances itself. We just grow so tired from waiting that we fall into a pattern of dulled expectations that strengthens each day. Soon we begin to withhold our gaze. He thought of all the houses between his and the junction. One contained a man perpetually drunk, another a low-grade smartman, another a diabetic mechanic, another a beekeeper whose wife had died in childbirth and who had grown old alone, another a woman whose husband had left her and her six children. He could go on and on until he reached the main road and there would be no improvement.

He passed his mother straight. There is nothing special about her. She is one of many. As am I. As is everybody. Thinking in this simple and straightforward manner, as a child memorizing the lines of a poem, everything made more sense. I was fat and unhappy and I had a brother. Then I became thin and happy with a wife and daughter. Then I became fat once more but without a wife and daughter and brother. Now I have lost my fat and my wife and daughter and my friend and my father and most of my mother. What have I gained in the meantime? A secure job and a woman. But Moon is not mine. I must let her know.

In the night, everything had seemed so simple and rational — like neon signs along a long road, he thought — but when, the following morning, he revealed over the phone that their affair could no longer continue, Moon misunderstood and launched a series of accusations. "So you get what you want . . . all my sweetness and you feel you could just call me over the phone and say, 'We breaking all the laws of the universe?' You wasn't breaking any law when you was deep inside me and bawling like a pig? Eh? And who is you to break up with me? Me. You ever take a look at yourself and ask why a woman like me will go with a man like you?"

"Why?" he asked obediently.

"Don't ask me any damn nonsense. You get what you want, you lick the kettle clean, and now you think you could just leave and go?"

Still caught in the simple and literal mood of the previous night, he told her, "Was you who was doing most of the licking."

She called him a snake and a dog and a *quenk*, a wild hog. Then she began to weep. Yes, it was her fault. She was too easily manipulated. She was weak and despairing. She gave in too easily to temptations.

She was shameless. He agreed with her, which caused a fresh burst of curses. Then she grew threatening and hung up.

She came into the office the next day. "How was the morning?" she asked as if the previous day's quarrel had never happened. She closed the door behind her. They made love with her against the filing cabinet, her hair spread on the upper drawer pulled open, one leg on the lower. Then she turned around and pushed him on the chair. She was rough and grunting so loud through her clenched teeth that he was relieved that Gums and Doraymay were in the field. As she was leaving she fiddled in her purse and brought out a tiny essence bottle. "Take this."

"What is it?" Orbits asked. The bottle had a pungent sulphurous odour.

"Something I make for you. Hing and googol. Keep it with you at all times. You could make a necklace and wear it like that."

After she left, Orbits chucked it in the filing cabinet. He felt it was anger rather than passion that had been at play during their love-making even though her departure was similar to her arrival in that it had ignored the previous day's argument.

And that was the pattern for the next three months, savage arguments followed by bouts of savage coupling. During one of their arguments, she clarified what had been on his mind for a while: she had chosen him because she knew that he would keep their affair a secret. He was friendless and safe and reserved although the disparaging term she used was *conumunu*. After every episode in his office, he would swear it would be the last, his determination strengthening as he drove to work the following morning. Then she would show up and all his promises would fall away, and in the aftermath, he would blame himself for his weakness. He went along with everything; his only faltering request was that she visit him in the early afternoons, when the other workers had already departed for a rumshop. Whenever she left and before the guilt took over, he would try to convince himself that what they were doing was normal, that he was a single man conducting an affair with a woman neglected by her husband, that nothing was given unwillingly by either party, that he was doing what his former wife had once done. Maybe, he thought, this is the balance Moon's husband had spoken of.

One Friday she showed up at the cook-up. Orbits was alarmed, and as she chatted with Doraymay, he wondered how she knew of this weekly event. When she came over to him, he noticed Doraymay watching them carefully, watching how she stood next to him, leaning against his shoulder intimately while making suggestions to Spanish, who was stirring the pot. Orbits folded his arms and tried to appear detached even when he felt the tip of her shoe scratching his foot. She accepted a drink from Gums and finished it in a gulp. Orbits, too, took a drink, drawing a little cheer from Gums, who said, "The one-drink man start and finish his dose."

But the drink loosened him a bit, and he felt that since he had not invited her, there was no harm in her appearance. Besides, she seemed familiar with everyone, laughing at Spanish's glum way of speaking and at Gums, who was trying to flirt in a deliberately ridiculous manner. Then Spanish began to talk of his spirits and she got quiet, and after fifteen minutes or so, she said to Orbits, "I still didn't get that thing."

Gums said, "What you waiting on, boy? Give the woman *that* thing."

"It in the office," he said, the rum in his head.

She followed him, and once in the office she was unexpectedly tender. She stroked his hair and pressed her hands against his cheeks, but when he loosened his belt, she held his hand, stopping him. She was making less sense than usual, and when she left abruptly after five minutes or so and he was returning to the cook, he tried to understand what she meant by saying, "I cast out everything. I clean." He was pleasantly surprised at this tamping down of their relationship that had recently been so volatile. Some of this relief was in evidence when he loosened up at the cook, uncharacteristically laughing loudly at Gums' description of "knife-and-fork people," which, he explained, was a term for country bookies who tried to imitate the mannerisms and habits of town folks.

He noticed Doraymay looking at him and stroking his moustache and drinking straight from the bottle, tipping back his head and banging the bottle on the table when he was finished. Later, when they were eating, Orbits told Spanish, "This duck tasting real good."

"Is the seasoning. People don't realize that is the seasoning, not the cooking, that is the commander in chief."

"You season anything recently?" Gums asked mischievously.

"Me? I am not a cook," Orbits replied.

"Yes, we know. You is the bookman," Spanish said.

"The bookman," Doraymay repeated with a viciousness that drew glances from the other men. He got up suddenly, scattering the food from his plate. "The blasted bookman." He reached for the bottle and finished it. "The bookman who feel that he so smart he could do anything. With anybody."

"Take it easy," Spanish cautioned.

"Don't tell me to take it easy, man. Is not me you should be telling that." He advanced towards Orbits, the bottle in his hand. Orbits noticed how red his eyes were. "I didn't do anything. Is he!" He pointed to Orbits and flung the bottle at him. Orbits felt the bottle whistling against his ear, and he was about to get up when Doraymay kicked away his plate and fell upon him. He received several jabs before Spanish and Gums managed to pull away the other man. Orbits steadied himself against the chair and managed to sit up. He wanted to leave but felt it would be inappropriate to do so now. Why did this happen? Was there something that I missed? Why was I and not the others the source of Doraymay's violence? The simple and childish manner resurfaced. He heard and saw the other men as if at a distance. Doraymay seems confused. Why is Spanish consoling him rather than me? Why is Gums still smiling? Is my ear still in place? He felt his ear and was reassured.

Eventually he got up. He felt a sharp pain in his left shoulder. "Where you going, man? It still have food in the pot," Gums said.

"Yes, man. Don't let the lime spoil like this." Doraymay had spoken without sarcasm or malice.

Don't let the lime spoil? Orbits thought. What the hell is he talking about after he nearly take out my ear? And the others? Did they witness the assault or did I imagine everything? He felt his ear. The pain was real. But the friendliness was fake. And suddenly he was enraged. "All of allyou witness what just happen." He advanced towards Doraymay, and Gums and Spanish came between them. "I never do him one damn thing!"

"Yes, is true. You never do *me* one damn thing."

Once again, Orbits could detect no sarcasm in the other man's voice, and this stirred his rage anew. He recalled the times when the bullies at school had smiled serenely whenever he complained to a teacher. "This not going to end here," he said. "I have a friend in the town. Portogee lawyer." He was too enraged to see the ridiculousness of the lie. "He going to hear about this."

Spanish put his hands around Orbits, and as he was leading him to the car, he said, "He will cool down by the morning. He going through a rough patch. It eating him up."

"And he choose me to get over his rough patch?" He wanted to break loose but Spanish — remarkably strong for such an old man — tightened his grasp.

When he was in the car and the headlights on, Spanish told him, "What Doraymay do was a stupid thing." He hesitated and added, "What you doing not smart either." Orbits wanted to tell the older man that his little affair was over, but his ear was hurting, he was still fuming with rage and he was not sure of anything at that point.

In the morning the pain in his ear had receded, but his left eye, which he assumed had been spared the blows, felt raw and itchy. In the mirror, he saw it was black and swollen. He placed his hand over his good eye to be certain his vision had not been affected. "Just like the shopkeeper," he mumbled, his anger now renewed. He wondered if he could really sue Doraymay but knew that the object of an assault was viewed with derision rather than with sympathy and the bad-john as a flawed-but-heroic rebel. The police could barely contain their amusement whenever reports were made. Women beaten by their husbands, children by their parents, students by their teachers, and the general consensus was that the victims somehow deserved their fates. The weak paying a price for their weaknesses. "This blasted place," he mumbled, using a phrase from his last weeks with Wally. He remembered, too, Wally saying that the island had been built upon violence. Tribes wiped out and their shackled replacements flogged into submission.

He did not go to work that day but drove instead to a Chinese shopkeeper who stocked all sorts of odds and ends, and he bought cheap sunglasses. He put it on and from habit glanced at the sky and marvelled how the world had suddenly become a darker and unstable place. The trees had a faint purple tint, the asphalt road seemed to be rolling in the distance and the pothound he almost hit looked decidedly green.

"Nice darkers, man," Gums said when he returned to work the next day. "It suiting you real nice. You looking like a real barrister now." Orbits walked to his office without replying; he had already decided he would keep to himself and not associate with anyone at the station. He didn't care that Doraymay, too, seemed changed by the incident. On succeeding days, he was either friendly to the point of fawning or sullen and silent. According to Gums, "The man singing sweet Jim Reeves tunes and all of a sudden he buss it up with reggae like if is the most natural thing in the world." From Gums, he heard that Doraymay's property battle with his brother had escalated, and, after losing that battle, he had picked arguments with arbitrary farmers. One afternoon, a fisherman who was as short and stocky as Doraymay was tall and skinny had pulled out his cutlass and threatened to slice him up. But to Orbits, Doraymay was unceasingly polite. The week of the incident with the farmer, he stood at the doorway to Orbits' office and said, "What happening to this place?" He smiled shyly like the Doraymay of old and added, "But I still walking. Just two years again for pension. Wifey looking forward to it. Have to get out from this commess before it too late."

He seemed to be looking for some sympathy. This enraged Orbits, and he asked him, "And why you telling me that? I look like I interested?"

Another day he told Orbits, "Really looking forward to retirement. Spend some more time with the family. Get to know them better. What about you?"

He smiled, and Orbits noticed his yellow teeth through his moustache. He snatched a nearby folder. "Me? I kind of busy right now." He only looked up when the other man had gone. Orbits couldn't understand Doraymay's game. Was he looking for forgiveness and now trying to strike a connection, or was it a trap, trying to draw him in with friendliness before another assault? In any case, he decided he would not bite: he had no intention of clearing the other man's conscience or falling into a crude trap. One morning, Spanish told Orbits, "Is common for friend to fall out after a little rum drive somebody head crazy. But they does always patch up. You know how much times me and Gums fall out? I know you is a different fella from we, but Doraymay trying."

Orbits felt his irritation rising. "Trying what? To draw me in with laglee like a semp?"

Spanish took this as a joke and laughed. "Alright, Mr. Bookman, I just saying."

The more Doraymay tried to be friendly, the more Orbits put up his defences. One midday he surprised himself by thinking, Chaos. That is the only way these blasted peasants know how to behave. All this knife-and-fork jealousy! It was an uncharacteristic assessment, and later in the day, Orbits recalled where he had heard the judgment; the man who had taken over the office following Wally's departure had mentioned it in a taunting, punishing way. "The bitch was right," Orbits mumbled. "He send me to a hellhole."

Orbits did not want him to be right, and he wished he could follow Spanish's advice. Yet each time Doraymay uttered a greeting, he found he could not respond with any equivalent cordiality. "Look, man, I busy right now." The phrase sprung out the minute he spotted Doraymay.

From Gums, he heard of Doraymay's other side, increasing outbursts in the rumshops as if he had found an outlet to make up for Orbits' aloofness. "He pulling rank," Gums told him one day. "Threatening the hunters now of all people."

One day Doraymay did not turn up at the office. Midday his wife called to say he had not been home that night. Gums told her that he was probably drunk in some rumshop, but in the afternoon, he told Spanish in a worried manner, "I call all these other places. It look like Doraymay went out with some hunters last night."

"But he don't hunt."

"Yes, I know. They say that he went out with a group who tell him that poachers had a camp full of dead ocelot and these tamandua anteater. But it was a setup."

"He went by himself? That is craziness. These hunters will eat him raw."

When Doraymay was found by a forest ranger the following day, badly beaten and bound to a tree, Orbits recalled his rebuffing of the other man and dragged himself along with Gums and Spanish to the local hospital. The sight of the disengaged doctors and nurses and the sound of groaning reminded him of the night of his daughter's birth, when he had run three miles to get to the hospital. He recalled his in-laws' treatment of him, and in spite of his earlier decision to be as polite as possible to Doraymay, he felt his mood souring. And when he saw Doraymay racked up on the bed, his head bandaged and his face blue and swollen, he wanted to rush out from the place. Doraymay turned to look at the visitors and a trail of red spittle ran down his neck. At the foot of the bed, a bloody bandage sneaked down like a battered snake. One of Doraymay's feet was slung up at an angle that was sure to cause more pain. Or maybe it was broken, Orbits thought, as he pretended to not notice Doraymay's beckoning gesture. He felt Gums gently pushing him in the direction of the injured man, and when he bent over the bed, Doraymay reached out, faltering, and Orbits saw one of his fingers was broken and twisted. Orbits stepped back; he felt overpowered by the odour of clotted blood and urine and antiseptic.

Chaos! Laglee! The bitch trap me!

He rushed away and ran down the steps. He took the following day off from work and when he returned, Gums said jokingly, "We thought you and all had gone to the forest." As Gums related his visit to the hospital the previous night and assured Orbits that Doraymay would recover and soon be at work, Orbits recalled the sour odour of urine and clotted blood. He spent half an hour in the washroom. In the evening as he was driving home, the odour returned, and he pulled to the side of the road.

ON SOME DAYS FOR no apparent reason and with no provocation, a deep panic overcame Orbits. It displaced his decision to keep to himself, to ride out the years, to manage. He tried to regain his temporary and troubled calm by repeating the phrases lodged in his mind over the last few weeks. I am forty-four years old. I have a reasonable job and an office. In sixteen years, I will retire with a pension. It could be said that I am secure. But this time the simple restatement of convenient facts, rather than bringing comfort, introduced more troubling concerns. I have done nothing of substance. If I die tomorrow, no one will miss my presence. I have no one. At times, while he was driving home, from habit he looked up and thought: I am just like these drifting clouds, turned this way and that by the wind and melting to nothing in an instant.

Day after day, he considered his circumstances. At intervals, he imagined finishing his course in meteorology or applying for another job, but he made no move. Instead, he thought of the house opposite the school in the cocoa village and more frequently of Wally and his family in Canada.

He knew that these options were unavailable to him because he could not leave his mother, who had also retreated into another world. One evening while driving from work, he had this image of finding her dead, and although he felt guilty and a little shocked at the relief this picture brought, he could not help but consider how much the tragedy would release him. Every evening he saw her on the porch, sitting on the chair he had brought, her gaze straight ahead, even when he turned the slight corner into the driveway. He felt he was trapped in a jail that grew smaller each day. Once he had read of inmates in solitary confinement remaining for months in a cell with the lights never turned off. He had felt that particular punishment did not seem too horrible, but this is how he felt now: perpetually agitated, unable to relax, shifting to untenable fantasies. Frequently he would stare at the walls for hours, not conscious of the time passing until there was a knock on the door. In the middle of the day, he would catch himself muttering for no reason. "The strands of cobweb over the cabinet look like a silky hammock. If they are brought together, they can form a strong rope. The patterns of the tiles on the floor resemble a diamond. But yesterday it was a pyramid. Can the inhalation of diesel cure the body of worms? Of cancer? Why was Doraymay so pleasant with me? Was his violence towards me karma or did it happen because I wished for it? What has happened to the woman?"

At odd intervals, he saw shapes on the wall that recalled his childhood fantasies of twisting the clouds into fluffy animals. But these new shapes were alarming: spiders that appeared to grow extra legs, freakishly bandaged serpents, baby animals that mutated into blobs of fat that wobbled helplessly because there was no skeletal structure. He tried to fight these bursts of paranoia by providing a countervailing delusion, ratcheting up his fantasies of flying through the clouds on his way to a country that he knew only from gossip and boasts. Gradually he began to see anything that potentially stood in the way of his repose as deliberate and malicious. In this manner, he wondered why his co-workers were holding a raffle to pay Doraymay's medical bills, why farmers and fishermen daily came to him with simple problems they could easily handle themselves, why his mother was still hanging on.

One morning while he was leaving his car for his office, instead of mentally reciting his now-useless statements, he counted his steps. Twenty to the front door of the building, nine to his office and three to his desk. Thirty-two steps. He wrote the number on the back of an application form. In the evening when he was leaving, he counted thirty. Why were there two less? Was it because he was in a hurry to leave? Did he miscount? He returned to his office and walked in a manner that he would match the morning's steps. When he got home, he did the same. Ten steps to the front step and seven to his room.

This measuring of his life — which is how he thought of it — intruded into and separated his fears, the simple ritual of counting numbing and then stabilizing him. He discovered that with his sunglasses he could mark his steps with no one noticing. He was aware that the little towns he passed on his way to work were filled with crazy people who marched about mumbling to themselves. He had heard Gums and the other workers talking about a former teacher who, fired from his job, walked around with the ends of cardboard boxes, writing equations and beseeching the onlookers to follow his calculations. "I solve the puzzle of life," the man would shout to frightened women and children. Orbits knew every small town had its own crazy person.

In one of these little towns, he met Moon. He was on his way to the bank and was annoyed that someone had called his name and disrupted his counting. He glanced back and memorized the last number. Fifty-five. Moon began talking. She and her husband had just returned from a family outing. Things were really good between them. She had visited a pundit who had removed the light from her head. She was now herself once more, the evil spirit banished. Fifty-five. Orbits tried to focus on the number. She had heard about the incident with Doraymay eleven months earlier. He had been her husband's drinking partner and now her husband spent more time at home. Did so much time pass? Orbits wondered. Eleven months? What was that number again? Fifty or fifty-five? She was saying something about her seven-month-old son. Seven, she repeated. They were now a perfect family.

"Fifty-five," Orbits told her and sped along.

But the spell was broken. He could no longer measure his steps; random numbers interrupted his summations. Most began or ended with seven. Reluctantly, he returned to the real world and immediately felt its burden, flattening and crushing. For this, he blamed Moon, who, viewed through his sunglasses, had seemed haloed by concentric rings of mauve and salmon. She had described their affair as a light on her head, placed there, no doubt, by her malicious aunt. Orbits knew she believed this completely, and with this immutable belief, she had been spared any guilt or regret. The spirits were to blame, and she was just a vessel. Did she actually say this, he wondered? Her belief in this unseen world was similar to Skullcap's view of his god. Blasted savages, he thought. Yet he wished he, too, had some invisible entity or deity in his back pocket, but the years of praying futilely for his childhood bullying to stop and the tormenters to be punished had erased every trace of religiosity. He was a nonbeliever not because of any rational determination, but because of what he saw as constant betrayals.

One evening when he got home, he told his mother, "Nobody willing to accept blame for anything."

It was the first time in months he had spoken directly to her, and although she maintained her gaze, he saw her eyes welling up. "I want to go."

"For a drive?" She shook her head almost imperceptibly and raised one hand tiredly. The fingers fluttered in a dismissive gesture. "You shouldn't be cooking any more. I will bring something every evening for us." Now she looked at him in a studying way. She drew circles around her eyes and cackled sadly. He put his briefcase on the floor. "What is it you always looking at on the hill? What is it you seeing?"

Her lips were still twisted from her grin, the features, like those of many old people, taking their time to transition. "Is my fault."

"Your fault about what?"

"My fault that Starboy get murdered. My fault that your father fall and damage himself. My fault that you not with your family. My fault with everything."

"When I mention that nobody want to accept blame I didn't mean you—"

"My fault. My fault."

"Ma."

She wiped her eyes and her face hardened once more, shutting him out. But he remained there, leaning against the railing until she got up and went into her bedroom. He tried to recall some pleasant memory from his childhood during which his mother had displayed a special affection towards him and, failing to recall anything, wondered if her affection had really been so one-sided. She had made fun of his weight, his fascination with clouds, his moroseness, even his humiliation, and he had seen her behaviour as either indifference or spitefulness, but now he considered it may have been simply part of her general bantering that included jokes about her husband's dentures and the junk he stored in every corner and, in his later years, his forgetfulness. Sitting alone in the dark, his sunglasses still on, Orbits was sure of only one thing: his mother had suffered enough. In this mood, unexpectedly, he was touched by the remembrance of the silliness that had once offended him at the dinner table.

In his office, he asked the farmers about cheap lumber and labour, and these men, eager to please, expecting some favour in return, descended on Orbits' house during the following weeks, and they pried loose and knocked away the slack boards and the railing around his mother. They waited until she went inside before they shifted her chair to complete their job. They did the same when they were building a new porch, hammering and laying railings around her and painting the ceiling above the chair Orbits had brought.

One evening when he got home, he saw that her hair matched the green paint on the ceiling. "You looking like that Joker man from the comics," he told her, but he was angry at the workers' carelessness. When he confronted them, they told him they had had no choice because it was difficult to communicate with a mute.

"She is not a mute," he said, but too softly for them to hear.

In the evenings, he could smell the fresh paint and he saw the print of her slippers on the floor. He bought a length of carpet that he laid from her chair to the door and potted orchids and dahlias that he hung from the rafters on the porch. He returned from work with pommecytheres and custard apples and papaws and pineapples, the fragrance of the fruits mixing with and then displacing the petroleum odour of the new paint. Mother and son sat side by side for an hour or so with no words exchanged. Now and again, he would imagine another car driving into the yard and his daughter emerging with her books and his mother standing to receive a hug before both women disappeared into the house. At times, too, he pictured his wife sitting on the couch and planning her lessons.

He linked these imaginary scenes with periods he had long associated with turmoil and distress, and he was surprised that he now thought of that time with fondness and even regret. His former wife planning her work on the desk while he studied on the bed. Even the drive to the cocoa village where she had condemned the house he admired as haunted and the school as abandoned. And he convinced himself that at some point, backward glances at these evenings he spent alone with his mother would unexpectedly be tinged with the same longing. In this way, knowing that soon all of this would be gone, that his mother would die and he, too, would grow old and feeble and wonder what had happened to his life, the hour or so with his mother became less an obligation than a period of appreciative calm.

Side by side they sat, not saying anything, and Orbits knew that a passerby might look at this forty-seven-year-old man sitting every evening with his mother on the porch and believe, in the village manner, he had nothing better to do. A *locho* and a *peong* waiting for her to die so he could inherit the property. Yet he began to look forward to these late evenings, just sitting there, watching the lizards sneaking into the space between the boards and hummingbirds buzzing around the orchids and semps and bananaquits alighting in a line on the telephone wires. He observed the swift drawing of night, grey clouds turning red before they were swallowed up by the darkness.

The approach of night was always signalled by a drop in the temperature, and during the occasional thunderstorms that came with such abrupt force, the gutters overflowed within minutes and the winds, hoarse and tortured, walloped the trees so that blowing leaves clipped the ground and rose at once in jousting funnels. Within this frenetic energy, it was easy to imagine he was in another country. But the fierce storms soon expended their energies and tapered into light drizzles, the patter on the roof so faint it seemed to be coming from a great distance. Orbits would look at the drenched orchids twisting like snakes lapping up the droplets and the birds returning to the telephone poles, flapping their wings and dipping their heads into their bodies, and imagine another scene. But this was a scene he could only imagine imperfectly because he had glimpsed it in movies and magazines. Snow, at once powdery and spongy, fluffing up the ground and red burning leaves hanging in the sky like frail jewels before they plummeted. Somewhere in the background was an ice-capped mountain, its reflection glistening on a lake. Into this imperfect scene, he imagined himself walking along a road, and because he was never sure of the colours, the landscape was, at intervals, white and bare and at other times vivid and sparkling.

On Christmas Eve, when from all the houses in the village came the sound of *parang*, a kind of Spanish Castilian music played on a three-string guitar, a *cuatro*, and the malls built with oil money and stocked with foreign paraphernalia were crowded with families, Orbits was returning to his home with fruits and gifts he had picked up at a small store. A lamp with a dimming switch, slippers, a light raincoat, a basket of aromatic oils, a decorative rug and a snow globe that enclosed a white cottage surrounded by two pine trees. His mother displayed no interest in the other gifts, but she took the snow globe and held it before her, tilting it from one hand to the other and watching the white confetti spread. He remembered her during past Christmas Eves when her entire family was around, chatting with her husband while she changed the curtains and decorated the tree and checked the oven. In the night, the aroma of sorrel and cakes and imported fruits drifted throughout the house, and he could barely wait for the morning when everything would be laid on the table.

On Christmas Day, he called his former wife and he learned that his daughter had left for Canada three weeks earlier. She had intended to call, but the last months had been a flurry of activity with foreign exchange and student visa and arranging for a place to stay. Orbits was deeply disappointed, but he told his former wife he understood, and it was okay, and he was happy her daughter had left because of the upsurge of crime in the island and because there were many other options for her in Canada. His wife remained silent and Orbits realized he was saying too much and none of it mattered. Eventually she said, "I am glad you understand."

"I have a friend there—" he began, but she had hung up.

He felt he needed to share this news with someone, so he told his mother, "Dee went away."

She clutched the snow globe, leaned slightly forward and nodded. Orbits was not sure if she heard or even if she remembered her granddaughter's name.

WITH THE NEW YEAR came the dry season. Now there were no rainy evenings and the humidity carried in the nights, so everything seemed clotted and dried. The green paint lost its lustre and began flaking out in tiny ribbons. Woodlice and ants burrowed behind the raised strips, and sometimes Orbits would stare at a lizard, still for more than an hour, suddenly leaping to life, its neck stretched up as it swallowed. This how life is, he thought. One swift moment of change shattering all the accumulated harmony. But maybe this setting things in order is the real harmony. At other times, though, he believed that change, when it occurred, was so sluggish it was impossible to trace its inception. In the nights, smoke, sweet and syrupy, from bush fires seeped through the house, banishing the odour of dead paint, and he would hear the distant cackling of bamboo and would wonder if men and women who lived in a war zone ever grew used to sounds like these. Then the rainy season came once more, washing away the dust and grime, and tiny green tendrils sprung from the dead vines and the flattened brown grass. Some evenings his mother would be so still that Orbits would worry she had died in her chair, then he would see the confetti in her globe shivering.

Soon the rain gave way to blistering heat and the cycle that led to the parched land and the forest fires continued. Orbits arrived at his work and left at the same times each day. He stayed an equal length of time on the porch and went to his bedroom at the same hour. He was aware of the passage of time, the days falling into weeks and the weeks falling into months, not only from the change of seasons, but also from the increasing frailty of his mother. Although she still insisted on cooking, her hands trembled as she lit the pro-gas stove, and sometimes Orbits, smelling the gas, would rush to the kitchen to turn off the valve. He bought food, soups and sandwiches that were at times untouched and fruits that were nibbled at the ends. She now had to support herself on the doorway and on the furniture as she walked to her bedroom. He bought her a cane that she accepted numbly as she had done the chair. He no longer wished for her death, nor did he think of her passing away; everything seemed to be playing out in slow motion, stretching and stretching in a kind of indifferent and neglected permanence. He guessed he was waiting, but for what, exactly, he had no idea.

Years earlier, his former wife had asked what he wanted from life and, not getting a ready response, had grown annoyed. Now, he still did not have an answer. He was neither happy nor unhappy, neither contended nor dissatisfied. Nor was he paralyzed with the lassitude that had fallen on him following his separation from his former wife and the departure of Wally. He did not hold the world at a distance, so he still felt a marginal sorrow at the retirement of Spanish, a tendril of regret when Gums left and a short burst of grief when he heard that Doraymay had been paralyzed and sent on permanent disability leave. He was aware of these feelings and reassured, too; he treasured these temporary eruptions because they were signs he was alive. Sometimes, late in the nights, he would catch a bit of harmonium music from a village ceremony, the sounds badgered by the distance and the wind, and he would sit up in bed, listening for a familiar note, the stirring of some melody. Frequently he would hear his mother coughing and during the periods of silence, he would relax only when she resumed. Her coughs were dry and harsh and had the rasping stridency of an accusation.

She remained on her bed longer in the mornings, and he would drive to work only when she emerged from her bedroom for the cup of hot, freshly grated cocoa and ginger — the odour strong and brisk — she had taken to drinking during the day. He finally got a home phone and instructed her to call him if she was not feeling well, but she glared from him to the phone as if it were a curse. The phone was a mistake, he soon realized, because he would grab the office receiver in alarm each time it rang. During one of these calls, which turned out to be from a farmer who was always crying down himself and berating his ungrateful children, six daughters in all, for shunning the hot sun and the muddy rice field, Orbits told the man that his application for subsidies had been approved and he could come to the office for the letter. He arrived just before closing, and Orbits, who believed that the farmer had castigated his family to emphasize his deservedness, listened impatiently as he launched a fresh assault on his daughters. One was wayward, the other light-headed, yet another rude and the rest hopelessly lazy. The farmer, who had a long trunk on short legs — his face with its big forehead and insignificant chin repeating this oddity — scratched his ear with his muddy thumb. "Eef they was good-looking I could have married them out *toute baghai*, but all of them take after they mother." They had all attempted various jobs but had failed. He mentioned the jobs — seamstress, fruit vendor, road worker, maid — and Orbits lost track of who had been fired from what. "The lagoon is the proper place for them, but they feel they foot too good for mud."

At the end of the conversation it was agreed that one of the daughters, for a salary of one thousand a month plus a room and food, would move to Orbits' place to take care of his mother. On his way home, he tried to recall whether it was the wayward, the light-headed or the rude daughter. He hoped it was not the lazy one. The father had arranged to drop the girl on Sunday; she would stay during the week and return on weekends. Orbits tried to prepare his mother for the appearance of a stranger in the house, explaining that the girl would help her clean around and cook but not mentioning anything about attending specifically to her. The mother just scowled at the snow globe.

On the appointed day, Orbits felt the father had changed his mind and had forced the poor girl into the lagoon, but about eight in the night, when his mother had already retreated to her bedroom, he heard the honking of a horn and saw the farmer's old van parked at the side of the road. The girl followed her father out of the vehicle carrying a suitcase in one hand and a bulky cloth bag in the other. He ran down the step to help her, but the father said, "She could manage. She could manage." The father, his long trunk striving for balance on his short legs, tilted forward as he walked down the slope, his hands slightly raised at the side as if he were riding an invisible motorbike.

Although the girl had a trace of her father's disproportionate shape, she had a pleasant face. "Where Grandma?" she asked.

Orbits was a little surprised by the girl's reference, but she had spoken respectfully. He told her as they walked up the steps to the porch, "She went to bed. She is up early and goes to sleep early too."

"This one here is the opposite," the father said. "She up late and go to bed late." Orbits wondered if this was, in fact, the lazy daughter. But the father added, "From small, I start calling her Moaner because she always moaning about something or the other."

"Only when I have cause," she said to her father with a little smile. "Only when *somebody* give me cause."

"Well, you better don't give these people here cause to fire you because it will be back to the lagoon for you."

Not wanting to be drawn into a family quarrel, Orbits said, "Mona. Is a nice name." He saw the girl glancing inside the house and he told her, "You will sleep in the middle room." He pointed to the room once used by Starboy.

When he awoke the following morning, the girl, Mona, was in the kitchen shifting around tins of condensed milk and salmon and beans in the cupboard and discarding fruits that had turned brown and soggy. His mother was at the doorway watching her with the wariness of an animal uncertain of its surroundings. "This girl came to help out," he told her. "Her name is Mona."

"That is true, Grandma." Mona stood up, cans in both hands. Her damp hair was loose and fell around her shoulders. She put down the tins, produced a clip from the pocket of her jeans, bunched her hair and fastened the clip.

The mother bent forward, her body even more crooked, squinting to get a better look. Then she slowly raised her cane and pointed it to Mona and to the front door.

"I have to go now," Orbits said to both women. And to Mona, "She likes ginger and cocoa tea in the mornings."

He left the office earlier than usual, stopping on the way to buy oranges and avocadoes. When he drove into the driveway, his mother was not at her usual spot on the porch. She was by the small side table pushed against the wall, where the shelf still had some of the dental material used by her husband. Her cane was on the table and she was holding both ends like a stickfighter. The girl peeped out from the kitchen and when she saw the fruits, she said, "Let me get that." Orbits placed the bag on the dining room table. "Grandma is in a bad mood today." She retrieved the fruits and held a papaw before the other woman. "You like this? Is nice and sweet. Look at the red and yellow colour." Orbits' mother turned and swished at the fruit with her cane. The girl jumped back and giggled nervously. "I think she is in a bad mood because she not used to me as yet. Not so, Grandma?" she asked in a high-pitched, cajoling manner.

The bad mood got worse. Each evening he returned to his mother pacing from the porch to the kitchen, knocking her cane loudly on the floor. And each evening she screamed to Orbits, "Send she back!" The girl, whose full cheeks and big eyes gave her a vague cherubic look suited to martyrdom, did not seem too upset and even treated the old woman's outbursts as expected and inconsequential, which only made matters worse. "What she doing here?" the mother asked one evening, pointing to Starboy's room. Orbits wondered if this was the cause of his mother's rage: the room had been unused since his brother's death, and maybe she believed her son had been shunted aside, memories of him no longer useful to anyone but to herself.

"She helping to . . . helping to keep the place clean," he told her.

"Yes, Grandma. Look how nice the place looking now. I want you to look the same way. You want me to comb your hair?"

"Get away!"

Mona followed Orbits to the porch. "Grandma just like my father. Getting vex like if is a habit."

"So, you don't mind?"

"Is only two weeks so far. I think she will come around."

"She wasn't always like this," Orbits said apologetically. He was on his way to his Kingswood when he returned and told her, "The two most important people in her life died." The girl looked confused, and Orbits had no idea why he had mentioned this. That day in his office he wanted to call the father and explain that things weren't working out, but the girl was right: maybe his mother just needed more time. Many old people were like this, he reasoned. Like some of the farmers who planted the same crop year after year in the face of falling profits.

He was surprised each Friday night when the girl would say, "I have to leave now, Grandma. Be a good girl when I not here, okay? Don't give this nice quiet son you have here any trouble." And his mother would raise the stick and point to the road. But the bigger surprise was his mother's relapse during the weekend, sinking into the old chair, sitting quietly, her eyes clouded, stroking the snow globe as if it were all she could feel. The minute Mona reappeared on Sunday night, his mother would rise from her chair, her eyes would sparkle, and she would be filled with malicious life as she followed the girl around, resting on her cane, watching her every move.

The father hung around on Sunday nights, chatting about his other daughters, assuring Orbits that they were just as worthless as Mona. "You need a cook or a bottle washer? Just say the word." Orbits was never sure if the man was joking or had fallen into the ritual of criticizing his family or if he really wanted to palm off his daughters to a man he saw as soft. So he was thankful when, invariably, the talk shifted to the pleasures of lagoon life. Not only rice, the man said, but dasheen, catfish, cascadura and conches. "Everything you want to eat right there in the mud. You ever study mud? Is the most useful thing in the world if you ask me. You could build road, repair house, make wares, plaster bruise. Anything you like." Orbits couldn't believe the man was so backward, and because he was uncertain as to whether this was all a put-on, he listened quietly and made neutral sounds. One night the man said, "Just now, people will have to eat mud. This money going to run out and everybody forgetting how to plant. Young people not interested in the field again. And people like Halligator waiting to eat everybody up. Just wait and see."

That week Orbits saw Mona on the front step with the potted orchid disembowelled. She was softening the mud around the roots and above her, standing with her cane, was his mother. He parked hurriedly. His mother was saying, "Stupid child. Foolish girl. Not like that. Look how you gone and spoil everything." She turned to Orbits. "This stupid child meddling with the flowers." She had a ghastly, lopsided smile. "I feel to knock she in she head."

"Grandma only full of talk. She like me too bad."

"Like you? Who will like you with you big bottom? Look what you gone and do." She laughed from somewhere in her throat, the sound caught and expelled with a rush of air. Orbits couldn't recall when last he had heard that sound from her.

Another evening, he saw Mona combing his mother's hair. "Grandma hair full of louse," she said provokingly.

"You give to me. Is you!"

When Mona got up, her skirt bunched at her waist and he saw her lower body silhouetted against the window's light. He looked away quickly; she was possibly twenty, the same age as his daughter. He tried to keep this in mind, and once he wondered if Starboy's life would have turned out differently if he had met someone like her. He had already concluded that the girl's amiability with his irritable mother was because she was accustomed to dealing with her father and his insistence on lagoon work. Or maybe she was just relieved to get out of that back road and had never known anything different. From his work at the station, he knew country people whose lives repeated those of their parents and grandparents, who could envisage no other existence, and who were annoyed whenever innovative solutions to their problems were suggested.

One midday he came home early and he saw his mother on the sofa looking at Mona, who was reading so intently she did not observe his arrival. When the girl saw him, she hurriedly put away her book and pushed some pages into a brown folder. He didn't ask her anything, and when he emerged from his room later in the evening, she was in the kitchen cooking the vegetables he had brought. During dinner, she cajoled the old woman. "Look at this nice pumpkin your kind son bring home. It not tasting nice?"

"I don't like pumpkin. It look like shit."

Mona covered her mouth with the back of her hand, trying to disguise her laughter. Eventually she managed to say, "That is a bad word, Grandma."

Orbits told her, "My younger brother used to say that all the time."

"You have a younger brother? Is he away?"

"People kill him. They kill him over and over!" She swept the table with her cane, sending the bowl of pumpkin to the floor. She got up and went to the porch, where she sat for the rest of the evening. In the night, Orbits heard Mona singing to her, a ridiculous nursery rhyme about a pot and a spoon.

It was close to a week before he told the girl, "They find my brother dead in the community centre. The police say he committed suicide because of the marks around his neck and on his wrist. But he had other wounds and my mother believe he was murdered."

They were on the porch waiting for the arrival of her father. "And they didn't do an autopsy?"

"My mother didn't want it. I don't think she wanted to know."

They remained silent for a while. Then she said, "The man from the shop close to where I live was killed last year. His eyes and everywhere else had been ice-picked. He used to beat his wife all the time and everybody saying is his own son who do it. Every other house it have . . ." She paused and added, "Sometimes I want to go and live in the town."

"Your father know about this plan?"

"He say that in the town these criminals just looking for country bookies pretending to be knife-and-fork people. But if you ask me, over here is no better."

Once he had listened to Spanish and Gums talking about the difference between country and town crimes. In the country it was mostly domestic violence and praedial larceny, they claimed, while in the towns it was drugs and gangs. "Is that why you are studying?" She seemed so guilty that he regretted asking the question. He told her, "My daughter is away at university."

"Oh, you have a daughter too? I didn't know that. What is she studying?"

He had no idea. Thankfully, her father pulled up and Orbits went to his mother and said, "Mona is going for the weekend. Tell her goodbye."

The mother removed her hand from the globe, and with her fingers bent as if she was turning a key, waved. But after Mona had left, she said, "That girl too fast. Why she want to know everything for?"

"She just want to better know the people she working for."

"And what you know about them."

"They don't have much money."

"They have family."

"Yes. Yes, they have family."

"Everybody together?"

"I believe so."

His mother made one of her guttural sounds that could be either scorn, uncertainty or approval. This conversation, though brief, was the longest he could recall since his father's death.

Sometimes he came home to hear Mona reading from her books in a childish voice to his mother. "Once on a dark winter's day, when the yellow fog hung so thick and heavy in the streets of London that the lamps were lighted and the shop windows blazed with gas as they do at night, an odd-looking little girl sat in a cab with her father and was driven rather slowly through the big thoroughfares."

His mother listened attentively, but when the girl was finished, she said, "That little girl too stupid. She going to get kill for nothing."

"Is not that kind of story, grandma. And why you want a poor little girl to get killed?"

Another day he heard her saying, "Don Quixote. Try to say it."

"Donkey Hotay." When his mother noticed him standing by the front door, she pointed with her cane to Mona. "Donkey Hotay. That is she name."

The girl looked embarrassed, and Orbits recalled his shame at the nicknames he had been assigned when he was a boy. His mother had used many of these and, in the fashion of the island, had seen nothing wrong with using a disability as a name. He felt a sliver of anger at her unstudied, reflective cruelty, but he said nothing. Mona must have noticed because she told him the following morning, "Grandma beginning to make jokes now. She coming out of her shell."

The girl's statement lessened his guilt about not alerting his mother that she should be more sympathetic to a stranger who — even for a salary — was treating her unusually kindly. He had heard horror stories of old people, helpless and alone, mistreated by care-givers whose sympathy swiftly faded as they were ground down by demands. Years ago, when he was working in the capital, he had listened to a woman on the bus say that caring for an old man was like taking care of an ugly wrinkled baby with diarrhoea and a bad temper and a horn in his nose. She had been speaking of her grand-father. A man on the opposite aisle who had been listening asked in a high-pitched way, his head bobbing like a pigeon, "You know why old people does snore? To make it easier to shoot them in the night." Those within earshot had exploded even though there were a few sighers.

His mother was lucky she had someone like Mona. Orbits was a bit confounded at the affection he felt for the girl and his desire to protect her, and once, when he was dressing for work, he imagined his daughter in Mona's place, sitting with his mother, reading to her, brushing her hair.

During the weekend, Orbits interrupted her father's talk of rice and lagoons to tell him that his daughter had been studying over the last months. The father became apologetic. "These children pick up all they bad habits from they mother." Orbits told him he did not mind; in fact, he was happy the girl was trying to further her education. The man was relieved; he began boasting in his unusual self-deprecating manner. "You know I tired warn these lazy children about they reading all the time. But they wouldn't listen. And Miss Moaner is the worst because all of them taking a example from she. Coming out third and fourth in test. Winning prize. What they will do with all that fancy-pancy education?" He paused for Orbits to answer the question, pushing his tongue in front of his upper teeth, sniffling and nodding as if he needed further convincing. "People does call me Cascadoo, you know. The mudfish." Almost as an after-thought he added, "I happy with my dunciness."

Soon Cascadoo began calling every other day, giving Orbits a rundown on his blockheadedness and pretending to deplore his family. "The teachers always say my head hard like banga seed and who is I to disagree. I reach till the two times table but ask me any-thing after that and is like you asking me what the sky make from." He always ended the conversation by saying, "My head too hard to encourage Miss Moaner, but a man like you with a ton of degrees she might listen to."

Orbits never confessed his own lack of qualifications, but he began to feel more obligated to encourage Mona. He brought her folders from the office and realms of paper with the ministry's stamp for her to write her notes. She accepted these shyly, almost suspiciously, as if she believed it was expected that favours should be returned, and Orbits, when he realized this, told her that he never had the opportunity to help or even witness his daughter's progress from high school to university and that he was just happy to assist someone with ambition. As he said this, his voice grew heavy and perforated with unstable pauses, and he realized that he was not simply making excuses to the girl; that he had carried this unexamined loss for a long, long time.

She got up, twisting her hands, her eyes on the floor. She wished her father was as encouraging. Orbits told her of his conversations with her father and he saw how her face lit up with surprise. Perhaps as a means of repaying Orbits' encouragement, she redoubled her efforts with his mother, who responded with more life, renewed energy, more inventive insults. "How long you going to keep she here for?" she asked Orbits. "Look how fat she getting eating out all we food."

"She not fat and she not eating out the food," he told her angrily. "You even know that she start back the backyard garden?"

"Start back what? The garden was good all the time. She just spoiling it."

Yet there were times when he returned from work and would watch his mother, her eyes closed, listening to Mona read from a book. Although the girl bore the assaults well, he wished he could find some way for his mother to relent, to treat the girl as she would a family member. In the meantime, Cascadoo always assured Orbits that his daughter was lucky to find her way into a decent family and, despite all his earlier condemnation of her, began to sneak in little snippets about her brilliance. "All these big plans that she have does just give me a headache. Teacher! I ever tell you how she use to line up she dolly like if it was a classroom and teach them arithmetrick and alzebra? Poor dolly and them." Then he would push his tongue between his upper teeth and lip as if he was searching for a bit of errant food and make his sniffling sounds, waiting for Orbits to correct him.

Orbits never knew what the father expected of him, and he was uncomfortable when the other man heaped praises on him, too, as if he were a scholar consigned to a village field station instead of a man who got his first real job *vaille que vaille*, through the sympathy and perhaps the rebelliousness of a lonely and frustrated official. He tried to see himself through Cascadoo's eyes and was bothered by the false image the other man apparently possessed. What would Cascadoo say if he knew that Orbits had failed exam after exam and had hated school for the taunting he had received? That he was less the man he appeared to be and had never truly rid himself of the fear of being discovered and humiliated? That he always felt he was one step away from being dismantled, the remaining bits of him rearranged to be the boy cowering before his bullies?

There were times when he would think of his unfinished course in meteorology and of his fantasy of reading the weather reports with a parrot on his shoulder, and for a moment, he would be stiffened with determination to improve himself. Then he would consider the fact that he was close to fifty and was living alone with his mother and her helper.

One Friday evening, he heard Mona reading on the porch to his mother: "When someone is crying, of course, the noble thing to do is to comfort them. But if someone is trying to hide their tears, it may also be noble to pretend you do not notice them."

"Who you see crying?" She raised her cane. "I notice everything because my eye strong like a crazy old bat." She cackled, short, high-pitched bursts that sounded scandalous in an old woman. Surprisingly, Mona joined in the laughter as if his mother had made a great joke. Her father pulled up then and from the car he, too, began to laugh, the sound like water gurgling through a bloated hose. Later while Mona was getting her things, he began to talk in his lugubrious way about happiness, claiming that he was too stupid to be unhappy and how he was glad that god didn't give him a brain to think too much ahead. "You know eef I dead tomorrow not a cyat or a dog will quack."

"You have a wife and children."

"Wife? Children?" He shouted to his daughter who was approaching. "You hear that Miss Moaner? You will miss me when I gone?"

Orbits by then suspected that Cascadoo's manner of pulling himself down was just a conversational ruse and he didn't mean a word of it, but the conversation lingered in his mind and he tried to gauge his own life. He was comfortable if not happy. But neither state had ever been a permanent fixture; for as long as he could remember, each period of calm had transitioned so smoothly into turbulence. He had learned to appreciate the quieter periods, to wait for the turmoil. He felt his old anxieties returning. He tried to still his mind by thinking that perhaps he had expended all the misery in his life and was now on a new track. I have a good job. I am secure. My mother is still alive. She has someone who seems to care about her. But he knew these were all temporary conditions and could change the next day. Doraymay's situation was proof of this fickleness.

>━━

ONE DAY AFTER WORK, he visited Doraymay at his home. The man was in his hammock downstairs with a crutch laid crossways along his body, the lower half of which was covered with a patched blanket. He greeted Orbits as if this were a regular weekly visit. "Come, come, sit man. You want something to eat?" He called and a young man pushed his head out from a shed at the back.

"What is it you want?"

"Visitor, boy. Important visitor. Fellow worker. Tell you mother to bring something with ice for this heat?"

"I busy," the boy said. "I going in the back to change the goat."

Doraymay called again, and Orbits heard a girl's voice saying from upstairs, "Mummy busy cooking."

"Well, you bring it then. Some soursop or sapodilla juice." To Orbits, he said, "The best thing for the heat."

The girl said, "I studying right now."

Doraymay laughed as if all of it was funny. "If I was still good

I would have carry you straight to the soursop tree and pick the fruit right off the branch. You want to see something?" He removed the blanket and Orbits saw the stump where one foot had been amputated. There were scars and indentations on the flesh, which still looked raw and unfinished like a badly baked piece of meat. "The strangest thing is I does still feel the pain as if the foot right here." He tapped the stump.

"I have to go now," Orbits said. "I just dropped in to say hello." He got up, imagining the odour of clotted blood and urine.

"Already? Wait, man. I have something for you to hear." He pushed up his back and felt around the hammock. Eventually, he fished out his harmonica. "I learn a new tune. All this time alone home give me plenty practice." He put the instrument to his lips and began playing the tune to *Adios amigo, adios my friend / The road we have travelled has come to an end*. He was not a good player, but all the gaps and pauses, the fluting inhalations and rasping exhalation that were not part of the song, all of these breaks seemed to reflect the sadness and the adjoining chaos that were a part of Doraymay's life.

When he was finished, Orbits told him quickly, "I dropped in to see how you doing."

"I understand, man. Drop in any time you want. We could have something to eat. Soursop ice cream. Pudding."

As Orbits walked away, he noticed the walkway had been freshly swept and the poinsettia, marigolds and crotons neatly arranged and pruned. Around Doraymay, the world was operating normally; everyone was busy with their tasks, everything taken care of. On his way back, Orbits wondered how he would operate if he were struck with some disability, if he would pretend as Doraymay or rage against everyone as his mother. But perhaps the other man was not pretending. When he was a boy, he had seen a troop of ants running around a dead comrade, climbing over the body, busily hurrying from one place to another. This is the normal way of the world, he thought. The weak are bullied, the sick pushed aside, the dead forgotten.

The next morning as soon as he got to work, he wrote on the back of an application form: "I am older and wiser and more experienced. I am better able to handle everything." (He had planned to write: "I am no longer a fat little boy afraid of the world," but he stopped when he thought that someone, perhaps one of the two young workers at the station, might enter and spot the words on the form.) He fell in and out of this mood, thinking one day that he was unnecessarily worrying and the next that disaster was just around the corner. Without realizing it at first, he began to prepare himself, little by little, day by day.

He checked his savings and discovered that the combined amount was thirty thousand dollars. The amount stunned him; although he allowed fifteen percent of his salary to go into his savings account, he never checked the total. He withdrew ten thousand from that amount, applied for a loan from a credit union, and finally bought a foreign-used vehicle, a green Wingroad station wagon. The Kingswood he sold to a grateful Cascadoo for one thousand dollars. He now had a vehicle that he assumed would last him for ten years or so, close to his retirement at sixty. The two workers, both in their mid-twenties, who had replaced Gums and Doraymay — Spanish's position unfilled — and to whom he had never paid much attention, he now began to see as slackers. As the senior worker, he devised a schedule to keep them both at the compound for the entire day. They both protested, but he brought out a copy of the job specification and explained how many of their duties they had been shirking. They began to make excuses: one said he was here just temporarily and was planning to do a degree in forestry at some university in New Brunswick, the other stammered about his coursework not preparing him for rough, dusty fields and drunken farmers.

He realized they were more qualified than him — though they

were not aware of this — and informed both they could apply for transfers, but in the interim they had to work for their salary.

"Salary? You call this a salary?" This worker had a moustache that was parted exactly above his missing tooth. It added a weird symmetry to his face.

The other worker, who had a repertoire of unstable rubbery expressions that gave Orbits the idea he was cruel to animals and would some day maim someone, added, "Why we have to go to visit them when they could just come here? What is the purpose of a field station?"

Orbits got out a brochure and began to read. The brochure was from the Ministry of Agriculture, where he had once worked. When he was finished, he told them, "We have to move beyond all that we learned in college and interact with these farmers. My diploma was in meteorology, but you don't see me locked up in my office staring at the clouds all day." He had no idea why he had mentioned this, but both workers seemed sullenly impressed. "From next week get your tall boots ready."

Ever since he had begun working at the station, he had been seen as the bookman and assigned to desk duties, but he now accompanied the two workers to the fields. His Wingroad suffered on the bumpy roads, and he winced whenever he felt the muddy ridges grating against his exhaust. He suspected the two slackers were deliberately choosing the impassable roads to discourage him, and weekly he grew more suspicious of how they had been assessing the farmers' suitability for government assistance. They had already understood they could coast through the job, collecting little bribes and doing the minimum that was required.

The agricultural areas they covered were filled with houses that were of board and galvanize, similar structures that were distinguishable only from the arrangement of trees and plants in the yards. All the houses were on teak posts with the downstairs blocked with a maze of scantlings and planks, some diagonal, some lateral, all make-shift and haphazard so that the construction seemed piecemeal and dependent on the mood of the builders. Intermittently, there were stretches of bananas on the hills, and in the valleys muddy lagoons, and beyond, shining fan-shaped dasheen leaves rising above the wispy rice. In these areas, there weren't houses but camps, rectangular areas covered with carat leaves and containing a crude bench and a fireside.

Before many of the houses were little stalls frequently manned by forlorn-looking children who briefly perked up when they noticed an approaching vehicle. Once he stopped to buy a soursop and a golden apple from a girl who was just seven or eight. The girl, her streaky hair almost hiding her eyes, counted the money slowly, and the two workers in their Land Rover honked impatiently. When Orbits got into his vehicle, he imagined that Mona had been forced also to stand in the hot sun all day to make three or four dollars. He returned and bought the entire mound of fruits.

During these field trips, he discovered that his eyes, accustomed to the gloom of the semi-lit office, could not handle the stinging brightness of the midday sun, and he resumed wearing his sunshades. In the nights, he had to place a damp handkerchief across his face to still the itch in his eyes and the headache that the day's foray had wrought. He bought even darker sunglasses that transformed everything that was green into purple and shifted distance so that he had to drive carefully on the unfamiliar roads. One midday, he looked up and instead of clouds, he saw an ocean of wrecked ships and jetsam floating around.

During another trip, he felt that the farmers had begun to resemble the crops they grew: the rice farmers were thin and wispy, the dasheen farmers wet and lumpy, the banana growers sly and filled with sweet-mouth. But they were all desperately poor, and they spent from morning to night in the field. He couldn't interpret their attitudes: they drank in the evenings and sang in the camps and spoke of their livelihood both as a blessing and as a curse. The government was not interested in agriculture, they said. Poor people from backward areas were always forgotten. Everyone now wanted expensive foreign fruits. The little money that was allocated to them took months in coming. There were always promises. Their parents and grandparents had managed and so would they. Yet they drank away the little money they earned. They verged between an unstable optimism and a more comprehensible fatalism.

Whenever Orbits returned from these trips, he considered that it was only a few lucky breaks, one of which had granted him his job, that separated him from this dispiriting fatalism. He could easily have been in a similar situation, living in a piecemeal house, buying goods on trust, borrowing from relatives, dependent on the weather and the price of produce and little subsidies. One night he dreamed he was alone and walking along a road filled with old, ramshackle buildings. He got up in a sweat, trying to recall why he had been alone and what he had been looking for. In the dream, his clothes were patched and ill-fitting, like one of the vagrants he had spotted in the capital, but he could remember nothing else. The old fear of his qualifications strengthened, and he tried to convince himself that there must be some statute of limitations that would prevent him from being fired.

He fought fear with fear: he might die before he was fired, a crippling disease would purge him of minor anxieties, he would grow into someone like his father with no memory of humiliation or no fear of the future. In the end, it was the contemplation of Cascadoo's casually fraudulent confession about dying with no one to recall his life that nudged Orbits out of the cycle of suppositions. The recollection of Wally's talk of duty, too, further eased him into a spurious notion of a mission.

It may be that some good deeds are not done through a generosity of spirit but because of a desire to rise above weakness and helplessness, a way of lashing at despair, and so Orbits decided to focus on those who were short-changed, scorned, helpless, oppressed, like he had been for much of his life. He began to understand dimly that there were men and women whose situations were worse than his had ever been. "Sometimes I does wonder eef I was like you, with so much book sense, how my life would have been," became one of Cascadoo's regular mamaguy.

Orbits moved beyond this mamaguy. He began to concentrate more on his job. He learned that the farmers' talk of corruption was not always, as he had assumed, just a pitiful ritual they had wrapped around themselves; during his field trips, he discovered that most of the subsidies were given to shopkeepers, grocers, clerks, postmen, even teachers: men who knew nothing about farming, had never ventured at the fields, but who all had the resources to bribe. One evening he called the two young workers and he hinted darkly that he had written the supervisor about the bribery that was taking place in the field station. The workers had been there for over a year; their sudden fear he attributed to their callowness. During the following weeks, he noted with some satisfaction their sullenness, the manner they slammed their doors when they got to the station, the way they dragged their feet on the road, their impatience as they listened to the farmers, their discomfort plain in the hot sun.

One midday it occurred to him that they fitted the profile of the bullies who had tormented him throughout his time in school. In this mood of accomplishment, he actually wrote to the supervisor. He mentioned that more than half the money allocated to the station went elsewhere and speculated it was the reason why the country had not progressed in spite of the money rolling around. A month later he received a terse and brief reply that alerted him how far up the chain of bribery went. The supervisor said if he had any evidence, he should take it to the police; in the absence of this, he should either keep quiet or fight elections. The last suggestion was sarcastic, he knew, and as he looked at the official paper and the official envelope, his anger grew. "The bitch," he said loudly, drawing out the two workers from their office. "Fight elections? Show the police?" Over the following weeks, he began to encourage the farmers to form delegations and associations and to channel their requests through these groups.

He went to these meetings and returned late in the evenings, the swimming spots in his burning eyes signalling the beginning of a headache. The farmers at first were suspicious of him and of his angle until he explained that he wanted nothing in return. Then their scepticism turned to puzzlement and finally to pity. What kind of man would *do* something for nothing, would *want* nothing from something? They actually spoke these words, and Orbits unexpectedly felt a slice of sympathy for his two idle fellow workers. He invited Cascadoo to the meetings that he insisted should be held either at a house or a camp rather than a rumshop, and while he was driving through the country roads, he often felt like turning back and leaving the farmers to their miserable lives. Once, in the middle of a meeting, he was reminded of a painting he had passed every morning at the Ministry of Agriculture. It had hung there for so long that the frame had splintered, cobwebs from the ceiling hung like a gauze over the top half, and the acrylic had chipped off the lower. It seemed so much a part of the neglect of the building that he had never paid much attention, but on the week of his departure, trying to observe what he may have missed during his years at the ministry, he saw that it had been done with attention to detail. The straw hat of the man collecting christophene was as carefully detailed as the mountain in the backdrop and the vines trailing from the trees.

When he was called upon to speak at the farmers' gatherings, he simply said, "Sometimes it's the things that we miss that really count. We must pay attention to little details." They weren't sure what he was talking about, but it sounded impressive, so they all nodded thoughtfully and clapped. Orbits didn't realize they were more struck by his reference to small things — which they interpreted as trivialities — to which they were always attuned.

The farmers were noisy during these meetings as if in familiar surroundings, among their own, they could unleash whatever false bravado they had strapped around themselves. Then they grew quiet and contemplative before they erupted once more. They tilted from one extreme to the other, and Orbits felt he was going around in a never-ending loop, and these men, in spite of all their protests, wanted nothing different. During one meeting, a man who wore cut-off pants that rode on his knobbed knees said, "Everybody eating apple and grape like if them is born and bred Cyanadian. I wonder what they will do if I stop planting orange and mango."

"They will continue to eat apples and grapes," Orbits told the man.

"Eh? Is so? You think them gullet design for foreign thing? Just wait till sugar or heart hook them up them, we will see who could eat what."

The other farmers nodded in agreement. Another man mentioned a relative who had migrated only to return with a host of health problems. The conversation shifted from gossip to a more philosophical discussion of the horrors of migration. Then there was more gossip. He was frustrated by their lack of interest in the rest of the island and their manner of treating villages just five miles away as if they were in other continents. Someone had actually mentioned this tendency to him, and he couldn't recall if it had been Wally or Skullcap the maxi driver.

It was a relief sometimes when he returned to his home and witnessed Mona tending to his mother with so much patience, as if looking after this cantankerous old woman was not an obligation but a joy.

Everyone have their own duty, he thought one evening on his way to a meeting. He had been thinking that his mission to help men and women who seemed weekly more undeserving of any intervention was useless. That evening, he drove through the usual back roads until he came to the only direction: a big water tank painted red next to a mango tree.

Too late he saw the house; the mango tree he recalled, but the red tank was new. He hesitated on the road before he noticed the group already gathered beneath the house. The husband of the woman with whom he had the affair was seated in the middle of the group of five farmers. His hands were on his lap and he appeared out of place among these rough men. He seemed so polite that Orbits wondered if he recognized him. The farmers' association was a good idea, the husband said. It's easier to take advantage of an individual than a group. The farmers needed to be organized. For too long everyone had been exploiting them because they could get away with it. There was still money in the country, but it was drying up. Time balanced everything, but now time was running out. If nothing was done, this rape of innocent people would continue.

He sat down, and Orbits was so flustered that he simply repeated the man's pleas. When he was about to finish, he saw a pair of legs on the stairs, and Moon soon appeared with a tray on which was a jug and a cylinder of Styrofoam glasses. Orbits felt a confused scatter of excitement that he tried to still by looking at the husband and smiling. The husband, now seated, had his hands on his lap once more and he was studying a crack on the ground, right beneath the hammock. Moon returned up the stairs; the farmers drank and wiped their lips with their hats' brims. The husband asked Orbits if he wanted to stay for dinner. Orbits told him it was difficult to drive in the night, which was true. The man nodded; he seemed relieved. Moon came down the stairs once more, but now she had a small child. She stood at the landing while Orbits and the husband walked to his car.

On the way back, Orbits was struck with a familiar mixture of guilt, shame and fear, and once again he wondered why he was getting involved in the lives of men and women who had been living in this manner for generations and who were suspicious of any change, good or bad. During subsequent meetings, petty rivalries stretched out into silly arguments about every trivial issue. Additionally, every proposal was met with scepticism. And Orbits' headache worsened following each meeting. "These kiss-me-ass people will never improve," he grumbled to himself. "I don't know why I wasting my time. I really don't know." Sometimes, though, he came close to the truth. "Doing all this just to feel better about myself," he said in a low voice to his mother one evening while they were waiting on Mona and her father.

He felt he was going around in circles, and he waited for the circle to end. But the farmers group miraculously persisted, and when there was talk of expanding it into a village council, he suspected it was the husband, quiet but respected, who had prodded them. But it was Cascadoo who had told the farmers, "Eef you ask me, he is just one of these crazy people who does help out for no rhyme and reason." He amended that later to include, "He have no wife and children. Poor fella."

"A big hardback man living by himself? What wrong with him?"

"Poor fella living with his mother," Cascadoo elaborated. "Madam pack up and gone."

And Orbits, brought down to their level, tainted with uselessness, was now viewed with sympathy rather than mistrust, and his proposals were no longer seen as opportunistic. So, for a few months, outfitted in his dark shades and white long-sleeved shirts, he sat among these farmers and patiently explained how the system worked. He drew from his time at the ministry in the nation's capital to describe the manner the money was disbursed and how genuine farmers, mostly invisible, were left out of the configuration. They already knew this: it was always part of their comforting beat about neglect and sacrifices and survival, but the force of the actual figures blunted the romance they had built up about their sacrifices. Orbits, propelled more by guilt than by any notion of success, never expected much from these meetings even when the informal gathering was transformed into a group that began to resemble a crude organization. The meetings were rotated at different houses every fortnight, and Orbits, not wanting to face Moon, suggested the relocation to the field station.

About three months following the first meeting at that location, he received a call from the supervisor. "Is you who giving permission like Lord Lalloo to hold meetings in the station?"

"It's only in the nights," Orbits explained. "When the station is closed."

"Yes, closed. You understand the meaning of the word?"

Orbits felt his temper growing. "Yes, I understand. And I beginning to understand plenty other things in this department."

The supervisor, caught off guard by the accusation, grew blustery. "Hello, Mister, you better don't play up in you ass with me, you hear. I call you to explain a simple government regulation and you hitting me with all this damn nonsense about what you know and don't know. If I say is no permission, then is no permission. End of text." As the supervisor sank further in his bluster, Orbits knew he was right; he could give and withhold permission as he pleased.

From then, the meetings were held at his place, and Cascadoo, during these evenings, fretted noisily and unnecessarily about the arrangement of the chairs in the driveway and the coffee his daughter brought out. He interrupted the meetings to call out to her and complain about the coffee dregs and the amount of sugar or milk. "All this book-busting making she forget the simple things," he said proudly. "Alzebra and hiss-tree. Jagraphy."

Orbits' mother looked out with interest at the farmers and one day, she said, "All these people sitting in the gap and drinking coffee like if is a wake. Like if they waiting for somebody to dead."

"Is a good thing they doing, Grandma."

"Good what? Just wasting time and muddying up the yard like fat chicken. Why you don't go and help them with you big bottom?"

"Oh lord, Grandma. That so rude."

"You rude." She held her cane before her, twisting her hand.

One day a small delegation came into Orbits' office. They were not farmers but businessmen, who got to the point quickly. They had heard news of this village council and all the other nonsense he had been putting into the farmers' heads. This had to stop. Orbits couldn't understand the source of their anger until one of the men, who smiled with one side of his mouth, the lips parting and revealing two gold teeth said, "Life is a funny thing when you really get down to it. If we get the money or the farmers get the money, it will end in the same place. In we rumshop self. It will just take longer to reach if the farmers get it. A funny thing as I say." When the man stopped talking he pushed out his lips, his sunken nose disappearing in his moustache. He wore an engraved bracelet on each wrist.

Another man, with his belly bulging out of his shirt and his neck threatened by heavy chains, said, "What Halligator say is true. This committee nonsense suit these hifalutin town people, not humble village people. That is knife-and-fork thing. We don't operate so."

"Every man for himself then?"

"You could say so. Yes, you could say so," Halligator said with his half-smile. "We know you would understand. Pass by my place any time you want. You like whisky?"

"I don't drink."

"Eh? You don't drink? I never hear that sort of thing before. Something wrong with you liver? Kidneys?"

His friend said, "My hardware have plenty more than drinks. You want to fix up you house? A little renovation? A spare room? Roof work? Check me out." He spoke in simple snaps like an advertisement. The group walked out talking loudly.

Orbits had been neutral during the conversation because he was not familiar with the visitors and he wanted to be as polite as possible, but he received a call the following day reminding him of his commitment. Again, he said nothing; he had lately grown a bit too involved with the farmers and had been thinking of a way to step back now that he had initiated the process. He had never really been comfortable with large groups, and he disliked the way these rough men argued about nonsense.

It's likely he would have dropped out if the calls from Halligator and the consortium of businessmen didn't continue, growing more insistent and threatening with each new message. "You opening a big condensed milk tin of worm and cockroach that will turn around and sting you," Halligator said during one call. "Just remember that a sting worse than a bite." And two weeks later, another voice he couldn't recognize: "Sometimes people does go barefoot in the lagoon and these *jangee* eel does be sucking they toe and they don't even know because they can't feel anything. But the jangee sucking all the time. Drawing out blood, little by little." Orbits couldn't understand why the man was telling him this until he added, "If this don't stop right now, we will put you in your proper place." The tenor of the calls began to remind Orbits of the period when he had been mercilessly bullied, and so he began to respond in a manner he had fantasized about during that earlier period. Fatboy fall down! Fat to last months! The cannibals will like that! Eat out every single plum on the floor! You useless, Fatboy! He told them he was not afraid of threats and he would report the matter to the police if the calls continued. The latter drew laughter from the callers; Orbits then lied and said he had contacts higher up the chain. "I have higher than you," one caller said after a while.

"Mine still higher than yours," Orbits replied.

"Well *I* will climb higher."

"And you will fall harder."

These childish exchanges excited Orbits, and he began to look forward to the calls, rehearsing all the lies with which he would surround himself. He placed the phone closer to him and would snatch it the minute he got a call. One afternoon, while he was filing away the accounts, the phone rang. He picked it up hurriedly. "I have a notebook here to take a note of every single thing, so go ahead. Let me hear."

But the call was not from a crooked businessman; it was from Mona, who managed to say that his mother had fallen asleep while she was combing her hair and she wouldn't awaken. He rushed to his car. When he got home, his mother was on the couch, her hands crossed over her chest and her eyes closed. She seemed asleep and her hands, when he felt them, were not cold. He called an ambulance and waited with Mona on the porch. Every two or three minutes or so she would return to the house and he would hear her saying, "You had a good sleep, Grandma? You better wake up now because you getting everybody worried." Then she would come to the porch and watch the road for the ambulance. It came two hours later. A well-dressed attendant with eyebrows that that met in a disapproving salute asked, "Where the sick?" He waited for the other attendant, who was rummaging around and cursing in the vehicle. Eventually the other man dragged out an oxygen tank. The well-dressed attendant went to Orbits' mother, felt her wrist and her neck, looked at his watch, opened one of her eyes, looked at his watch once more and said to the other attendant, "Carry back that in the ambulance." To Orbits he said, "Who was the old lady? Mother? Well, she travelling."

Orbits, in his confusion, could not understand what he meant and asked, "Travelling where?"

"That part I can't tell you. To another planet. To up they." He glanced at the ceiling. "Down here." He tapped the floor. "The only thing I could tell you for sure is she not here right now."

Mona began to sob, pressed her face against the wall, her hands on her head. "How you could do this, Grandma? How you could go so easy like this? You never say a single thing and you gone. So easy . . . so easy."

Orbits was not sure how he should feel, and he suspected that his lack of emotion was due to shock and that he would soon break down like Mona. But the girl's words stuck. He put his hand on her shoulder and said, "She went easy. You right. She didn't suffer."

It had been such a straightforward statement from the girl, yet it simplified everything and provided a way out of guilt and grief. But during the wake Orbits came closer to the truth: his mother's death had finally released him from all obligations and he was, at the age of fifty, finally free.

And the change was so instantaneous, it felt as if he had been waiting for this moment his entire life. For two-thirds of his life, he had longed for lasting connections, and now that the last attachment had been removed, he felt as if a yoke had been lifted. As the bamboo was dragged into the yard by farmers and as the tent went up and Mona and her sisters made coffee, Orbits, still searching for grief, was met only with this new liberating sense of acquittance. He had surrendered nothing and now, removed from the world, feeling no real ties to anyone, he began to observe it more carefully. He had always been prone to fantasies, but these fantasies were weighed with deceptions and without the reflectiveness that allowed any insight into himself or his place among others. During the wake, he observed how the farmers towards whom his sympathy had been receding organized almost all the details of the funeral. He didn't say much, and they assumed he was suffused with grief. He saw the businessman Halligator, too, among the crowd, standing back, and he thought: he must believe I am drenched with grief, so why don't he come now with his proposals? Later, during the readings that went on for seven nights, he listened to the priests offering their inadequate interpretations of the dead, one lecturing that they were now transformed into malevolent spirits that could only be kept at bay through a dose of personal chants and charms, and the other claiming their final destinations were planets and asteroids unknown to anyone. Orbits saw the farmers nodding and their wives scraping their chairs closer to their husbands. On the final night, the astronomer-priest told Orbits, "Watch in the sky for any falling star and say this immediately." He gave Orbits a folded sheet that was stained with saffron. "Make sure you facing the east though. All the favourable planets in that position."

The other priest came up a few minutes later. "Crying after death is a strange thing. It does keep away the spirit, and it could draw them in. The scriptures not too clear on that one. Maybe a little tears now and again, just to be sure."

Orbits told him, "Grief that doesn't announce itself is more genuine than grief that blaring like a trumpet."

He had no idea why he said this or if he had heard it somewhere, but the priest said, "Eh? A trumpet? That might work but it better if you use a conch shell and say the chant loud and clear."

During that final night among the small group, Orbits saw Moon and her husband. The husband's legs were crossed in a relaxed pose and he was watching the canvas canopy meditatively while Moon was sitting upright to gaze at Mona, who was alone, the snow globe in her hand, her sisters and father in the row behind. With the smoke from the pitch pine and burnt butter blown this way and that, it seemed as if they were all at a distance, at some other ceremony unconnected to him. Following the ceremony, with the mourners gone, he saw Mona still on her chair, her sisters still in the row behind. Orbits wished to be left alone to sit by himself, but Cascadoo came up to him and began to talk about his daughter and his worry about her future. She was smart and intelligent and ambitious, he said repeatedly. Orbits recalled the time, a year or so earlier, when he had offered the opposite assessment. But he understood. He told Cascadoo that Mona would stay until the end of the month, during which time he would help her get a job. Cascadoo seemed surprised and almost touched. He said, "I did always know you was the sort of man like that. Some jealous people was saying why I putting me young daughter in the house of a single man, but I did always feel that if something had to happen, it will happen." Orbits knew that Cascadoo, fastened with the simple idea of removing his daughter from poverty, had possibly expected more, but that he was relieved that she, one of six, had not been cast aside. He agreed when Cascadoo asked if another of his daughters could stay during this period. He said Mona would be scared staying in the house all alone during the day. And sleeping alone, he added.

A year earlier, Orbits had fallen into the habit of counting his footsteps to convince himself he was alive and everything was real; now, he saw all that he had missed and avoided. He saw the world not in imperfect silhouettes that shifted their frames according to his mood, but rather in stark relief with jagged angles that, from a distance, did not seem bruised but united in a pattern that never changed. He saw this on his way to work, too: old bricks gaping from newly layered concrete, sharp sand and gravel flattening beds of croton, dangling bamboo scaffolds weaving around unfinished verandahs, incomplete houses awaiting the next oil boom. His Wingroad had a CD player with a radio, and during the morning programmes he listened to men and a few women regularly calling to complain and boast and bluster, their tones so similar they could have been reciting, day after day, from the same prompt. Sometimes he felt this perspective was a reaction to his growing vision issues, a conscious attempt to counteract this loss, and at other times he believed it was something less deliberate; that after half a century, he had achieved the balance Moon's husband had spoken about. Not by taking any steps to remedy his condition, but simply by waiting.

He suspected this latter attitude was not unlike the farmers' fatalism, but he also knew that he expected nothing, and so if nothing was delivered, he would not be disappointed. It was this attitude that carried him during the local elections when the village council members insisted he contest Halligator for a county councillor position. The businessman was well funded and in the days before election, he delivered hampers and bottles of rum during his walkabouts. During one of these walkabouts, he encountered Orbits, who with Cascadoo was giving out flyers. "Take care you don't strain yourself with all that heavy weight you carrying," he told Orbits. He himself had hampers in both hands and his supporters, trailing him, had bags hoisted on their shoulders.

A supporter said, "Just you and Cascadoo? A real big party you have they, man."

Orbits told him, "An alligator with a proper tail." It was a simple observation spoken aloud, but it drew a rippling titter from a group of lochos who were watching from the roadside.

During a meeting held at the junction, a heckler shouted, "A man wearing shades in the night. You blind or what?"

"If I was blind I wouldn't be able to see a man making a complete fool of himself right in front of me."

"Who you calling a fool?"

"I will be the first to admit my mistake. I meant a jackass."

And another night: "Orbits, you better come down from space."

He had been talking about self-help groups he had in mind if he were elected. He told the heckler, a known supporter of his opponent, "And Halligator better come out from the swamp."

These wry statements fell neatly in the island's appreciation of *picong*, a kind of cutting riposte. And Orbits' delivery, mechanical and swift, added to his reputation. People came to his meetings and provoked him just for these dry insults, and they were never disappointed. He didn't care about the laughter because it was not his intention to be humorous. A week before the election, Cascadoo, who had positioned himself as his campaign manager and had inducted all his daughters in the campaign, told Orbits, "A scholar like you wasting time with this local election. You should go up for the big general election."

He knew that Cascadoo was thinking of his children, and although he saw nothing wrong with that, he told the other man, "I not interested in anything else. I just want to help out the farmers and I couldn't do that in the field station. So I only doing my job."

Cascadoo jostled between scepticism and admiration and on the night prior to the election, he told a small group of farmers gathered in a rumshop, "I know this man for so long and I still can't figure where he coming from. Sometimes I does believe that he not in this for himself."

"You really believe it have people like that?"

"Sometimes I does feel that his own self don't know what he want."

If Orbits had been listening to that conversation, he would have agreed with Cascadoo's assessment, but he was alone at home, wondering what the boys from his school days and the teachers who mocked him would think of their easy target — Fatboy — putting himself up as an independent candidate against men like Halligator who were affiliated with established parties and who were well funded. He lived alone, had no friends, no contacts, no experience in politics, no inclination to bribe. Prior to his marriage, his wife, mistaking his shyness for stoicism had mentioned that he was like one of the actors in a western. He wondered if she and her parents knew of his political ambition, and if somewhere within that family there was a twinge of pride and regret. He thought also of his daughter, who had never seen this side to him and who knew him only as an absent parent. He contemplated the reaction of everyone who had pushed him aside, not with any satisfaction or joy, but to understand the island and his place in it. He didn't expect to win, but for the first time he had stood his ground.

He won in a landslide.

✦

IF, ONE YEAR EARLIER, someone had asked Orbits how he expected his life to turn out, he would have said that he would work at the field station until retirement, and if his mother were still alive, he would be living with her. He would not have foreseen her sudden death nor the freedom it would bring; nor would he have anticipated the manner that this distance with which he now held everything would lead to an undertaking for which he had no preparation and for people for whom he only felt a slight sympathy.

He would not have foreseen the sudden attention and respect at which he remained unmoved, the brief power to set things in motion, the competition for his attention, his growing realization that he was unsuited to the position. Once he had heard Mona reading a story to his mother. It was of a serpent that had been imprisoned in a basket and, overcome with starvation, was just waiting out its days. Then a mouse bore a hole and fell into the basket. The serpent promptly ate the mouse and, now energized with the meal, escaped through the hole. His mother had clapped at the end and said it was good for the stupid nosy mouse, but Orbits could make no sense of the story. What was the moral? Was the mouse supposed to be an object of sympathy or a character in a cautionary tale? There was really nothing to be drawn from the fable, and that was how Orbits felt about his life. He could be either animal. At an earlier time, he would have considered this abrupt shift in his life and wondered if it was some deep need to compensate for the neglect that had blighted his childhood, or if in fact there existed some nobler vein buried so deep he had never sensed it before.

His office was set in the upper floor of a building that housed, at the far end, a pet store with a small sign — *My Family and Other Animals* — at the centre a locksmith, the doors perpetually shuttered, and a bookstore, the Book Swami, specializing in local self-published tracts. From his window, he could see across the road a dentist's office and a fast food place, and during his first month at the site, he was fascinated whenever he saw men and women holding their cheeks and rushing from one of these places to the other.

Not far away were three rumshops situated in a sort of triangle and he was fascinated, too, at the transformation of the men filing into his office, these men who, when sober, were bashful and agreeable but were demanding bullies after a few drinks. Sometimes he heard them arguing with Mona, whom he had hired as his secretary, and she, who had been so good with his mother, wilted under the assault of the drunkards who wanted landslips and potholes fixed, water delivery stabilized, roads cleared, drains cleaned, boundary disputes solved, pests eradicated, jobs for their children, promotions for themselves, reproval of their competitors. When they brushed past Mona into Orbits' office, he patiently explained the protocol for getting things done, the sluggish bureaucracy, the limits to his position, the problems that could be handled without his help. Still they brought bribes of fruits and vegetables that he gave to Mona, and the next morning she would bring him a container of the cooked vegetables or the fruits sliced and sprinkled with salt and lime.

During the first months, he believed that he was learning the ropes and would gradually understand the correct protocol for getting funds from the various ministries, but he soon discovered that everything operated according to party lines. He had been the only independent candidate elected in the entire island, and there was no one to whom he could turn for assistance. At the monthly meeting with the other councillors, he witnessed the hardening of these party lines, the excuses and the rancour, the downgrading of serious issues into rumshop bacchanal, the violent outbursts, the trivialization of tragedies.

The chairman of the constituency, a tall, dark man whose age was difficult to guess because of his long curly hair that flopped around his ears and his stylish glasses and bright silk shirts, seemed bored with the meetings, only coming to life when a reference was made to the prime minister or when a question was levelled directly at him. It was Orbits who asked most of the questions during the first couple months, but he could never fully grasp the man's responses. Once Orbits told him, "Some of the people in my constituency have been complaining about the road workers bursting the water mains and the water repair workers leaving big potholes on the road. It's like two opposing armies."

There was a little titter at his description, but the chairman said, "All this da-da-da" — he twirled his fingers above his ear as if trying to pluck out a word — "happening all over the island so we have improvise and da-da-da the best we could. People have to decide if they want roads or if they want water."

"I think they want both," Orbits mumbled.

And during another meeting, six months later: "Mr. Chairman, nowadays, increasingly, we have the situation of young women working in the town and getting back late in the nights. If we can get a couple streetlights on the back roads it will make everybody feel more secure."

He glanced at Orbits sleepily. "If we put streetlights on all these back roads we won't have money for any other da-da-da. Landslips and school repairs and drains and rubbish removal." The fingers began twirling. "Oil money done. We have to da-da-da and da-da-da."

Sometimes Orbits felt on the verge of storming out of the meetings. But the chairman was right in one respect: the money which had sustained all the vices of the island for more than two decades had dried up. Windowless glass-domed buildings, incomplete stadiums, sprawling hospitals and schools with no equipment were scattered all across the island like relics from another place. Some of the empty buildings had been occupied by squatters and vagrants and in others, the plumbing and electrical fixtures were stolen. But it was not just the money; the projects begun by one party were always abandoned by the other, which had its own grandiose plans, its own monuments to construct. And this had been going on for as long as Orbits could remember.

He began staying in his office after Mona had left, testing and rejecting solutions. He was preparing to leave late one evening when a man entered. He was a farmer who Orbits knew was genuinely poor. "I don't understand how you operating so," the man said almost apologetically. "We vote you in and you doing nothing for we. Maybe we should have let things remain the same. The last fella use to thief plenty but at least he would give help every now and then." Orbits explained the operating finances of the county council had been halved and furthermore, in order to get an immediate hearing, he would have to operate from the rumshops, passing bribes along an endless chain that ended somewhere in the capital. He explained this to the man who, clearly unsympathetic, asked him, "So what you drawing a salary for if is not to help we?"

"I will do my best," Orbits promised.

Each week, he was reminded of traits he had forgotten. He saw how quickly flattery was transformed into impatience when he explained the limits of his authority, how impatience grew into annoyance when he offered facts and figures, how annoyance blossomed into rage when he suggested alternatives to bribery and shortcuts.

As the months passed, Orbits discovered how much he was unsuited for the position and frequently he left the councillors' meetings without saying a word. About a year after he had been elected, on his way back to his house, an old and familiar feeling descended on him. He felt that his job was a sham, he was not doing anything and soon he would be discovered. He tried to fight this mood by considering his recent successes. He had fought the election with many disadvantages, which, if he had rationally considered, would have encouraged him to drop out. And he had won. Some people still respected him, and Halligator's cronies still came with their demands that he felt pleased to deny.

One midday he saw Mona helping an old disabled man on the corridor. The man had one arm around the girl's shoulder and the other was clutching a wobbly cane. One leg of the man's trousers had been folded to the knee, exposing a scarred stump. Orbits got up and rushed out to help the pair. "Don't worry," the man said, and Orbits saw it was Doraymay. "I just glad I reach up these stairs before the place close."

"Sit down, Uncle. Look how heavy you breathing." Mona steered him to a chair.

"When I had my two good legs, I use to sprint up places like this in no time."

"So how everything?" Orbits asked awkwardly.

"Good, good, man. Daughter married and move out and son get a big job in the town." As Doraymay continued talking, it emerged that things weren't that good after all. His wife spent most of the time at her daughter's place and he had not seen his son in months. Orbits asked who saw about his meals. "I build a nice little kitchen downstairs," he said. "Have everything right there. Pro-gas, sink and a toilet in the back. Board up everything. You remember the place? You must drop by sometime. Will cook a nice curry goat for the two of we. You forget I was the seasoning man for Spanish?" He looked down at the folds of his trousers. "I should leave now," he said abruptly.

Orbits and Mona helped him down the stairs, and Orbits, who initially assumed he had come for help, could not understand the purpose of the visit. Was the request really couched in the description of his situation, the abandonment by his family? Was he too proud to ask directly for assistance? Orbits looked from the doorway at his old co-worker hopping down the street and for a minute felt he should run after him. He actually made a few steps before he hesitated. In no mood to return to his office, he climbed the stairs at the other end of the building.

The pet store owner sitting behind a desk bookended by aquariums glanced up. His wavy hair was neatly parted and he wore thick donnish spectacles. "Just looking around," Orbits said. "I have an office at the other end."

"The councillor? I thought you looked familiar." Now the man got up, and Orbits saw that his merino was rolled up to expose his hairy belly. He recalled a trip when he had remarked to his mother that the picturesque upper half of a scene was tarnished by the dereliction beneath. "Only fishes and a few birds here. Too expensive to import." He sniffed into his merino, wiped his hand and added, "Had a time when you could get all these birds locally but too much hunting. You know people eating alligator tails now? Eating everything. Damn savages." For a minute Orbits saw only the upper, refined half of the man. He was obviously educated and sensitive. Then the man said, "You want a puppy?" He walked to the end, reached behind a row of boxes and produced a trembling, skinny little thing. "Father was a hunting dog. Mother got bounced down." He placed it on the ground and it tottered and almost toppled over. "Does call it Magaboy on account of how it so skinny. But with the right master it will spring up in no time. I wanted to take it home, but these guard dogs I breeding will tear it up."

"I really don't have the time—"

"You ever see these movies where a skinny little dog pull somebody out of a fire? Or run for help like Lassie?"

Orbits smiled, his mood momentarily lifted. But once more in his office his mind turned to Doraymay. He was still thinking of the other man during the next meeting of county councillors. He told the chairman, "So far I am completely useless in this position. Why exactly am I drawing a salary if I can't help anyone?" He saw the chairman's fingers preparing to twirl and he added quickly, "And I don't want to hear any da-da-da nonsense." The chairman, his response pre-empted, reached for a file, flipped through its contents roughly, threw it aside and scratched his forehead, his finger tracing the deepening lines.

The next day Orbits visited the MP for the area. His office was in a town choked with high, narrow shops competing for attention with a multitude of roadside vendors congesting a pavement that dropped suddenly at spots. The concrete barriers placed erratically on the street slowed traffic to a crawl, and there was the constant honking of horns and inventive curses as pedestrians and stray dogs weaved through the vehicles. The MP's office was on the upper floor of a health food store with a billboard promising to cure cancer, diabetes and menopause. The MP was a small, benign-looking man outfitted in a white shirt and blue tie and a jacket several sizes too big. Orbits sat and described his frustrations. The man listened carefully, blinking sleepily and nodding. When Orbits was finished, the MP adjusted his tie, leaned forward on his desk and locked his fingers. The gesture was gentle, but the minute his fingers locked, his expression changed: his lips turned down and his eyelids narrowed. He seemed to recede into his jacket like a morrocoy retreating into its shell. He began to speak in an exceptionally reedy voice. "We have to move forward one step at a time. We must not look at our destination but at our feet. Where will it take us?" What the hell is he talking about? Orbits wondered. Has he been infected by the store downstairs? Orbits heard him saying, "We are puffs of smoke and the prime minister is holding the cigarette in his hand. He exhales the smoke and the wind blows it here and there. Do you think the PM actually cares? He has done his part." Unexpectedly Orbits thought of his old friend, Wally. What would he have made of this?

In the weeks that followed, Orbits tried to think of ways he could circumvent the roadblocks placed before him and help those who were genuinely afflicted. He discovered that less than half of the people he saw had legitimate concerns, and to this group he began to suggest alternative routes to solving their problems. He tried to explain that they should not expect everything from the government and that they had been trapped in a cycle of dependency that had cemented their helplessness. "I can't control the price of rice or dasheen," he told a group of villagers one afternoon. "I don't have the power to do that. All I could do is to advise you to plant some more profitable crop. What about pineapples and papaya, for instance?"

"Pine and papaya in a swamp?" The men slammed the door on their way out, scaring Mona. Still, he visited their farms and made promises he knew he could not keep. During these trips he listened to the complainers and mamaguyers on the radio and the lengthy advertisements sponsored by an assortment of quacks and psychics. "We have the cure for anything from A to Z," ran one while another featuring a man who called himself Doctor Stand promised marital bliss with his concoctions. One evening he heard an immigration consultant boasting of the men and women he had managed to get into Canada and America through some bogus refugee scheme. His mind ran to Wally and he thought: I should really pack up and leave this madhouse.

Instead he got the puppy from My Family and Other Animals. The pet store owner was delighted. He brought the animal from its box and Orbits saw that it had barely grown in the weeks since he had seen it. "Come Magaboy. You get a new owner." To Orbits he said, "You know the minute you stepped in my place I know this puppy was for you."

He brought over the animal to Mona and in the evening while he was preparing to leave, he saw her scratching her arms and legs.

Each morning he left Magaboy on his porch with bowls of water and chow, but it always managed to escape, and he would return to find it sniffing around his mother's backyard garden, now a tangle of lastro. Once it returned with a tiny iguana, and he recalled the pet store owner saying the father was a hunting dog. In the nights he heard Magaboy yapping, and although his sleep was disrupted, he was comforted by the presence of another living thing.

THREE MONTHS AFTER HE had purchased Magaboy, a delegation that included Halligator came into his office. Orbits was confused as to what they wanted; then it emerged that an emissary had been sent previously with a proposal. He was still puzzled: which emissary and what proposal? But he listened and he gathered that the man in question was a plainclothes officer who had forwarded requests from Halligator for government contracts to build roads and repair schools. At the end of the conversation, Orbits explained to the group that there was a bidding process. "We don't have time for any kiss-me-ass bidding," Halligator said. "We is busy people. Just coming to you today mean that five business had to close. What else you want from we, man?"

Orbits thought of the question. He opened a drawer in his desk and withdrew a folder. "This is the bidding form." He slid it across the table.

The plainclothes officer, tall and burly, read the form. "What is this?"

"Could someone read the form for him?" Orbits said tiredly.

"This is a joke. This is a joke," Halligator sputtered. He snatched the form from the officer and flung it at Orbits. It sailed harmlessly at the side of the table.

Another man said, "You know who you playing with? Allyou fellas does get a little power and feel allyou is Barabbas. I hope you know what happen to him?"

"Making threat in a government office is different from the commess in the rumshop," he told the group.

"Nobody making threat," Halligator said, smiling with one side of his mouth. "Threat is only talk."

Orbits saw Mona looking through the door and told her, "It's okay. Go back to your work." And to the men, "Don't waste my time with this nonsense again." His voice was even and he was not angry.

Two weeks later, he got a call in his office. He got into his Wingroad and drove hurriedly to his home. The left of the house had been destroyed — the bedrooms that had been occupied by his parents — but the kitchen and living room and two bedrooms had been spared by the fire. Joe the mechanic, who was gathered with a small group, told him, "The fire brigade come a whole hour after I call it."

"Did you see a dog?" he asked the other man. "Magaboy," he shouted as he walked through the rubble and the spared rooms.

"That dog gone long time," Joe reassured him. "Most likely it hiding inside they." He pointed to the forested area opposite the house. "Must be done eat up two-three snake by now. Ay-ay, where you going?"

"To look for it." Orbits crossed the road hurriedly. He struggled through the blacksage and the drooping guava trees closed in by vines, calling the dog's name. He remembered this area, but soon he came to a decline that led to a shallow ravine. On the other side, about five hundred yards away on a hill, was the old community centre. By the time he got to the building, his shoes were soaked and his pants and shirt were covered with burrs. The community centre had been built as a split level to follow the contours of the hill, and from the back it was a jumble of rotting walls and posts. He climbed to the front, which bordered a gravel road now abandoned and overgrown with para grass.

He pushed open the front door and walked inside. There were three men squatting around a box. They got up immediately, and Orbits, if he was not so beset by the fire and the loss of Magaboy, would have noticed that one was holding a knife. They were all shirtless and as they advanced, one of the trio asked, "What you doing here?"

"Looking for a dog."

"It don't have no dog here. What is you name?"

"Orbits. I live down the hill. Did you see a dog?"

"I tell you it have no dog here. What you doing here?"

And another, "You come to spy? That is what you doing here?"

Now he smelled the weed and noticed the knife. "I just told you. I live down the hill."

"We never see you before." Two of the men were on either side and the one with the knife was directly in front.

"Look, I had a brother who used to come here all the time."

"Nobody else come here. What is his name?"

"Starboy."

The men fell silent. Then one of them said, "Don't talk shit. You is really Starboy brother? You don't look like him. He was a pretty boy."

"Yes, yes," Orbits said impatiently, not catching the change in the man's tone and the danger that had just passed. "And I looking for a dog."

"It have no dog here, brother. The only thing here is the three of we and them snakes up in the rafters." He lit a joint and inhaled. "So you crazy like Starboy?"

"He wasn't crazy," Orbits said.

"I don't mean it that way, brother. He was too bright for this place. Sometimes he used to talk in parables that only he could understand."

"Like the time he say that people afraid to shut up because the minute they get quiet everybody wondering what scheme they up to."

"You remember that thing he talk about shame? How every man-jack grow up with a ton of shame on his head. I can't frame it nice like Starboy, but I think that was what he mean."

"Starboy brother, eh. You know after all this time we does still talk about him."

"Like when the rain sliding silky-silky down a dasheen leaf we would play this game by guessing how Starboy would frame the scene. Or if the sun peeping through the cloud. He use to talk about the sky a lot."

"As if he lost something up they."

The men grew quiet and awkward as they slapped away mosquitoes. Orbits felt the tingle of the burrs on his flesh. He asked the men, "You all know how he died?"

They took their time in answering. Then the man with the knife said, "For we he didn't die. He still around."

When he returned to his house, Joe, still there, followed him through the destroyed porch. The rafters in the bedrooms had been burnt and the aluminium sheeting, twisted by the heat, dangled over the floor. The sky, through the holes, looked pitted and broken, the clouds sliced by the angles of the dangling sheets. In his father's bedroom, the iron filing cabinet had been saved, and when he opened the drawers, he saw clotted parcels and bottles of dental material. Some were even older tonics with the handwritten words "shake well" on their labels.

"You remember when everybody use to think it really had a doctor name Doctor Shakewell because all the bottles from the drug store had this description?" Orbits did not reply. He noticed an old rusted iron box that he assumed contained more dental material. In his mother's room, the roof had caved into the bed and onto the dressing table, the mirror shattered and lying on its side. But the closet seemed unaffected, and when he pulled open the solid teak door, he saw her clothes, remnants from another time, dresses and gowns and the strange attire she had worn during his former wife's visit. Pushed to the side were a dozen hangers with clothes he recognized as his brother's. He walked to the other side of the house, to the rooms that had been spared. He pushed open the door to his brother's old room and sat on the bed.

Five minutes later Joe shouted from outside, "You find something inside they? Is the dog?" When Orbits emerged, Joe looked at him and said sympathetically, "Don't take it so hard. These things happen. Thank god the house was empty." He followed Orbits to the living room. "From the amount of smoke, I thought for sure the house was gone for good. We try to dash some water from the hose on this side and it help a little bit. Nothing permanent damage when you really look at it, so it shouldn't be hard to rebuild. Maybe you could put some brick walls outside and cedar inside. On the roof, you could put some of these green tiles that so popular nowadays. Sliding door and louvres will look nice. Sometimes these things is just a opportunity, I always say. Labour not so expensive again since the oil money start dripping away. Just a opportunity, as I say."

He continued with his suggestions, but Orbits had stopped listening. Finally, he told him, "You right. Is an opportunity." He almost added: I have to move away from this place.

⤙⤚

THE HOUSE HE HAD seen more than twenty years earlier, first when he was in a bus with Skullcap, the place transformed by the tourists' appreciation, and later lowered by his former wife's more level-headed view, remarkably, was still unoccupied, still abandoned, the fruit trees and flowers now overtaken by lastro but yet as appealing as when he had first spotted it. The village, too, had not changed; if anything, it appeared more abandoned, but there was an old grocery beneath a concrete house, the cantilever and the raised blocks and the fretwork and balusters above mocked beneath by the heavy slats, the plain unpainted walls and the yard bruised by knotgrass. Dangling from the fretwork on the upper porch was a sign saying "Soongsoong Japourie. Licensed Grocer." In the grocery, a smallish man who seemed to be in his sixties with moustache and eyebrows branching in several directions and huge knobbed knuckles that seemed transplanted from a bigger man, told him that the owner of the house had once owned a cocoa estate in the village. The owner had hoped his children would take over the estate, but they had all migrated. "The fella sell out the estate but he hold on to the house. Don't ask me why. Maybe he was hoping." He slapped down a fly and Orbits jumped back. "But then it get too late to sell the house," he said, examining his hand and flicking his finger limply like a dancer. "Nearly everybody leave the village and gone to the town. But I still here. You want to ask me why I never leave?"

"Why?"

He scratched his chin as if he had been caught off guard by the question. Finally, he said, "Go where? And for what? I have the most important thing right here in the shop." He gazed around his empty shop sadly. "Peace and quiet. You must be confused by the name on the sign, not so?" Orbits was about to tell him that he was not when the grocer said, "Father buy the shop from a old Chinese man who went back to Shanghai. Fella name was Soongsoong, and father wanted to leave the old signboard because everybody in the village was already accustom to the name, but these bitches from the county council office come down hard on him. They say that is fraud to use another man name on your business. So father combine two names. Soongsoong and Japourie. End of text. Case for the crown. You interested?"

Orbits tried to be polite. "Is a nice story."

"I mean in the house."

"Very interested," Orbits told him.

The shopkeeper seemed disappointed. He walked wearily to a stack of bills, tore off a sheet, examined both sides and wrote a name. "This is the owner of the house. Will surprise me if he still living but you never know. Sometimes these half-dead people like to hang on until they see everybody else go. Is bad-mind, if you ask me. My own parents was different, you know"

Orbits took the paper. "Where I could find this fella?"

"That is a good question. Try the said house."

"He still living there?"

The shopkeeper laughed shyly, hiding his mouth with his hands. "Once a month somebody does open window and door. Don't know who and don't know why." He scratched his chin. "But is a good question. Why at the end of every month? Something wrong with your eye? And how you have them black patch on two side of your face?"

Orbits left him to ponder the answers to his questions, but he returned to the village at the end of the month. He pushed the gate and walked into the yard. When he knocked on the door, a hefty woman stepped out and he saw, through the open door, a frail, yellowish man, slim, tall and clad in pyjamas and slippers. Before he stated the reason for his visit, the old man beckoned him with long fingers. "Do I know you from before?"

"I don't think so." Orbits told him.

"Come, sit here." He motioned to the narrow space beside him on the couch, but instead Orbits pulled a chair from a table. The woman sucked her teeth and said something he could not catch. "Are you blind?" the man asked, drawing circles around his eyes.

"No. I wear the glasses for . . . for cataracts."

"Ah yes, cataracts. Have you ever been in a catamaran? Now, tell me what it is you want."

"I am interested in the property."

The man looked up and laughed in three sharp spurts. Orbits saw his Adam's apple jumping as if it had loosened from his body. "You are interested? That in itself is interesting, wouldn't you say?" He laughed again. "And what do you propose to do with the property once you have purchased it?"

"I plan to live in it."

He called to the woman and told her, "Did you just hear that? This gentleman with cataracts who I have never met before plan to live in the house." The woman sucked her teeth and Orbits felt it had been a mistake coming to the place. "Did my children send you?"

"I don't know who they are."

The man leaned towards Orbits so that he was almost parallel to the cushion. "And let's keep it that way." The woman straightened him and walked out the front door. "Now, tell me what you want?"

Two hours later Orbits stopped at the grocery. "So you meet him?" the shopkeeper asked. "From what I know he used to be a important man. Sail all over the world but he a little bit *malkadee* now. Have a lady who does take care of him. So what happen?"

"He agreed."

The shopkeeper appeared alarmed. "What you mean agree?" Orbits explained that the man had agreed to sell the property, but he didn't reveal to the shopkeeper that a search for the deed had to be made at the Red House, and they had not finalized a price, and he had not really inspected the house. The shopkeeper then asked why he was moving into this abandoned village, and Orbits revealed his house had been destroyed by fire. "So you jumping from the fire into the frying pan?" the man asked, brightening up. "You walk through and inspect the house? The backyard and thing? Sometimes these houses does rest on the edge of a caveland and all it take is a little breeze to push it down. Sometimes the wall does look nice from the outside and the inside swimming with woodlice. Who could tell if the door and windows clamp down and electrical wires get chew up by rat."

"Maybe not."

"Eh? Maybe not? What sort of negative attitude is that?"

At an earlier time in his life, Orbits would have changed his mind about the purchase. He would have surrendered to the scepticism of the shopkeeper or to the advice of Joe the mechanic and Cascadoo and simply rebuilt the old house or finally given up during his frustrating trips to the Red House to get the deed, or even at the late stage in the lawyers' office when he was about to sign his name on the deed. He would have considered the size of the loan and the fact that his position as a county councillor would be up in three years, and deliberated over his status, a single man of fifty-two buying a property. Intending to live alone with no one to share, no one to inherit.

But he had stopped fighting the world. He sensed that his attitude of stolidity, of being unruffled by events, was not the detachment he had first assumed but simple and uncomplicated acceptance. He thought of this during the seven months he lived in the partially burnt house, wondering whether this acceptance was along the same resister as the villagers he met in the constituency office, the farmers he had seen at the field station. One morning on the Wingroad's radio he heard a politician known for jumping from one party to the next excusing himself. "It better to go with the flow." So when the pet store owner asked about Magaboy, he said it had grown independent, and when he discovered that wasps had built a network of nests on the burnt rafters, he avoided that area rather than getting rid of them. Once he told a goat farmer who had come to complain about a landslip threatening his pens, "Life is like that." He no longer bothered to make excuses he could not keep.

On his last day in the house, while he was packing his belongings in the Kingswood he had sold to Cascadoo, Joe walked by. "I have something to tell you," the mechanic said.

When Joe was finished, Orbits repeated the words he had spoken to the goat farmer.

The mood carried when he moved into the green bungalow, and

he thought of the passiveness into which he had fallen not as gazing impassionedly at some distant room from afar, but as living in this room and watching things melt and reform around him. As he set about repainting the walls and fixing bits of the sagging fence — for the house, surprisingly, did not need much improvement, and he was determined that it should retain as much of its original appeal as was possible — his mind drifted back to the conversation with the mechanic on the day of his departure. Joe had mentioned, almost as if it were part of his general advice about relocating and had no special significance, that Orbits' father, when he had found him wandering more than a mile from the house, had been mumbling about his son. "At first, I thought it was you he was talking about," the mechanic had said. "But when he start talking about how the boy gone and kill himself, I remember your other brother. Nice polite fella. Good-looking too. Always hail me out when he cross my gap. You father was saying that he cause the boy to go and take his life and how on that very said day he had chase him away from the house and tell him to never come back and how he was dead to him." Joe had moved on to comment on the cheapness of concrete as opposed to wood before he added, "Poor old fella. Talking out of his sense."

In his office, Mona, misunderstanding Orbits' frequent moments of reflective silence, frequently asked about his new residence and the drive to work. She mentioned at times some memory of his mother and more than once, she told him, "Grandma would have been so happy to see you in this big job." Another day, she asked, "You don't miss the old house a little bit self?"

He knew she was trying to get him out of what she assumed was a lengthening fugue. He told her, "Is just a burn out shell now with snakes and bats. I should try to sell it."

The next day Cascadoo came to his office under the pretense that he was dropping off a lunch container for his daughter. But a few minutes into their conversation, Orbits realized what he was up to and he told the other man, "I will sell it to you for the cost of the land because the house is useless unless you prepared for plenty renovations. Two lots in all." He recalled Mona's attempts at making his mother's last years comfortable and he added, "Just pay me for one lot."

The next evening, he walked through the property with Cascadoo, who said, "You know I could build a nice mud house on this spot. The foundation and the back still here. *Lepay* it good and proper. Nobody know how to lepay again, but them mud house was cooler than anything else." While he was walking around the property looking for the red bound-flower shrub that demarcated the boundary, Orbits wandered around the house. The burnt and blackened cedar, the twisted iron that was once part of the porch's railing, the flat-head nails swept by the rain into neat piles, the mounds of coal on the ground, the open sky above, made him think of a derelict jail. This house was never a happy place for me, he thought. Maybe for my parents, but they, too, were despairing at the end. It certainly was not happy for my brother. He recalled Joe's confession and abruptly he walked out from the house to the yard. He was surprised to pick up a whiff of woodsmoke, the burnt cedar battered by the rain and the heat but the aroma still there, a faint presence, like slippers dragging in the mud. He had no idea why that image came to him as he looked out at the slight hill opposite the house, the wild guava trees covered with vines and, higher up, the community centre's red roof visible between the palmiste. "I find this in a drawer." He turned to see Cascadoo holding the iron box he had seen after the fire among his father's other denture materials and had left behind. "You want me to put it in the car." He nodded.

Early the next morning as he was leaving for his office, he saw the box in the back seat and he wondered why his father had secured his plastics and polymers and acrylics in a locked box. Perhaps in his declining years he had forgotten about it as he had everything else.

From his office's second-storey window, he could see the patients filing into the dentist's office opposite. He recalled when he had been apprenticed by his father and his horror at the dentures swimming in the pot. "What you see so funny in the dentist office?" It was Mona who had heard him chuckling.

"Something I remembered. Dentures inside a big pot of boiling water and looking like crabs." He glanced at her puzzled look and added, "You have to see it to notice how funny it is."

"I don't have that imagination like you." He was about to remind her of the stories she had read to his mother when she added, "Daddy always say that in his next life he want to born back as a crab because they live so long and I always tell him that is a curse not a blessing to be hang up for days in a stall and put in a fridge for another week and then to get throw into a pot of boiling water and still be living through all of this. Who would want to go through all that torture? If I was a crab and I know the life that was in store for me, I would crawl out in the road to wait for the next truck. Better to die than to put up with all that heartache that in store down the stretch. Daddy always saying that animals have an instinct that tell when they going to die. You think these poor crabs have any idea?"

"I doubt it."

In the evening while he was driving home, he recalled her simple determination and felt a twinge of worry for her. At his home, he got out the iron box and placed it on the floor of the kitchen, next to a pile of tools he had used to renovate the house. He was about to cut a barbadine fruit when he stooped and used a hammer and a flat-head screwdriver to pry open the box. It was shut tightly, and not from the rust as he had assumed, but after some solid taps the top gave way. Stacked neatly were his father's implements: his pliers, needles, bowls with hardened resin, clamps and drill bits. In a plastic bag he saw cuff links and tie clips he had never seen on his father. Beneath these, he saw a copy book, its cover smeared with some fibrous fruit.

He expected to see a list of his father's clients when he unrolled the copy book, but the writing was unfamiliar. It was not his father's or his mother's. Puzzled, he began to read. *When the day closes I will stand before the night. When the night falls I will stand against the morning. When the world ends I will stand alone.* There were scratches that made the rest of the poem or whatever it was impossible to read. On another page, he saw: *The boy saw the dead body washed up on the beach. He walked up shyly to begin a conversation. He was thinking of what to say when the body spoke. I have been waiting here for six months. Each day I look at the sand and wait for you. Have I been dead that long? the boy asked.* Once again there were scratches over the following lines. And on another page, *The boy told his father he could not believe in god. All lies he said. I see, replied the father. If you are so smart to come up with this nonsense and you believe everything is a lie I also want you to relate to me a lie the first thing each morning. But it must sound like the truth or you will be punished. Each morning the boy related a lie to his father. The father was disappointed and angry because the lies were all perfect. One lie was bad people were always punished and good ones rewarded. Another was to live for today and tomorrow will take care of itself. Yet another said to know yourself and others will glimpse what you have discovered. The father's patience was fast running out. Yet he could not help feeling a trace of admiration even as the simple lies grew more puzzling. Morning after morning he heard aphorisms like, Pain that is shared ceases to burn. Then one morning the boy left a note instead. It said, death is simply a place not yet visited. Aha, said the father as he rushed into the boy's empty room. This can neither be true nor false because it cannot be proven nor disproven.*

In this case the cryptic story or parable was incomplete because the bottom of the page had been torn off, and Orbits wondered what the father may have felt when he uselessly, frantically searched for his son. As he flipped through the pages, he noticed guava seeds stuck on the inside cover and at the centre, between the staples, mango threads that looked like an intricate tattoo.

He took the book onto the porch. It was 5:30, the sliver between day and night that Orbits appreciated because all the brisk colours that instigated his headache were muted, the sounds then only of the distant parakeets and, closer, a carolling semp or blue jean. There was one sense enlivened during this half an hour before night dropped its coat, and usually he would close his eyes and try to separate the tart aroma of guavas from the pulpy sweet fragrance of Julie mangoes and cherries and plums.

But this evening he kept his eyes open, his focus not on the book on his lap but on the sky. The lobe-shaped clouds ignited by the setting sun looked like metallic bubbles poised ominously in the sky. He recalled a name. Mammatus. It was a strange name for a cloud formation, and during his time with Baby Rabbit he had been tempted to write this name on his weather prediction sheet just to hear Lilboy, the all-purpose janitor and traffic warden, screaming it aloud.

This celestial spectacle lasted five minutes at the most, and soon the sky was grey, then black. Yet he kept looking up, and he felt he saw, on this vast black screen, his brother walking to the guava patch lastro opposite the house, a copy book shaped like a funnel in his hand. His mother had assumed the trip was a replacement to using the toilet, his father ascribed another, more private vice, and Orbits felt it was simply to smoke. He recalled one of his brother's casual criticisms about no one possessing any imagination, but he assumed that had been just an aspect of his morose and sarcastic personality.

He turned some of the pages of the copy book and looked at a couple of cartoonish drawings, done perhaps at an earlier time, and he wondered what it was about his family or the village or the island that had stolen the life of someone who could imagine his own future. Maybe Wally, who had criticized the short-term vision he saw everywhere, had been wrong. And maybe all these singers, the calypsonians and village bards, were right when they sang of feting and wining and drinking rum until they were stunned into blissfulness. He recalled a stanza from a calypso: "Drunk and disorderly / Always in custody."

Late in the night, on the porch, he wished he had known his brother, who had died a stranger. Maybe his brother knew him better though: on one of the pages, he saw a cartoon of a boy sitting on a cloud. Beneath was a smaller figure, looking up, his hands outstretched, either waving or trying to hitch a ride.

He did not go to his office that week, and as he had done following the deaths of his parents, he waited. He felt along his entire body weariness as stroking fingers one moment, as a crushing hand the next. He was not sure on what he was waiting, but the tiredness dipped and resurfaced during those days. He wondered what would happen if he just sent in a letter of resignation even though he knew it was not easy to resign from an elected position. But these were idle thoughts. He was waiting for the moment he would feel grief and sadness and guilt, and from this mix, he would perceive some new way of looking at this world: a vision that was temporary and deformed and fraudulent, but one that would allow him to carry on.

As a preparation for this epiphany, he imagined the world was filled with suffering that served some mysterious purpose. He then reflected as to whether there was no grand purpose but just a series of coincidences and random events that made men and women either lucky or blighted. He recalled his mother's view of the reincarnated form's existence as payment or punishment for the last life. But these were all beliefs he had read or heard of, so they came to him impersonally, as a remote conversation or drained words falling off a page. They offered none of the personal anguish for which he was searching, and which would agitate a sudden insight that was so simple and obvious it would clarify everything.

He barely ate during the week and on the morning of the third day, he felt a ravenous hunger he had not experienced since his time with Wally. There is food in the kitchen and I am famished. But I am not eating. Why? He waited. Other questions arose. Some so digressive and childlike, he could barely understand their purpose. Why did the previous owner sell the house and where is he now? Was he waiting all the time for someone like me to make an appearance? What will happen if I allow the vines along the trees to continue growing? Will it soon cover everything? And he waited and waited. His hunger increased until it felt like a solid thing, a metal ball caught beneath his chest, rolling up and down like a pinball. Soon he could no longer feel it, and he feared it had looped somewhere else, hiding above an organ, waiting for him to fall asleep. One night he awoke in a panic; the ball had splintered and was crushing him from inside, hollowing him out. The following night, he was jolted by another nightmare in which a former teacher was telling him, "You brought down everybody in your family with your lickrishness." He sat up in his bed. A teacher had actually used those words. He walked outside, close to the road, facing the abandoned school. How did I, of all people, manage to escape? What will be the cost I must pay later on? I blighted everyone and everything I touched. But I escaped. Why?

He stood there for hours until the night faded, the morning light filtering through the trees, weak and unsteady, bringing the old school into relief. He imagined the sounds of children's laughter, the scraping of chairs, desk covers opened and closed, chalk on a blackboard. He pictured a slim little boy walking alone, his body straight, watching the games, three-hole marbles and hoop, briefly interested in one game before moving on to gaze at another. No one was interested in him and he returned their indifference, this frail child. At that moment, Orbits felt such a tenderness for his little brother that his knees buckled and he was forced to squat on the road. Eventually, he went to his closet and took out his white shirt and khaki pants. His hair was damp from the dew and his one-week beard was flecked with grey.

Later in the morning, Mona asked him if everything was okay, and he told her that he was thinking of the end of his term in office so he could retire peacefully. She seemed relieved and explained her worry that he was regretting the sale of his burnt house. When her father had bought the property, her sisters were overjoyed they could finally move away from the back road, she told him. Her father, though, insisted he would remain in the old house. "He is really like a cascadoo fish, you know. If you take him out of the mud he will begin to gyap." She tittered and returned to her desk. She returned a few minutes later to say, "I wonder what grandma would have thought if she knew I would be living in her house. Maybe her spirit will still be around, telling me, 'Girl, you and your fat bottom. You better keep the place nice and clean.'"

How did I manage to escape? Over and over the question came to him until he sometimes felt like a fraud and pretender, not because of his qualifications or his job but because he had survived.

FOR HALF A YEAR, Mona daily gave Orbits an update of all that her father was doing in the property: demolishing the old structure, building a new frame, putting up the cedar walls and laying the mahogany floor, installing doors and windows, running electrical wires and copper pipes, dropping the roof, painting and varnishing everything. During all this time, Orbits was brought back to one question: What will be the cost I must later pay for escaping from my family's blight? Will the torment unfold slowly, dragging me along, or will it fall swiftly, with no warning? His constituents mistook his malaise for disinterest, and in the rumshops they speculated on the reasons. He had been bribed by Halligator. He was just waiting out the end of his term. His true colours were finally showing. Among the farmers, Cascadoo offered a sturdy defence. "Eef he was interested in bribe and money why then he sell the old property to me for next to nothing?"

"Who could tell," a neighbour responded once. "Maybe it have spirit roaming around. The house take three people from what I hear. Father, mother and brother. And a dog. Nearly take him too with the fire. You better make sure you bless it good and proper before you move in."

One afternoon, as Orbits was about to leave, Moon entered his office. With her was a child, a boy of about four or five. "I thought you had packed up and gone," she said in the brash manner he recognized. She was dressed in tight jeans and a halter top and Orbits, just for a minute, wondered if she had made herself up for this visit.

"My term is not up as yet. What are you doing here?"

"Listen to you," she said in an amused manner. "Asking me these questions like if you is my husband. I had to take the boy to the doctor."

"What's wrong with him?" The boy was looking around in a disinterested manner at the folders on the shelves and the photographs of the prime minister on the wall.

"Shots." She noticed his gaze and added, "He look just like his father, not so?"

"Where is he?" Orbits asked uneasily.

She laughed loudly, and Orbits noticed Mona looking through the doorway. "Exactly where you expect him to be." To the boy, she said, "Did you hear what that man asked?" The boy nodded so rapidly that Orbits wondered if he was right in the head. "Tell him that your father is a councillor." The boy nodded again, and Orbits noticed that his feet were close together. He thought of the bobbing toys he had seen on the dashboards of taxis. "Tell him that your father is out campaigning and just now this office will be his. Would you like to visit him when he begin to work here? Look, there is a dentist office." She picked him up and walked to the window. "Over there." To Orbits, she said, "He is my little pet."

Be careful. The world is a cruel place.

"What was that? What are you talking about?"

Orbits realized he had spoken aloud what was running through his mind. "Little pets grow up and . . ." He tried to complete the thought. He saw the impatience on Moon's face. Mona was still watching through the door. She moved aside when Moon stormed out.

"Did that woman want you to help her husband?" she asked.

"I can't help anyone."

"That is not true. You help your mother so much. You help me and my father and my sisters. And all these people who you encourage to stop depending on the government. Why you don't pass by the house and see all the construction going on. So much noise!" She placed both palms against her cheeks and imitated the sounds of hammering and nailing.

She kept this up over the following weeks, almost as if she suspected that he liked the descriptions of old things pulled apart and replaced, bit by bit, with more durable materials. He listened carefully to all the little details and Mona, when she noticed this, described the lath and plaster and sidings and the tools and carefully outlined all that was still to be done.

"One day a old bald-headed mechanic come up and tell him, 'Mister you have a whole army of daughters building this house for you. Mixing concrete and hefting big-big plank like hardback men. I never see anything like it before.'"

On the day she mentioned the furniture, tables, dressers, cupboards and safe that the daughters had built themselves, she once more wondered aloud what his mother would have made of this new building. He had begun to view Mona's updates as unwitting interventions, the only time his mind was released from increasingly despairing speculations. Now she seemed to be waiting for an answer, so he said, "She would be glad that a happy family living there now."

"Happy? You don't know the amount of quarrel that take place every day. What colour to paint the wall. How much drawers to put in the safe. How big to make the cupboards. Who sleeping in which rooms." She smiled as if at some memory. "Who would ever imagine?"

"Imagine what?"

"I don't want to say. Is bad luck to talk about good luck."

Eleven months after he and Cascadoo had walked through the property, Orbits was invited to the house-blessing ceremony. In spite of all that Mona had described, Orbits assumed that the new house would follow the fashion of the back-road structures with a boxy top on poui logs, a shallow gallery at the front and misaligned louvres on all the walls. Beneath he expected to see a hammock strung on two posts and a table nearby. At the back there would be a chicken coop. But the structure he saw from his car was concrete with a shingle roof and an L-shaped porch that reached around the left of the house where a garage had been built. The ceremony was in the garage, and when Cascadoo saw him he rushed out from the small group to escort him around the house.

For the first time he spotted the wife, whom he had pictured from Cascadoo's descriptions as someone made hard and unattractive by the rigours of unending pressures, but instead he saw a handsome woman with a twist of a smile that gave the sense that in her younger days, she might have been prankish and playful. The daughters he had glimpsed at his mother's funeral; he now noticed their resemblance to their mother.

The family trailed him until the arrival of the priest, a tall, slightly hunched and slow-moving man. Orbits sat on a chair next to farmers he knew from his time at the field station and listened to the priest chanting and instructing the family to scatter the zinnia and hibiscus flowers, light a fire, sprinkle incense, bring scented water to their lips, take a brass cup around the house, offer little saffron cloth satchels to the fire, touch their foreheads, link hands, think of a secret wish. He spoke slowly, grimacing with each word but murmuring tunefully as the rituals were carried out. The smoke curled lazily upwards and carried the scent of the burnt offerings, the incense and pitch pine and camphor and clarified butter, and Orbits, who had so often ascribed the stagnant lives of the farmers to practices like these that celebrated solemnization instead of innovation, for the first time in almost a year, felt a quiet drip of peace. In closing, the priest said to the family in English, "Before we finish here, I want you to offer your thanks to everything you see here." He mentioned particular plants and animals and the sky and the weather and the materials that went into the house. He paused, consulted his book and mentioned several more.

Over the following weeks, Orbits tried to understand the manner by which grief could be shuttered and the mind offered a temporary repose through the sanctification of every trivial thing. So often he had seen this stunned gratification drawn from rituals and signs as a mark of backwardness. He had compared the adherents to rain flies briefly energized and given flight by the rain before falling to the ground to be carted away by wingless insects. He had thought of Doraymay, who seemed so accepting of his situation.

One night while he was on his porch, the rain beating down on the roof and the water gurgling down the spouting and crashing on the landing, he decided to simply accept the reprieve from a year of despair. I tried to do what I could, he thought. I, too, have been scarred. But I survived. Why? He repeated the sentiments aloud, in the same chanting voice used by the priest, as if an answer would be forthcoming just by imitating the other man. He closed his eyes and heard what sounded like the distant whoop of a water fowl although it could have been the wind tugging at the trees and the creak of the bamboo. Breeze funnelled through the half-opened jalousie and he imagined he could feel the coldness slicing at his hands and chest and face. This is a strong old house, he thought, surprising himself with the arbitrary determination. It's older than I am. It will outlast me.

As the days passed, he began to appreciate the solitariness of this almost hidden and abandoned village. There was no definable crop, cocoa long gone, and the few men and women he spotted on the roads, who showed no interest in him, were old and most likely holdovers from the exodus to the towns over the years. He drew comfort from the coolness of the nights, the shade of the day and the lush quietness broken only by the birds on the guava and pommecythere trees at the back of the house and the lemon at the sides. Maybe all over the world there were forgotten places like this village, untouched by progress yet hanging on, stuck forever at a point between desolation, neglect and permanence.

He stopped dwelling on his purchase of the property and particularly in the nights he was reminded of his first sight of the village. Yet there were times when, resting on his bed, he felt the soft slap of loneliness. During those moments the night sounds were transformed so that the drone of the crickets took on an ominous note, and when a sudden ruffle of breeze disrupted the cacophony, he imagined that the night birds were screaming in anguish and the frogs moaning their distress. He missed, then, the continuity of a conversation, the softness of a woman, even the promise of a trivial argument. And he supposed that while he was alone on his bed, in other houses couples were engaged in intimate acts. He envisioned these acts, torturing himself until disgust took over and unexpectedly he began to worry about his former wife and about his daughter. What if they were in abusive relationships? So he fell asleep worrying, but when he awoke the world seemed a different place.

In the early mornings he was awakened sometimes by the distant howling of dogs, and when he went to shut the window he would be met with the tangy aroma of citrus leaves and the fresh smell of grass, and he would change his mind and stand there watching the sun emerge from the bamboo grove at the back of the school. The light through the trembling leaves resembled flickering embers that had dripped from the blood-red clouds. During these moments, ten minutes at most, the sky appeared unstable and convulsive, and once Orbits felt this was how the world had looked during its creation.

One evening he walked to the back and saw an iguana slinking around in the water grass. The animal looked at him warily, but secure in its camouflage, it did not bolt. He wondered if there was a family of iguanas close by or if he had chanced across an adventurous specimen that had crossed the bamboo patch at the back and, beyond that, the abandoned cocoa estate. He gazed at the animal for three or four minutes until his eyes began to pain and he took off his shades. Then the animal dashed off and he saw only the ripple of the grass to mark its progress. On an impulse, he followed the animal's trail. He came to a ravine with conches stuck onto the smooth pebbles in the water. There were two bamboo trees leaning across the ravine, and tiny blackish crabs rose from the water to disappear into the plant's hollow trunk. Farther up, he spotted flatter water pebbles and he wondered if the ravine had once extended to that area.

Soon he came to an area of cocoa, the abandoned trees still bearing fruits, still shaded by tall immortelle and sandbox. On the ground, he noticed the dolphin-shaped seeds of the sandbox. At his primary school, some of the boys had polished and fashioned these seeds into necklaces. As he walked along, he thought: I missed out on all the activities of normal boys because I had no friends. Maybe I should now roam around the bush collecting seeds and making bamboo bows and guava tops.

"You see a 'guana running this way, Uncle?" He jumped. Two men, each with a gun, emerged from the bushes. He pointed in the direction the animal had fled and hurriedly retraced his steps.

Appreciation turned to alarm. The place was much too alive. The air was thick with insects and predatory birds. There were big bumble-bees above him. Crickets and bugs leapt off leaves as he approached. Mysterious things scurried away from the grass and the dead leaves. When he got home, he locked the doors and windows.

The next day he mentioned his encounter with the hunters to the shopkeeper, who said, "This village used to have real hunters one time. Not these little boys who can't hit a manicou if it jump right in front of they face." He looked at Orbits with some amusement. "You can't get frightened of every little thing all the time. I wanted to be a stickfighter, you know. *Cahraying* in the *gayelle* like a real bad-john. Then I realize that it would take just a single busshead to rack me up. Dreams is a real funny thing. They does sound nice in you head, but once they jump out they could cause plenty drama. I happy in me little old shop." He gazed around at the bees circling the bags of sugar with a tragic expression. Orbits wanted to believe him.

＞━━━

HE HAD NEVER LIKED driving, but on the route to his office, he passed through other small villages and stretches of forest that always seemed peaceful. Sometimes he wondered why these places infused with such a melancholy beauty were still derided with names like Hardbargain and Dogpatch and Ketchass Village. During these times, he was brought back to the trips, years earlier, when he had been confused by the foreigners' appreciative murmurs whenever they passed places like these. Maybe now that money was gone, the original inhabitants would return from the towns. Yet he hoped they would remain there and not puncture the tranquility of the village.

He appreciated the distance from the confusion of his office, too, and it was this distance from everything that was familiar that gradually allowed him to consider the questions of a year and a half earlier.

It was a cold and brutal assessment. His brother had killed himself for reasons that would forever be unknown, but the fact that he had been coddled so mercilessly by his mother had most likely given him an incomplete view of the real world. Orbits had been saved from that. His parents had arrived at their tragic ends because neither had made any preparations for loss. From this, too, he had been saved. And thinking in this manner, Orbits was able to look at all the unsatisfactory events of his life with a kind of wonder, seeing the losses, the shame and deprivations not as tragedies but as preparations. He suspected this was not an accurate rendering of his life, and that he had failed many people who depended on him, and that he was far from fulfilled, but it introduced a notion of wobbly balance — of his life tilting this way and that but still moving forward. Somehow, he had managed to hang on.

For the first time, he did not feel like a fraud or terrified that his job would be suddenly pulled away by an irate and threatening official. In fact, he now looked forward to the end of that phase of his life. He had learned to cook, using the old sturdy gas stove left by the previous owner. And the pleasure he got from seasoning and chopping and cooking was not unlike the hedonistic joy he had derived from eating. He spent long periods cutting and carving away the spiky pineapple's knobs or peeling mangoes and slicing papaws that he took to work in an icy-hot container. In the late evenings when he got up from the porch, he would cut chunks of breadfruit and tubers like dasheen and yam, and if he had bought carite or kingfish on his way home, he would either make a broth or steam everything with pinches of shadow beni and thyme and lemongrass and wedges of lime. The aroma of the herbs lingered in the house, and one night he wondered whether his sense of smell was growing to counteract the black spots that were always swimming in his eyes like bunched, drifting cobwebs.

He had discovered, soon after he moved in, a trove of old

hardcovers packed neatly in a cardboard box beneath a bed. The covers were either red or green and on the frayed cloth were titles like *The Sea Wolf* and *The Cruel Sea* and *High Wind in Jamaica*. He had never liked fiction and could never fully immerse himself into a world he knew was not real — and one in which he could never place himself — so those he returned to the box, and in the nights he would read, until his eyes began to complain, a chapter or two from *The Nautical Quarterly*, lavishly illustrated. He moved on to other books like the *Voyager's Tales* by a man with the unpronounceable name of Hakluyt. He learned of sailors who were trapped by enemies, caught in terrible storms, shipwrecked, rescued sometimes and still ventured out for other voyages. He was reminded of his fantasies at Baby Rabbit's place of diving into the eye of a hurricane or chasing a storm, a kind of recklessness that seemed unreal, but here in the books were men who had actually done more.

One night he returned to a book by Charles Kingsley that he had put aside because he recalled his brother reading a fantasy tale by this author. *The Water Babies* was the title of that book, but the one to which he now returned he soon saw was not fiction but an account of the writer's voyages through the Caribbean. In this book, *Westward Ho!*, he read of visits to his island by Walter Raleigh and Blackbeard, of revolts and naval battles, of plunder and treasure, and suddenly the place seemed more important, fought for by all the powers of Europe. He read from the book each night, and as he learned of the intrigue and cruelty and heroism, he recalled his boring history classes filled only with dates and laws and treaties and the horrors of slavery and indentureship.

So, late in his life, reading these books, he began to reflect not on his own condition, as he had always done, but on a bigger, more impersonal history to which he was still connected. Wally had used the word "transients" in describing his family, but the description could fit almost everyone in this side of the world. Old civilizations gone, new ones built on the ruins. And this process would be repeated over and over. This was the way of the world. An order to the chaos that could not be seen from within. He wondered whether it had been old, forgotten books like these from which Wally had gotten his knowledge. Or whether his knowledge had been passed down from generation to generation. During his conversations with the other man decades earlier, he had been impressed with Wally's facts and slightly ashamed of how little he knew. At that time he did not understand that it was the way of the village to pass down fables and myths composed many centuries earlier, time and distance bestowing on them a rhapsodic quality that could never be matched by remembered history. Those fables were part of a long, unending grind, of cycles of death and rebirth, of millennia enclosed always by a predetermined fate that rendered personal accounts useless.

Sometimes, late in the night, he would place the book on his chest and would recall his frustrations with the farmers who had to come to the field station and with the constituents to his office, and he would think that to these men, the fables, composed at a different place and time, held a significance he would never understand. Like with so many other situations, he had been shut out. But more and more, after he had finished his reading, the stillness occasionally pierced by the cry of a jumbie bird or a bat ruffling above the rafters, he would think back on his time with Wally, exploring the capital, talking about Canada as if the world were new and they would find their places in it just by being aware, but he knew that these recollections, tinged with nostalgia, were really the recollections of a stranger; the young man he desperately wanted to be. Sometimes he considered, just briefly, that his life was bereft and purposeless compared with these brazen sailors. And then he would wonder if his decision to forego his office was because he knew he would not retain his seat or because of some hidden fear of Halligator and the other goons, who had simmered down since his house had been burnt, guessing he had learned his lesson. They had stopped coming with threats when he had made public his decision to end his brief fling with local politics. So, too, did many of the villagers who, thoroughly disappointed with Orbits, turned their attention to the men and women lining up to replace him.

One of these men, a divorcee in his late thirties, came to Orbits' office one day. He was polite, and Orbits suspected the man wanted his endorsement. He told the visitor, whose prematurely grey hair seemed odd above his flat and baby-like face, that he was done for good with politics.

The man appeared embarrassed as he told Orbits, "Is not your endorsement I want, boss. In fact, is the exact opposite."

"So you don't want my endorsement?" Orbits wondered why then the visitor had been buttering him up.

"I will get to the point, boss. I want you to endorse somebody else." He called the name of one of Halligator's associates and, surprisingly, that of Moon's husband.

Orbits was taken aback by the request. He told the man, "As I mentioned, I don't want to get involved in this election. I finish with that."

"Yeah, I know that. Things wasn't easy, eh?"

He thought about preparing the candidate for demand upon demand, but this man had just requested him to support another candidate because he was so toxic. "All I will say is that I am relieved that my term has come to an end."

"Plenty pressure, eh?"

"I think it was my fault," he said suddenly.

"Eh?" The visitor was unaccustomed to this tack from politicians. "Your fault?"

"I set my sights too high."

"So what you saying is that I shouldn't promise anything? But how I will get elected then?"

"That is for you to decide. Do what your duty tell you."

"You know ever since I was wearing short pants, I see myself in politics. Crazy, eh? Anyways, I sorry to barge inside your office without a appointment. When I get elected I will . . ." He seemed undecided about what to say, this indecision on his baby face registering as childlike wonder. "What I mean to ask about is what you just mention about promise and thing. How you manage to deal with all these people over the years? What tips you have for me?"

"Well, let me see." Orbits mentally went through the list of his frustrations over the years. They don't like to be corrected. They believe that any apology is a sign of weakness. They believe that rumours have more weight than facts. They argue not to prove a point but to show off. They are offended by trivialities. He saw the expectant look on the visitor's face and added, "I don't think I was suited to the job." After a while he said, almost as if he was talking to himself, "I don't think I was a complete failure. If nothing changed during my time it was because nobody wanted anything different. Maybe everybody happy in their own way." A few minutes later, Orbits heard the man chatting with Mona. He walked out to the front desk and told the man, "This girl father is a influential man. You should get to know him."

Mona was blushing, and Orbits couldn't figure if it was the praise for her father or the conversation he had interrupted.

SOON THE CAMPAIGN GOT under way and Orbits was forgotten. This was a relief. The baby-faced candidate came into his office frequently, but only to talk to Mona, and he seemed embarrassed whenever Orbits stepped out to ask about his campaign. From his window, he spotted the mikes set upon vehicles, and he could hear the blaring of pre-recorded messages. Each lamp pole was pasted with photographs of the candidates. More and more, he began to miss the quiet of his bungalow, and he began to count down the weeks before the election. He also imagined improvements he would make to his property. The bungalow he would leave alone, but he could dig a pond at the back and plant a variety of fruit trees.

One midday from his office he heard over a loudspeaker a candidate promising to install traffic lights at every intersection if he was elected; on the following day an opposing candidate questioning whether his opponent was also planning to build an animal college to teach bison and buffaloes to understand traffic signals. Soon after, he wandered to a small congested pharmacy to get eye drops. He heard the chairman of the meetings he had attended saying over a loudspeaker, "The people from the other party only promising a set of da-da-da, but while they only promising, I want to ask who you trust to build your roads and bridges and da-da-da." His speech was frequently interrupted by applause. So it went, day after day, and Orbits sometimes felt that if he were observing this from a distance, he might even find the ridiculousness funny. Yet there were these coded racist taunts, too, made by all the candidates, and Orbits was sometimes puzzled that he had managed to win as an independent candidate close to four years earlier.

In his last month as a councillor, he was visited by a man of advanced years who still possessed an athletic figure and a full head of white hair. Orbits recognized the man immediately, and he waited for some equivalent gesture that suggested the visitor also knew him. But he sat in the chair opposite without an invitation and said, "I want you to do something for me."

"What you say? I didn't hear you," Orbits said, trying to control his voice.

The man leaned back to withdraw a rolled-up sheet of paper that he pushed across the desk. "Read it."

Orbits was usually patient with the villagers, who he knew could be quite brusque, but he told the man, his former teacher, "I don't have the time. What exactly is it?"

"You don't have the time?" He still had the look of stabilized frenzy as if a spiral of divergent emotions had smashed into his face. It was that look that had made him such a feared teacher and he had lived up to it, soothing one minute and maddened the next. "So I waste my time coming here?"

For a second, Orbits wanted to reveal the reason for his uncharacteristic curtness. He still couldn't understand why the man had not recognized him even though it had been more than forty-five years earlier and in another village. Orbits had been eleven or twelve at the time, the period during which he had been trying to persuade everyone to call him Orbits rather than Fatboy. He was not the only one picked upon, but the others could run away from the bullies while Orbits' awkward attempts at escape only drew more laughter, so he just stood there and pretended he had heard nothing and was looking at the clouds.

That day Orbits had been chewing at the warts on his fingers and the teacher had hauled him to the front and brought down his rod ten times, each blow on a different finger. The warts, perhaps softened by the blow, dropped off soon after, but for months the taunt — *Fatboy fall down* — had followed Orbits. Later, in another class, the teacher had begun a story about a land called Fatlandia from which a stupid fatboy had been banished. He had been sent to the world of normal people as a punishment for not obeying the rules and not paying attention. In this normal world, he would be perpetually mocked and scorned. "Look at the cannibal. You think we should send him back to Fatlandia?"

"Yes," the class chorused.

Orbits had begun to sniffle, and the teacher had asked, "What you say? That you missing Fatlandia? I didn't hear you."

Now, more than forty-five years later, this teacher was before him, and in spite of all he had achieved and all the years that had passed, Orbits felt a mixture of anger and shame at the instigator of this childhood humiliation. Perhaps if the teacher had not maintained so much of his old arrogance, Orbits' reaction would have been different, and when he took the cylinder, removed the rubber band and read of the constant digging of the roads and the dry taps and the failure of the water trucks to maintain a regular schedule, he told the teacher, "I can't help you. That area is developing and roads have to be built, so——"

"So what you expect me to do? And where you expect me to go?"

Fatlandia. No, Oldlandia. But he did not say what was on his mind. Instead, he told the teacher, "You can go wherever you choose."

"You expect a pensioner, a man almost eighty, to suddenly pull out and relocate? That is the advice you giving me? You know I spend nearly my entire life teaching and that some of the children who pass through my hands holding very important positions? You know that?"

Orbits replaced the rubber band around the sheet, snapping it in place. "Then you should take this issue to them. I am sure they remember you." He got up and held the sheet before him.

"I know people like you," the teacher said, looking past the proffered sheet and straight at Orbits.

"And I remember people like you."

He stood up. "You think just because you holding this important position you could talk how you damn well like?" The teacher was furious. "I hope you know that one day all of this will get taken away and you will just be an ordinary man walking the street. A blasted ordinary man."

"And I looking forward to that day."

"You know if I was twenty years younger, I would——"

"Would what?" Orbits asked, raising his voice. Other questions raced through his mind. Strap me? Make me eat all my warts? Laugh at me? Give everybody an excuse to say "Fatboy fall down" again? Tell me what you would have done.

The teacher glared at Orbits for a full minute before he said, "I would have handled everything myself and wouldn't have to depend on any blasted councillor who can't understand his duty is to people like me. Duty! The word fill with shit now." He turned stiffly as a soldier, as he had done at school, and walked out the door.

Mona came up from her desk outside his office. "Who was that mister?"

After a while he told her, "An old man who want me to do my job."

After he closed his office, Orbits walked down the hall to the bookstore, the Book Swami. The owner, who was usually hunched over a chair too low for the table, his furtive eyes magnified by his thick glasses, seemed startled, as always, to see a visitor. "Anything in particular, boss?" the man asked in a rustling, almost sinister voice. Orbits glanced around the shelves stocked with slim period-icals and tracts, almost all self-published, almost all written by the owner of the store. "Something for the glands? Something for the brains? I have plenty of those. Or if you interested in lists I have plenty of those too." He gestured to a wall with books bearing titles like *The Complete Lists of Things to Do, The Complete Lists of Things Not to Do, The Complete List of Good Foods. The Other Complete List of Good Foods.*

"Just looking around," Orbits told him. "Any visitors today?"

"Yes, man. A old fella was here not too long. He buy a book on deading properly. Not one of mine and I never did expect to get it sell. You know I have a book on exercises for the eyes. I notice like you don't see too properly with them darkers you always wearing." Orbits left the store with *The Complete Book on Seeing and Blindness.*

At his home, he flipped through the fifteen pages of cartoon drawings with accompanying injunctions like "Watch the sun. Watch the ground. Watch the sun again." On the last page was an illustration of a bearded and bespectacled man sitting cross-legged. Above him was a comic book balloon saying, "Watching the sun is like watching god in all his glory. The Book Swami."

Orbits placed aside the book and thought: if I had a book like this in primary school, I could have used it as an excuse for staring at the sky. It was a funny thought, and it reminded him of his teacher's visit and of his time in primary school. It was a period he hoped had been pushed aside and buried for good, but the appearance of the teacher had dislodged the memory of those torturous years. He had had no friends and was always suspicious of anything resembling friendship because it had often been a ruse, a preparation for some trap. Maybe there were other students he could have drawn close to. A boy everyone called Sixtoe Changoe, who had been dropped into a ravine. A girl who sucked her thumb until she was seven or eight. A stutterer whose father was a mute shoemaker. There were others, too: quiet, furtive boys and girls who kept to themselves and hurried to their homes. He recalled how often he had scanned his new classes for children like these, not with the intention of forming any bond, but hoping their presence would remove the target on his back.

Unexpectedly, Orbits felt a gentle tap of sadness that, as always, was tinged with a grainy, undefinable regret. He was not sure if it was the memory of his own beginning or that of other misfits whom he had studiously ignored and whose distress may have been equal to his own, or if it was the visit by the teacher, so feared and respected, now broken down by age and disease. He recalled Starboy's brief fascination with comic books like *X-Men* and *Suicide Squad*, which he had seen around the house. Orbits had liked the idea of orphans and misfits and the despised rising up against big, powerful bullies, but he could never get any sustained pleasure from fantasies that were so far removed from his own condition. Once he had come across a superhero called Bouncing Boy who, as his name suggested, had the stupidest power and shape in the world. That had ended his brief interest in comic books.

Starboy had persisted with the comics, and Orbits had always believed it was because his good-looking and confident brother could, however dimly, still see himself reflected on the pages. One night, with a book of mutinous sailors on his chest, Orbits recalled the incident where his brother was on the ground with a bigger boy on his chest, pounding away, and his brother's split-second glance at him among the onlookers. Did his brother somehow sense that he had been too afraid to get involved, to step in and part the fight, or did he see it act an act of betrayal? It was Starboy's first year at school, so he must have been five, and that afternoon walking home alone, Orbits expected to be chastised by his parents for his indifference. But his brother never mentioned it to anyone.

Over the following weeks, Orbits was brought back to those years while he was arranging his belongings in cardboard boxes, while he was expressing his gratitude to Mona, while he was marvelling at the way the years had flown. The mood followed him to his bungalow, and he recalled his fantasy of floating over the clouds, away from his parents, his brother, everyone at his schools. That dream had lasted longer than he had anticipated, and now Orbits wondered how many other awkward children like him had devised fantasies that gave them the power not to punish and destroy, as in the comic books, but to escape. He wished his younger self could meet others like him far away from the gaze of the bullies, maybe in an abandoned village like this, and he tried to imagine what they would talk about apart from the wish for invisibility. He recalled instead a scene from another era, when he was in high school and the teacher was talking about a book in which a man had bemoaned his invisibility. Orbits had misunderstood the writer's point and couldn't understand why anyone would see this as an affliction.

This foray into his childhood was something Orbits had always avoided, and in the nights, he walked out to his gallery hidden from the road by ferns and ornamentals. When he switched on the outside light, insects, as if they had been patiently waiting, began scotching around the bulb, bumping against the ceiling, their arcs briefly illuminated so that the scene resembled a distant fragmentation. His mother would have liked it here, he felt, even though she might have complained about the obscured view of the road. On some mornings as he stepped into his car, he speculated on what exactly her gaze had been fixed on during her last months. Maybe she had been seeing her dead husband on the road and beyond, Starboy returning from the guava patch. Or perhaps she had chosen a single insignificant object rooted to a single spot to constantly remind her she was still alive.

Occasionally he stopped at the shop on his way from work. The owner perked up to ask if the electrical wiring had come loose, or if he had discovered termites on any of the walls, or if the water tanks at the side of his house were empty. Orbits said the wiring was fine, there were no termites, and the tanks were filled although he was not certain of this. Then the shopkeeper would ask if he had checked the voltage of the plugs and the water for *kiwi*, mosquito larvae and tadpoles. He seemed affronted with each of Orbits' assurances that everything was satisfactory. He would open a soft drink in a sulking and exaggerated way and take a tiny sip, wiping his lips with the side of the bottle before he pounded the cap into place with the flat of his palm. Once he said, "I surprise that the mister decide to sell it, if you ask me. But who know what in people mind. Maybe it was haunted. It look to me like the sort of house that no spirit will pass straight. Sometimes when I passing in that direction I does hear children laughing from the school opposite even though that place shut down forty years now. The thing about spirits is they have no rhyme and reason. They willing to tangle with anybody." He paused and looked over Orbits' shoulder. "Ay-ay. Long time I didn't see that preacherman. I wonder what he want?"

The man who entered the shop seemed to be in his late sixties. He was bald and had a white beard on his chin, but his upper lip was clean. It was his voice, slightly trilling as if there was a bit of nervous gaiety at the centre of all his words, that seemed familiar. He stood at the end of the counter while the shopkeeper rummaged through his fridge for the requested drink.

"Skullcap?" The man turned and Orbits remembered this was just a private nickname he had given the man. "Baby Rabbit? Remember?" He looked at Orbits without recognition. "I too worked at the place."

For a minute, Orbits felt he had made a mistake, but the man drew closer, looked him up and down and said, "Not the matter-rologist? Eh?"

"Yes, yes, man." Orbits was so excited to see someone from his younger days that he was uncharacteristically effusive. "Is me self. You remember we use to go for drives all across the country."

"Come, brother." He hugged Orbits. "Listen, I know hardback men don't like to hug like this but is nice to see you. In darkers and thing. You was a youth in them days. How long that was? Twenty years?"

"Thirty maybe."

"Thirty and twenty is the same amount," the shopkeeper murmured. "Is just a difference of ten. Take out the one from ten and it leave zero." He tittered.

"Time does fly in your old age. So what you doing in these parts?"

"I living in this village now. In the green house opposite the old school. What about you?"

"Here and there, brother. Here and there."

"Guess who maxi I was in when I first see the house?"

"You joking! With all these tourists bundle in the back and bumping they gums about how nice the place is." He laughed sadly. "Was a different time, brother. A different time. Baby Rabbit gone and get diabetes and now he park up in some nursing home. Rich people disease, brother. You remember Lilboy? Get bounce down and remain on the road for hours from what I hear. That is what happening to we people now. Nobody watching out for the little man. Money melt away but sweet teeth remain. Foreign this and foreign that. Foreign crime, too. Kidnapping and ransom. That is why it have so much thiefing. The end times, brother."

Orbits wanted to change the topic. "So what about the outsides?" Skullcap seemed startled with the question, so Orbits added, "We visited a family. A little girl at the time."

"Ah, yes. She not so little again. In fact, she in America now. I does visit from time to time to help out with the grand but that place not for me. Shaitaan, brother."

The shopkeeper, who had been listening, said, "For years I trying to get a visa but every time they ask about bank account I does come to a complete full stop. My bank account is my and mine damn business. I applying for a visa, not getting married, I tell the officer the last time." He tittered.

Skullcap shifted away from the counter and spoke in a lower voice. "So what about you, brother? What you up to these days?"

"I worked in a field station for a few years, but I is a councillor now. In a village about twelve miles away. I almost finish there."

"Good, brother. I always thought you would reach far. You remember all these questions you used to ask me? About every little thing."

Orbits could not recall and he wished the other man would continue, but it was the shopkeeper who said, "So you is a councillor? You never mention it to me. Don't ask me why but now that I know I wondering if you could do anything about the drain in the back of the shop. Everybody rubbish does come to a full stop right behind me. Never know rubbish could be so bad-minded."

"Is not in my jurisdiction," Orbits told him.

"Jurisdiction. That is a very big word you using on me." He returned to his corked drink and gazed sourly at Orbits while he sipped daintily. "Joo-risk-deek-shan."

"Look, brother, I have to push on," Skullcap said. "Was nice meeting you." He seemed set to leave before he asked, "I making a trip to the town next week. If you want to come is fine with me. Will be like old times."

Orbits suspected the invitation had been issued through politeness, but he was curious about Skullcap's mention of questions during their trips together. So he said, "Sure. We could meet right here. What time?"

Skullcap took almost a minute before he said, "Wednesday. Ten in the morning."

"Okay. I will take the day off."

When Skullcap departed, the shopkeeper said, "I wish I could take a day off. But I not so lucky. Ask me why?"

"Because you are self-employed and I never see any children around the place."

The shopkeeper took a long drink, his eyes on Orbits. "No madam, no children, no close family. Sometimes I does ask myself why I standing behind this counter day in and day out." He raised a leg to kick away a fly and almost lost his balance. "Because is the only thing I know. The parents die out before they time and all of a sudden everything fall on my lap. No time for romancing and liming. You could say that I marking time. Yes, you could say that. So when you bringing the people to see about the drain?"

"This area have its own councillor. You should talk to him. He might—"

"But don't feel sorry for me. I had a craft once, you know. Real pretty and sexy." He put down the bottle and traced a wavy shape with both hands, stopping to adjust his hands further apart. "You have anybody?"

"Parents passed away."

"Anybody else?"

"My wife and I separated."

He bent to blow on his knuckles but kept his gaze on Orbits. "The first time I set eye on you I tell myself that you and the madam run into some problems. Ask me how I know that?" When Orbits did not respond, he said, "You have the look of a man who toting feelings. A man with a bag of cement on two of his shoulders and a solid concrete block on the other two. What I was talking about before? Oh, yes. Father never approve. He say the girl was from the wrong family. Maybe he was right. Maybe he was wrong. Who is to say? Sometimes I does blame him for that and sometimes I does feel that my script get write long ago. Which remind me. That old friend of yours was mixup in some bad business."

"What sort of business?"

"Is not for me to say. I just repeating what I hear. Something with the law." He slapped away a fly and glanced suspiciously at Orbits. "What you all going to the town to do?"

"I have some business there," Orbits told him. "Government business."

The statement was just to terminate the shopkeeper's curiosity, and on the appointed Wednesday, when he saw Orbits with a folder in his hand, he asked, "People drain business?"

"An old teacher came with a problem."

"So you does help out old teachers? Drain?"

"I just dropping the form for him. He too old and sick to travel."

"Sick? What disease?"

"He never mentioned it to me and it was not my place to ask."

"But you is a funny sort of councillor. Not your place you say and yet you doing big-big favour for him. Ask me what disease I battling with?" When Orbits remained silent, glancing at the road, he continued, "Heart. But the thing with the heart is that it real bad-minded. When it start getting ownway it does pull down everything with it *toute baghai*. Lungs, liver, kidneys." He counted on his fingers. "I leave out anything? Is four it had the last time I check. You know the preacher fella who was here the other day say that time does fly in you old age, but in my case, it dragging on. I wonder why he say that? You think is because old people have plenty years in the bag to compare with? I not that old you know. Guess."

"Your age?"

"Make a pick. Any number from ten to fifty-five." Thankfully, at that moment Skullcap drove into the gap. "Fifty-four!" the shop-keeper shouted as Orbits got into the car.

During the trip to the capital, Skullcap was talkative the way Orbits remembered, remarking on the direction the country was heading, the growing gap between the rich and poor, the flaunting of wealth, the corruption at every corner, the arrogance of those in power and their reluctance to annoy the wealthy. "The money bring new vice but people didn't forget the old ones. It had a time when I use to wish for a hurricane or earthquake to run through the place just to remind people that it have a big man upstairs watching and he don't like what he seeing."

During a break in his sermon, Orbits told him, "It look like you should have been in politics rather than me."

Skullcap laughed and said, "Sorry, man. I didn't mean to throw all this on you. I hope you don't mind." But as he continued on about the absence of god and the wickedness all around, as he made the world bigger and more consequential, Orbits saw his own four years as a councillor stripped and reduced. And when Skullcap asked him about his "own good works," it was not false modesty that was attached to the simple statement "I try to help out some of the poor people in the area, but I didn't make much progress."

"But you try, brother. That is the thing. You try."

"Sometimes I feel I didn't try hard enough."

Orbits had spoken in a deliberately lugubrious manner, offering the statement in a joking way, but Skullcap said, "That is honest, brother. Not much people like that again. That is what I always liked about you. You used to lay you cards on the table even as a youngboy working with Baby Rabbit. In the coming battle fellas like you will always be on the right side."

As Skullcap spoke admiringly of men like Orbits, his subject was at turns flattered and reminded of his frustration with the long bureaucratic chain that sputtered and stopped before it reached the capital, forcing him to restart the entire process over and over until he gave up. Skullcap continued to preach about god and morality, and when they approached the capital, Orbits told him that he had some business and would take a bus back to his place.

When Orbits got out of the vehicle, Skullcap told him, "I was telling you before that for years I was hoping that god would send a earthquake or hurricane to remind people, but what he was really sending was messages. Not from goat or cyat and thing, but real message. Smallman getting murder and bigman walking free. All these moneymen walking around like they own the damn country." He recited his messages in a singsong way, like an old-time calypsonian, and Orbits felt he had used this speech before. "Big shot with no cover for they mouth. Children borning with chicken foot and pig snout. So it does go. It take a time before I was able to decode the message and them. You know what the message tell me? It tell me that all a madman need is people to encourage him. That when a madman back against the wall is then that he is the most dangerous. Alright, later, brother. Keep fighting the good fight."

Orbits walked around the capital marvelling how much the place had changed. There were new buildings everywhere, ugly structures that borrowed from arbitrary styles that made them seem bullying next to the small older wooden buildings squashed between all the concrete. The new structures had pushed the vendors closer to the streets, so that some intersections were almost impassable. There was constant honking of horns and everyone looked either miserable or violently impatient. Cars were speeding by, cutting dangerously close to the vendors selling every imaginable thing, it seemed. Thirty years earlier, there had been a few vagrants, but now he saw them everywhere, young, muscular and aggressive. The boom years had given the capital a vanity that extended even to the lowest.

"You could spare some small change?" a young man asked him. "Twenty dollars and some coins. I want to get a little something for the belly. Kentuckys." Orbits, always uneasy with brashness, slipped his hands into his pockets and walked away quickly.

As he came to the Savannah, he realized he was less than twenty minutes from his old workplace, and he headed in that direction. He recalled his forays in the capital after he had lost his job with Baby Rabbit, a secret he kept from his former wife. He had been overjoyed when Wally had offered him the position, but his former wife had asked about contract and salary. He wondered how his life may have turned out if they had not divorced, if he had had the benefits of her practical side as the decades rolled by and they both grew older. As he approached the street, his mind drifted to Wally, whose company had blunted so much of the distress of the time. He had kept up his pretense about his life, but before Wally's departure, he had revealed everything to the other man.

The building was exactly as he recalled, and from his time at the station, he knew that the money from the boom years had passed that ministry straight. But the workers were new, and they seemed more harassed than the men waiting on a long bench and glancing at their watches. From their clothes, Orbits knew these were country folks, most likely farmers. When he walked to the front desk, a young man with a tie said in a rough voice, "Mister, join the line please. Why allyou people so?"

"Allyou people? How long you working here, boy?"

"Who you think you calling boy?"

"The person who just mention allyou people. Do you understand what I am saying?"

Now the young man put down the magazine he was reading. He was not accustomed to this reaction that could stem either from ignorance or from a position of authority. He studied the man before him; his clothes, neither country nor town, offered no clue, but his hands were not a farmer's. Just to be safe, he asked, "What is it you want?"

"I want your attention."

"You have it now. What is it you want? As you could see, we very busy."

"Yes, I know very well how things operate here. I used to work in this same building at one time."

"Yeah? I never see you before. Must be a long time ago." His voice was now more cautious. "What is your name?" When Orbits told him, he said, "Hold on." He walked over to a young woman who was polishing her nails and then to the filing cabinet that Orbits remembered so well. "I think these is for you." He returned with a bundle of envelopes tied with a string. "You know how much time we nearly throw them away. Is lucky for you that the old supervisor who retire mention that it was from his old boss. Say that was to one of his good friends who move to a field station. The letters keep coming year after year, mostly at Christmas. You have any identification." Orbits saw the letters were all from Wally, and he was so moved that he sat on the bench next to the farmers. He glanced at the stamped dates and he saw they spanned a period of twelve years and had stopped sixteen years earlier. Wally had not forgotten him; year after year, he had written. Orbits glanced at the date of the last letter and wondered if his old friend had died or, not receiving a reply for twelve years, had finally given up. Perhaps somewhere in Toronto, he, too, was sitting in some old building and wondering if his old friend had died.

"You okay?"

The question was from one of the farmers, and Orbits saw a splatter on the top envelope's stamp. He wiped his eyes hurriedly. "From an old friend. I thought he had forgotten."

A man sitting on the far end of the bench said loudly, "It look like these people who working here forget *we*."

Orbits got up. "Some things never change," he said to the people watching from behind their desks. "One day all of you will be without a job. A few of you might be alone wondering where the time went and the others will be looking for favours from people in the same position you in now." He walked out of the office and diverted to the department, where he dropped off his old teacher's application. He had not been entirely sure what he had intended to do with the application, but he was in a good mood.

He tried to see the city from this mood. In the book he had discovered in the cardboard box, the writer Charles Kingsley had described the city more than a hundred and fifty years earlier as a sort of paradise, with a botanic garden organized in the English fashion and trees transplanted from every part of the world. There were cavorting animals and magnificent birds and flowers of every hue. Orbits tried to see this as he walked along the Savannah, and although there were still traces of what the writer had described — grand old samaan trees and flowering poui and castle-like structures — the city had moved on. The old structures seemed forlorn in this setting; the trees, no longer spreading, appeared hunched and tremulous, the gingerbread houses defensive and frightened. Soon he came to the rumshop where, the only time in his life, he had attempted a bribe. The proprietor, who was also wearing dark shades, did not recognize him, and Orbits explained that he and a good friend had come to the establishment almost every afternoon. He pointed to a table in the dark corner. The letters were from his friend who was living in Toronto. Twelve in all. The proprietor was not interested but he nodded and said, "That good," without feeling. For old times' sake, Orbits ordered a rum and continued talking; the proprietor shifted away.

"You *must* remember him," Orbits insisted. "He used to be here all the time. Big fella. Portogee."

"It have no Portogee in this place," the barman said. "You want anything else?"

Orbits took out a photograph from one of the envelopes and held it before the barman. "Look. This is the fella I talking about. The one in the middle. He had more size at the time you know him, but the face is the same."

The barman came closer and pushed up his shades with the insides of his wrists. With his fingers spread above his ears he looked completely demented. "I thought you say Portogee. Nearly everybody in the family look mix. All the women and little children." Orbits had not noticed that, and he turned around the photograph so he could look more closely. "What you trying with me?" the man asked impatiently. "You is a health inspector or something? What is it you really want? If is a bribe then come out and say it straight."

Still looking at the photograph and with the rum in his head, Orbits said, "I want to know if you and the wrecker fella still running allyou scam. You catch me good and proper about twenty-seven years ago." In spite of his tone he was not angry.

The barman lowered his shades and peered at Orbits. His eyes, yellow, inflamed and rheumy, looked like leaking eggs. "If I catch him I will dismantle him from beak to gizzard. He disappear with more than a thousand dollars in bills." He moved away to consult a thick notebook, cursing his former accomplice as he added and subtracted.

Ten minutes later, Orbits left the joint. He felt that if Wally were here with him, the proprietor would have surely been friendlier. Wally had that way about him. During the journey back to his place, he went over what he would say in his reply to his old friend. First, he would apologize by explaining he had never received the letters and so had no idea of Wally's address. He would express his shock . . . no, his joy, that Wally had written him year after year. He would obviously give him an update on all that had happened since he left the ministry.

He would reveal that both parents had passed away — one from an undefinable grief and the other from anger at what the world had wrought — and he was now like the person Wally had imagined himself to be with no family around. His would mention the arson that had destroyed his house and the frustration with his constituents who expected too much and grew annoyed when he explained his limitations. He would hint at a belated understanding of his brother.

By the time he dropped off at Soongsoong Japourie, he was a little surprised at the lack of joy in all that he remembered. He ordered a soft drink and the shopkeeper brought it over. "Plenty letters," the man said. Was this the extent of his life? What had he done to leave a mark? Who would remember him with affection? The woman with whom he had had an affair believed it was as a result of a light on her head. Most of his constituents felt he had failed them. "It look like you fixing up plenty people business." The mood of the last months, pretending to be satisfaction, hinging at acquiescence, had swept away all his failings, all the gaps in his life. "You didn't come back with the fella who pick you up. I ever mention that he was in some trouble with the police?"

Orbits was brought back to the present. "Yes, but you didn't say what sort of trouble."

"Is not for me to say." The storekeeper stamped on the floor, disappeared behind the counter and emerged with a squashed grasshopper. He flicked away the insect and sniffed his fingers. "Was planning some kind of coo, a nice little coo." He whispered the words as if he were sharing a tender secret. "Is what I hear so don't quote me on it. These fellas always talking about god like if they alone know his address. Always jumping up and down and never satisfy with anything. Me? I does go with the flow. I ever tell you about the nice craft that father reject? Now I will satisfy with anything. Even a old fowl self." He moved away to serve a customer, an oldish man asking for torchlight batteries, and Orbits left with his letters.

He read the letters on the dark green couch on which he had first spotted the original owner of the house. The first letters were filled with hints that Wally had made a terrible mistake in moving to Canada. He missed the limes and the rumshops and the laughter and the confusion. "I wish I was with you right now, boy. Coming out from a rumshop and walking around the Savannah with all the poui in bloom and the fresh smell of coconut water leaking from every cart and the aroma of cassava pone wafting from a parlour." Orbits was surprised at the descriptions — almost poetic — of all that Wally had remembered and all that he missed. They sounded almost like those of the old English traveller, and Orbits wondered whether this view was possible only from a distance. But there were no equivalent descriptions of Canada, nothing of his family or details of his life there.

Letter after letter followed this style, and Orbits felt that Wally had been expecting some reassurances that he had made the correct move to be with the family he had spoken so often about. But it was too late for that now; the last letter was posted sixteen years ago, and he had most likely found his own way. Still he knew he would write his old friend.

Three hours later, he reread what he had written and realized he would never post it. He had sought to console Wally by telling him that things on the island were getting worse and he had made the correct choice to leave. He wrote about the oil boom that had granted sudden wealth to people unprepared for this new freedom and who mostly feted away their money or saw it stolen by a new breed of criminals, younger and more vicious. He mentioned all the government projects — given fantastic comic book names like "The Amazing Five Year Plan" and "The Magnificent Highway Project" — that had run out of money so that there were these incomplete stadiums and glass-domed buildings all over the capital and highways that led to nowhere. He mentioned the excuses and the passing of blame onto people who were long dead or no longer in power. It was an impersonal letter that could have been written by The Seerman, a regular writer to the newspapers. He had ended by saying that the place Wally missed so much no longer existed, and maybe it never had. After two pages of this, he realized he would never post the letter, and so he began another. Here he congratulated Wally for pursuing a vision. He mentioned the frequency with which his friend had spoken about leaving the island and his own doubts, years earlier, that Wally would actually abandon the comfort of his job for a place he knew nothing about. In this letter, he praised Wally for his persistence and ambitiousness and offered his own life as a stumbling alternative.

The first letter had been essaylike and impersonal, but the second ran to five pages and when he reread it, he was surprised at the eloquent bitterness of the tone. "Unlike you, I could never see any purpose to my life," he wrote. "In spite of your little complaints in the rumshops, you saw a destination that you reached for in the end. I made the mistake of thinking it was just rumshop talk, but you were serious." He ended by stating, "Among the billions of people in the world, there are just a handful that are useful and show the way forward. But what of the others? Are we just leeches of no consequence? Or does the world need this mass to create a forward momentum pushing towards this promised land? Maybe we in these islands are just floaters and cloud-gazers. We have nothing to contribute so we simply drift along like passing clouds, hoping for the best."

This letter seemed written by a stranger, and he realized that his lament was a hodgepodge of complaints Wally himself had made, but in rereading it, he began to see his childhood fantasy of floating above everything as the one connecting thread along which everything in his life was strung. This fantasy had never left but had remained hidden, pretending to be something else. He was no different from everyone he knew, no different from his parents, the farmers, his constituents, the passengers on the buses, from Gums or Doraymay or Spanish — no different from anyone in the island.

Maybe it was impossible to possess any real value in this place. People who preached about making a difference either spoke in an exalted and impractical way or were like Skullcap, whose confused sermonizing sounded like frenzied banging against tightly shut doors. How often he had heard that babble from the powerless! How often he had been struck by the same powerlessness. He thought of his brother.

On his last day at work, the local election scheduled the following day, a group of men smoking outside his office entered after a few minutes. "You already pack up?" one of them asked.

"Yes, I finish here."

"So easy you going?"

"Is better to go easy," he replied.

"So you say," one of the men said. "So you say."

His companion asked, "No farewell party? Not a drink self? Nothing for the throat?"

They seemed reluctant to leave so Orbits told them, "I have to clear out everything in an hour."

"Fete in all the rumshop. We going to one now."

"We plan to hit all of them before the night finish. All the candidates buying drinks."

"Except for the one talking to the girl in the front. You know last week he was reading a speech and when people start to heckle him, all of a sudden he break down and start bawling.

"I never see anything like that. Anyways, we going now. You sure you don't want to join we? Plenty action. Two days aback a fella put a good licking on Halligator for calling him a miscreant. Don't know what the word mean and I sure the fella who *planass* Halligator don't know either. Miss-creant. Sound like a bigshot lady if you ask me."

Orbits knew they were angling for a free drink. He took out two twenties from his wallet and said, "Take this. If I find the time, I will join you."

They left immediately. Orbits looked through the window at the people going in and out of the dentist's office and he thought of his father's place. During a visit there, he had seen a woman, her legs apart, utterly helpless while his father drilled her. He hated the office for its smell of rubbing alcohol and the rusty clamps and pliers and the vulgar bawling of the patients. But his father seemed happy in the place. His mother, too, had been happy during that period. A perfect family on the surface, yet he had suffered through the first two decades of his life and his brother had, at some point, turned his back on the world. How was it possible that his parents could not notice any of this? How could they feel all of this was natural? One of the men he had met in the community centre mentioned that Starboy had spoken of shame as an ever-present affliction. He assumed his brother had escaped, but maybe he was doubly afflicted.

A van with clearly drunk men waving banners drove by, almost hitting a woman who had stepped out of the dentist's office. She watched the van roar along and held a palm against her cheek as she crossed the road to the chicken and chips joint, where she passed two men sitting on cardboard ends. One of the men had his hands out even though with his head down and his eyes closed, he seemed to be sleeping. Another van with banners from an opposing party screeched to pick up a group from the chicken and chips place. An old man walking with a cane stopped and looked up at the building where Orbits' office was housed. He watched for a full five minutes before he moved on.

Orbits remembered the scene at Doraymay's place and the image of ants crawling around and over their dead comrades. During the visit, he had felt that it was the natural way of the world for the injured, weak and helpless to be pushed aside and forgotten. He recalled a conversation with Cascadoo, the other man speaking about reincarnation, which he was convinced extended to animals. "Eef you see a cockroach mash it one time. Eef you see a dog in the road bounce it down. All them animals paying for their sin in they last life." He had moved on to impoverished men like himself, and Orbits was uncertain if Cascadoo wanted him to argue otherwise. But Orbits had seen how other men had used this belief to stave off guilt or passivity. "How I could change anything that set by higher powers? The script already write." Did someone actually say this?

A pickup truck with Halligator and some other men standing on the tray drove by. Halligator's hand was bandaged and he was waving with the other at nobody in particular. If he had glanced up at the office he was hoping to soon occupy, he would have seen Orbits looking through the window, but he was focused on the men and women on the road. Already I am forgotten, Orbits thought without bitterness. He hoped the new councillor would be more helpful to his constituents than he had been. He had swiftly discovered that the men who barged into his office were not always the sad, oppressed peasants he had first imagined, but often the architects of their own tragic lives. He had seen how much they were bound by tradition, comforted by its rituals, softened by familiarity but always, always trapped by the rules. They had excuses for everything: excuses that had been handed down from generation to generation and that had lost all meaning.

He heard a knock on the door and saw Mona. She seemed anxious, and Orbits recalled the promises he had made to her father four years earlier. He had not seen Cascadoo for a while, and he guessed the other man was busy campaigning for one candidate or the other. He prepared himself to console the girl, but it turned out her anxiousness had nothing to do with her job. She thanked him for helping her, a complete stranger with no qualifications, first by giving her a job as a caretaker and then at his office. "I still remember Grandma, you know. How she used to pretend to be vex all the time when all she wanted was a little attention. Somebody to show she that she still living."

Orbits, overwhelmed, told her, "She was lucky to have somebody like you."

"She was lucky to have somebody like *you*." And Orbits reacted as he always did, with unexpected tenderness; he felt his eyes burning. He hugged the girl. She said, "Don't worry about me. I will be okay." She told him that he could stop at the house whenever he wanted.

The owner of the bookstore came out to look at the pair, and when Mona was gone, Orbits walked across. The owner pretended surprise at his approach. "So you come to pay a last visit? How was the book on blindness that you buy? Sometimes these books work and sometimes they don't work. That is the thing about cures. They don't obey any rules. I have some good books here for a man in your position. *How to Retire and Relax*. *How to Retire and Keep Busy*. *How to Forget the Past*. *How to Prepare for the Future*." He walked through his tiny store, pointing out this and that book. Orbits wondered how he managed to survive with so few customers. "So what you going to do now?" the owner asked.

"I not too sure," Orbits replied. "I will take it as it come."

The owner looked offended. He repeated the phrase in a sarcastic way. Eventually he said, "I have exactly the book for you." Orbits glanced at the title. *How to Live*. But beneath the slim tract was another. *How to Die*. "Take your pick," the owner said, shuffling both books.

The book Orbits bought for thirty-five dollars was *How to Live*. It was just sixteen pages, each page representing a decade and on the opposite page, an accompanying illustration to the statement.

"What will happen if somebody live past eighty?" Orbits asked.

"I been thinking of that and I already have a sequel to the best-seller in your hand. *How to Live Past Eighty*. You think is a good title? Or how about *How to Live. Part Two*? The title of a book is the most important thing, you know. Is like if you see a pretty girl and you fall in love at the first sight. You know I always had my eye on that secretary of yours, but she didn't have any time for me. People does see me as a big writer and bookstore owner and feel I could make sweet magic, but sadly, that is not the case. Going to write a book about that one day. Already have the title. *How to Force People to Like You*. But maybe that too strong. I should choose something like *How to Trick People to Like You*."

Orbits left him to speculate on the titles. On his way home, he spotted scenes of merriment in every rumshop. In the morning, half these men would be happy and the other half disappointed. Winners and losers. Soon, some from the losing side would jump ship and others who had supported the winning candidate would grow frustrated and regret their support.

As he passed the villages he knew he would probably never see again — the houses with their gardens of crotons and zinnias, the roadside stalls from which he had often brought fruits for his mother, the limers idling by the bridges, the little landmarks: an overdecorated temple, an old Presbyterian church on a hill, a parlour perched on the edge of a precipice — he considered he would never again have to make promises he wouldn't keep or be subjected to bouts of reproach and anger. His mood lightened as he got closer to his bungalow and he calculated how he would spend his free time. He would build a pond at the back of his house and fill it with fishes. He would plant a variety of fruit trees. Caimites, sapodillas, soursops and tonkobeans. In the nights, the aroma from the fruits would seep into his house as he was finally completing his course on meteorology. Then he thought of the tiny tadpoles swimming in his eyes and the waviness of distant objects, and he decided he would visit an eye doctor. Maybe he would surprise his daughter with a visit, and one evening he might disembark in Canada and see Wally waiting at the airport.

He was fifty-seven; in three years, he would receive a pension. He had saved enough money to last until then as he had no real expenses. At Soongsoong Japourie, he told the shopkeeper, "Today was my last day in the job."

"So what you going to do now?"

"I have plans," Orbits told him. "Plenty plans."

On page twelve of the book Orbits had bought from the Book Swami was an illustration of a man floating on a cloud and looking down at stick figures. On the opposite page was the statement *When you hit sixty prepare to see the world again*. He liked both the illustration and the statement. See the world *again*, he thought. He tried to imagine both Florida, where his daughter lived, and Wally's Toronto. "I going to visit some foreign places soon," he said to the sceptical shopkeeper. "But first I have to plant my fruits and dig my pond."

"You know sometimes I does wonder why I slaving out in this place day and night. Who I leaving all this to? No children, no old fowl."

Orbits understood what he meant, and he had thought of this himself. He told the man, "The important thing is to occupy yourself with a plan." He had actually read that from the Book Swami's tract. "A bucket list."

The shopkeeper tittered at the term before he grew serious. "Sometimes these plans don't work out as planned. The bucket does tip over and break you crown. You hear about you friend in the radio? The one who pick you up a few weeks aback." When Orbits shook his head, the shopkeeper said, "The police find a ton of guns in his place. Look like he was planning something serious. A coo." Each evening, he walked across to the shopkeeper and listened to news of Skullcap, who had clammed up in the police station. "I hear he tell them lawyers that god will tell him when is time to talk. Like he and god have a special line. If god use to study all these crazy people he wouldn't have time for anything else. Like building new planets and shaping new animals and thing." During these visits, Orbits mentioned amendments to his list, irritating the shopkeeper, who felt this was an unnecessary and trivial distraction from the news he was sharing.

"I finish with all that," he told the shopkeeper one evening. "I have my bucket list."

Some of these he actually accomplished. He phoned Cascadoo and stood in the backyard garden while the other man dug his pond. This is good mud you have here," Cascadoo said. "Sapatay. You could do anything with it." From Cascadoo he heard that Mona was engaged to the baby-faced candidate who had visited his office and who had lost his deposit. Moon's husband had won the election, and Orbits wondered how soon Halligator and his band would come to him with their demands. Maybe the thugs would meet their match in his delusional but strong-willed wife. After a week, Cascadoo told him, "I finish here. All you have to do now is throw some cascadoo in the pond. Not me, eh. The real cascadoo fish."

The fruit trees Orbits planted himself. He was not accustomed to manual labour and he had to rest frequently to calm the pain in his chest, but as he gazed at the rows of plants, the mud fresh at their roots, their buds shining and tender, he felt fulfilled, as if he had completed some great task. In this mood of accomplishment, he contacted his wife. He revealed he had bought the house in the little village they had once visited. She could not remember until he mentioned it was on the day she had driven in her Bluebird to his work. "Ah yes," she said. "I recall it now." She sounded exactly like her mother, and he asked about her parents. Her father had passed away and her mother had occupied herself by joining groups concerned with the education of girls. She planned on taking the same route herself when she retired from her principal position, and Orbits recalled she was a year older than him. He was also impressed that she was now a principal even though he had always expected it. He mentioned this to her, and in the moment of her silence, he asked for Dee's address.

That night he wrote his daughter a long letter in which he used phrases like, "Don't put limits on yourself," and "We can accomplish anything once we have a plan and we stick to it. Know yourself. That is the most important thing." He also wrote Wally an even longer letter in which he outlined all his plans. "I finally going to finish that course in meteorology," he wrote. "Straight on to part four." It was a cheerful letter and he did not reveal the pain in his chest or his growing vision problems that had made driving impossible. His daughter replied within a week. She had visited the island a couple times, but because of her job at a hospital, her visits were limited to just a few days. She had her own place in Florida, and if Orbits visited, he could babysit his granddaughter. Immediately he began to make plans. Two weeks later, he got a letter from Wally. "You wouldn't recognize me now," Wally wrote. "After my heart attack the doctor put me on a strict diet. Massive attack in a mall. I roll down an escalator and I could swear before I pass out I hear somebody saying, 'Get me a harpoon fast.' But I in recovery mode now."

ORBITS' HEART ATTACK WAS not as dramatic. He had just finished clearing the weeds in the backyard and was looking at the reflection of the sky on the pond, the water disrupted by the fishes that rose to the surface; and when he noticed the rippling patterns seeming to fray, the clouds shattering and reforming much too quickly, he felt at first it was just an atmospheric disturbance. Afterwards, he realized his luck in looking up at that moment because he fell on his back rather than forward onto the pond. He wrote to Wally, adopting the joking tone of the other man's letter. "It look like me and you will end up side by side in the same hospital room remembering all the good old times."

But first he had to visit his daughter. He suspected his daughter's unexpected cordiality, expressed through her letter, was because she was now a parent. Maybe she really needed him to babysit. Regardless, he would finally get the opportunity to draw closer to her. During the trip to Florida, he looked through the window and recalled the flight following his honeymoon when his former wife, not knowing of his long-lasting fascination with clouds, had lightly mentioned how real they seemed. Now, because of his deteriorating vision, they appeared dotted with tiny black spots that looked like the mile-corbeaux he had seen, as a boy, high up in the sky.

During the first days in Florida, Orbits was continually surprised by the coolness of the nights, by the number of car dealerships as they drove through the place, by the mix of cacti and familiar tropical plants, by the animals wandering around without a care, by the formal but genuine affection between Dee and her husband, who was not, as he had assumed, the Chinese-looking person he had spotted at his father's funeral, but a lanky, balding American minister, quiet with everyone but his daughter. "The cutest little thing in the world, isn't she?" he asked Orbits one night.

"Her mother was just as cute," Orbits replied. He felt embarrassed with the statement, but he could see that Dee was pleased. He couldn't connect this grown woman with the girl who had been irritated with him during their scheduled visits and who had cut him off altogether later on. Five days after his arrival in Florida, following a visit to an ophthalmologist, she asked him if he would consider spending more time with the family. Both she and her husband were working and it would be good to have a relative seeing about their daughter rather than a babysitter. "It's how these Cubans and Mexicans operate," the husband said.

Orbits was overjoyed. "The minute I get back I going to make preparations," he told her. And he did. He would visit later in the year, maybe before Christmas, where he would get the opportunity to celebrate with his family. The bungalow he would rent or lock. Perhaps he would fix his eyes and his heart in the hospital that employed his daughter. In the evenings, in his backyard or on the porch, he would marvel at this unexpected and satisfying end to his struggles. Sitting on a wicker chair on his porch, listening to the shrill cries of the parakeets blending with the musical notes of the bullfinches, observing the scattering of the evening, the night percolating through the bamboo, the coolness separating the fresh clinging odour of the para grass from the astringent aroma of the lime and lemon, Orbits could finally feel that he was satisfied. He owed no one, was obligated to no one.

He had seen the island move from poverty to obscene wealth and, when the price of oil fell, the money long squandered, back to poverty. But he had been untouched by these fluctuations. For all his life, he had had little idea of what the future might bring; he never planned for anything, and whenever a slice of luck fell his way, he briefly imagined it was the world settling to balance the torment of his early years. Now, for the first time, he began to see the opportunities within his grasp. The fastidiousness that had marked his time at the Ministry of Agriculture returned: he began to calculate and apportion — groceries, renovations, flights, surgery, presents, clothes for himself.

He wrote to Wally of his visit to his daughter, using phrases about fate and destiny he would have once scoffed at. He mentioned the visit in Florida to an ophthalmologist who had referred to the black specks as floaters. "It looks like I can't escape from floating," he wrote. "Maybe the man upstairs is granting me what I always wished for. If I can't get to the clouds, he bringing the clouds to me." He also revealed his plans to the shopkeeper, who countered with his own problems in getting a visa and who mentioned plane crashes and foreign diseases.

It was a heart attack rather than a foreign disease or plane crash that ended Orbits' plans. He had been describing to the sceptical shopkeeper all the animals he had seen roaming about in Florida, armadillos and deer and opossums, when the pain in his chest shot through the left of his body and then spread everywhere else before it leavened into numbness. "Ay-ay, what happen to you?" the shopkeeper asked. "You fall asleep just so?"

Half an hour later, he told the ambulance personnel, "The man talking about a deer he spot behind his daughter house and before he could tell me if he shoot it or not, he just kilketay on the counter here."

"You know him?" the personnel asked.

"Was a councillor. Just the other day he see about a man drain. Teacher or something. Look at how people does go, eh. Easy-easy. One minute he talking about deer and thing and the next minute he just cal-laps. Life is a funny thing. I don't know what going to happen with his bucket list. I warn him about that."

"You know his address?"

"A house not too far from here. I tell him the house was haunted but he didn't listen."

Orbits' funeral was held in the house he had desired for half his life. Cascadoo came with his daughters and a few farmers. He showed them the pond he had recently dug and the fruit trees, many already with fresh buds. Mona came, too, with her new husband, who seemed badly affected by her tears. The couple had seen about most of the funeral preparations and had contacted Orbits' former wife.

Moon, the woman with whom he had had an affair, did not attend, but her husband, the newly elected councillor, made a speech in which he said that during moments of greatest distress, one should never despair because it is simply the world restoring itself and righting the balance. Dee, who had flown down with her family, nodded as if it were a wise statement. During the cremation, her daughter, one and a half years old, looked at the blue smoke from the pyre curling upwards and disappearing into the clouds and she put her little hand out as if she could touch it. Her grandmother, who was holding her, said, "You can't touch it, sweetie. It looks real but it's just smoke."

Her son-in-law took the girl and pointed to the clouds, "That's where your grandpa went. Can you see him?" The child nodded, pointing from one cloud to the other.

Acknowledgements

I WOULD LIKE TO THANK Hilary McMahon, my agent at Westwood.
I would also like to thank Laura Pastore, Tania Blokhuis, Jessica
Albert, Avril McMeekin, and my editor at ECW, Michael Holmes.
Forever grateful to Dianne Martin.

RABINDRANATH MAHARAJ is the author of six novels and three short story collections. His fifth novel, *The Amazing Absorbing Boy*, won both the Toronto Book Award and the Trillium Fiction Prize. Previous books were shortlisted for various awards, including the Commonwealth Writers' Prize, the Chapters First Novel Award, the Bocas Prize for Caribbean Literature, and the Rogers Fiction Award. In 2013, Maharaj was awarded the Queen Elizabeth II Diamond Jubilee Medal. He was born in Trinidad and now lives in Ajax, Ontario.